WATCHER OF THE DARK

WATCHER OF THE DARK

JOSEPH NASSISE

TOR®

A TOM DOHERTY ASSOCIATES BOOK

NEW YORK

This is a work of fiction. All of the characters, organizations, and events portrayed in this novel are either products of the author's imagination or are used fictitiously.

WATCHER OF THE DARK

Copyright © 2013 by Joseph Nassise

Edited by James Frenkel

A Tor Book
Published by Tom Doherty Associates, LLC
175 Fifth Avenue
New York, NY 10010

www.tor-forge.com

Tor® is a registered trademark of Tom Doherty Associates, LLC.

The Library of Congress Cataloging-in-Publication Data is available upon request.

ISBN 978-0-7653-2720-8 (hardcover)
ISBN 978-1-4299-4565-3 (e-book)

Tor books may be purchased for educational, business, or promotional use. For information on bulk purchases, please contact Macmillan Corporate and Premium Sales Department at 1-800-221-7945, extension 5442, or write specialmarkets@macmillan.com.

First Edition: November 2013

Printed in the United States of America

0 9 8 7 6 5 4 3 2 1

For all the fans who have supported my work for the last ten years:
This one's for you.

WATCHER OF THE DARK

1

I bolted awake in the shitty little motel room I'd been calling home for the last three weeks, with my heart jack-hammering in my chest and my skin coated with a thin sheen of sweat. The room was as dark as an oil slick thanks to the way I'd taped the drapes, already as thick as medieval tapestries, against the wall behind them to keep out even the faintest glimmer of light. In that darkness, however, I had no trouble seeing Whisper standing beside my bed, watching me with a flat expression on her usually animated face.

Whisper's real name was Abigail Matthews. She'd been dead for a little over three years. Not that that was a problem for me; I can see the dead as easily as I can see the living.

Once upon a time, I was just an average Joe living the American dream. Life might not have been perfect, but you wouldn't have caught me complaining. I had everything I'd always wanted. I was married to a good-looking woman who loved me as much as I loved her. We owned a house and a good-sized piece of property in a nice little neighborhood in Boston, not far from the law firm where my wife Anne had made partner and within easy commuting distance to Cambridge where I was on the fast track for tenure as a professor of ancient languages at Harvard University. We had a bright, precocious daughter, Elizabeth, who was the best of both of us combined into one. We were happy, content, and as oblivious to the reality of the world around us, to the dark things that move within it, as an ant is to the theory of relativity.

We were living the dream, so of course reality had to rear up and bite us on the ass.

Hard.

Our daughter disappeared one day, just vanished without a trace from her second-story bedroom. I later learned that she'd been snatched by the supernatural equivalent of the man with a thousand faces: a doppelganger, or fetch, as they were sometimes called, that could take the form of any creature with which it came into contact. That took five long years and what felt like a lifetime, though. In the beginning there was just confusion, guilt, and a desperate need to find Elizabeth and bring her home.

In the aftermath of Elizabeth's disappearance I'd tried everything I could to discover what had happened to her. When, after a few years, I'd exhausted the usual methods, I'd delved into more esoteric ones. Things like divination, witchcraft, and black magic. That's when I met the Preacher.

To this day, I'm not sure what he is. Sorcerer? Demon? Something worse, maybe? I honestly don't know. Not knowing hasn't stopped me from bargaining with him for what I want, however. He's appeared to me twice and each time his assistance has proved crucial in resolving what seemed like an insurmountable problem, but, like Faust before me, I always paid a price.

The first time that he appeared, the Preacher offered me a book claiming that its contents would help me find my daughter if I was brave enough to follow it. Inside that book I discovered an arcane ritual, one that was supposed to allow me to see that which was unseen. I performed the ritual, but it didn't work out quite the way I'd expected. Rather than helping me locate my missing daughter, it altered my sight, changing it in a way I never would have imagined possible. From that day forward daylight has been like darkness to me, the light preventing me from seeing anything but endless vistas of white, like an arctic explorer caught in the whiteout of a winter storm. In the light I was effectively blind and was forced to learn how to navigate through a world I could no longer see.

What was even more terrifying was the fact that the change stripped away the Veil that keeps humans from seeing the true nature of the creatures that move among us like wolves among the sheep and revealed the supernatural world around me in all its hideous detail. The world is a cesspit full of creatures you can't possibly imagine, all waiting to devour the hearts, minds, and souls of those careless enough to get in their way.

That night I discovered the monsters in our world and they, in turn, discovered me.

It was Whisper who rescued me from the near-paralyzing fear that the discovery had caused. She's been my comfort, my rock, which is rather ironic given she's no more substantial than a wisp of fog on a cool summer night.

I hadn't seen her since the night I lay dying in a New Orleans drainage canal with an FBI agent's bullet in my guts, when she and the ghost of my dead daughter, Elizabeth, had appeared to me in a vision, showing me the horror about to descend on the Big Easy.

She'd played the harbinger of doom that night, and, given my current reaction to her appearance and the expression of concern on her usually jovial face, I had to believe she had now returned for a repeat performance.

>—+—<

Whisper stared at me with those ancient eyes, eyes that had seen far more than I could ever imagine, and then she spoke.

"He's coming, Hunt," she said, in a voice that dripped omens and shook with an angel's might. "Run. Run while you can."

My mouth fell open in shocked surprise; in the three years that I'd known her, Whisper had never said a single word. I hadn't even known she had the ability to speak.

The raw power in her voice had the hair on the back of my neck and arms standing tall in response, and I realized that in that moment I was afraid of her. The fear, her message, even her very presence had totally flustered me, and it took a few seconds to wrap my head around it all. I must have looked like an idiot, propped there on my elbow with my mouth hanging open, but finally my brain caught up with what was happening and her words registered.

I sat up and swung my legs out of bed, suddenly, irrationally afraid of the emptiness of the room around us, as I asked, "Who? Who's coming, Whisper?"

She glanced toward the door and then back at me, a look

of such empty sadness on her face that I wanted to weep at the sight of it.

"Too late," she whispered and then abruptly faded from view.

No sooner had she vanished than the door of my hotel room was kicked open with a splintering crash.

2

There's nothing that hones your reaction time like living with the constant fear of discovery, especially when you know that those chasing you are more apt to shoot first and ask questions later. *Much* later. I left New Orleans with both the local authorities and the FBI gunning for me and had been waiting for weeks now for one or the other to figure out where I'd gone to ground, so I was up and moving before the remains of the door had time to bounce off the carpet. I snatched the baseball bat I kept by the side of the bed off the floor as I rushed past, headed for the bathroom and the window it contained. The early morning light was pouring in through the now-open doorway, stealing my sight away from me, and, even as I squeezed my eyes shut in a futile attempt to block it out, I watched the world in front of me disappear behind a gleaming curtain of white.

Thankfully, it didn't matter; I didn't really need to see to know where I was going. The motel room I was staying in wasn't much bigger than a walk-in closet and I'd taken the time to pace out the room and the area outside it when I first checked in, mapping it all out in my head, just in case something like this happened and I had to make a hasty departure.

I kept expecting someone to shout "Stop! Police!," but the fact that such calls never came didn't slow me down any; I was getting out of there no matter what. Of course, that should have been my first clue that this wasn't the U.S. Marshals come to drag me back to Boston.

As soon as I felt the bathroom tiles beneath my bare feet, I spun around and slammed the door, jabbing the lock button down with my thumb. Something heavy slammed into the other side half a second later, but I wasn't waiting around to find out who, or what, it was. With barely a pause I crossed the room, felt for the window, and then used the bat to smash out the glass. I tossed the bat out ahead of me, snatched a towel off the nearby rack, and laid it over the sill to keep me from slashing myself to ribbons on any leftover glass that I couldn't see. Preparations finished, I hefted myself through the opening headfirst.

Or, at least, I tried.

Hands suddenly grabbed me about the ankles with a grip as tight as a vise. I almost let go of the sill out of sheer surprise, as I'd been too wrapped up in what I was doing to hear the door give way behind me. One good yank was all it took for whoever it was to haul me most of the way back inside the room. I was stretched out over the bathroom floor, my hands latched in a death grip on the windowsill as my assailant steadily pulled me backward by the ankles.

I could hear several voices coming from the direction of the bedroom and knew that reinforcements were on the way. I had seconds, at best, to get free or I was going to be in a shitload of trouble. I had no idea who these people were, but it was a safe assumption that they didn't have my best interests at heart; you didn't kick in the door of a man's motel room to invite him out for a venti caramel macchiato. In desperation, I began kicking and flailing my legs, trying to dislodge my would-be captor's grip. To my surprise it worked; my left leg popped free. The person behind me was shouting in a language that sounded suspiciously like Russian as I brought my knee up and then sent my foot hammering back down with all the force I could muster, using the other's voice to hone in on my target.

Something crunched beneath my heel as it collided with what I hoped was his face. There was a sharp yelp of pain and then my legs were free. I scrambled for a few seconds and then my right foot found the edge of the toilet and I used it as a brace to push myself forward.

I tumbled out the window, landing hard on the second-floor walkway outside. Countless little shards of glass, the detritus of the window I'd just smashed to smithereens, jabbed into my bare flesh, but I ignored them, compartmentalizing the pain to be dealt with at some later point, knowing that if I didn't get my ass out of there I probably wouldn't live long enough to bleed to death anyway. I scrambled to my feet and reached out with my hands, searching blindly for the rusty old iron railing I knew was there somewhere. When I found it a moment later it was with my left hand, which told me I was facing back toward my room. Given that was the last place I wanted to be, I spun around, put my right hand against the railing as a guide, and took off as fast as I could go down the walkway toward the stairwell at far end of the motel.

It said something about the kind of place I was staying in that no one moved to stop the near-naked tattooed guy dressed only in his boxer shorts running helter-skelter down the length of the second-floor walkway leaving bloody footprints in his wake, which, when it came right down to it, was probably best for all involved. After all, I couldn't see a damn thing; if some-one had stepped out in front of me I would have simply slammed into them full speed, and I had little doubt that the collision probably would have ended with one of us tumbling ass-over-elbows over the railing and falling an entire story to the unfor-giving cement of the parking lot below.

Not anyone's idea of a successful escape.

I'd taken less than a dozen steps before shouts behind me let me know that whoever it was that had broken into my room was now in hot pursuit.

Again, there was no order to stop, no cries identifying my pursuers as law enforcement of any kind. I was starting to think I might be in more hot water than I'd originally suspected and pushed myself to go faster while trying to figure out a way out.

The stairwell would take me to the ground floor. If I could get to the bottom ahead of my pursuers, I might be able to get to the motel office where I could hopefully scrounge up some help or at least find a place I could hide long enough for the cops to show up.

If anyone had bothered to call the cops, which was *not* a foregone conclusion by any means in this part of town.

Still, I knew there was no sense in worrying about it; what would be would be. I just needed to get my skinny ass down there and hope for the best.

Thirty-five steps.

That was the distance from my bathroom window to the stairwell at the end of the walkway by the corner of the building. I was counting my steps off as I ran—*fifteen, sixteen, seventeen*—using my hand on the guardrail to keep me moving in a straight line.

Eighteen . . .

Nineteen . . .

Twenty . . .

I'd walked this exact route dozens of times already, and I knew that I had to slow down around the twenty-eighth step to keep from overshooting the stairs. Once I made the turn onto the stairwell I could speed up again, but making that turn without falling down was crucial to getting away, so I was totally focused on the numbers reeling out inside my head.

Twenty-three . . .

Twenty-four . . .

I was still ten steps off my count when I felt the railing disappear beneath my right hand, signaling the entrance to the stairwell. I heard someone shout, "No!" from behind, but it took my brain another precious few seconds to catch up with what my body was telling me: I'd gone too far, too fast.

My legs hit the railing in front of me at midthigh and carried me right over.

I screamed like a girl all the way down.

I thought I'd been pretty smart, pacing out that distance and knowing exactly how far I had to go if the shit hit the fan. A little too smart, as it turned out, as I hadn't taken into account the difference in my stride. Walking that distance was one thing; doing it pumped full of adrenaline and running hell-bent for leather to save my hide was another.

All of this flashed through my head as I plummeted downward, and I found it more than a little ironic that I had managed to defeat a sorcerer and his pet fetch, live through a full-fledged throw down with an embodiment of the Grim Reaper himself, and escape from the FBI only to wind up killing myself because I suck at math.

Sometimes, life just doesn't seem fair.

Fully expecting to splatter myself against the unforgiving

ground, I was shocked for a second time that morning as I plunged into the freezing waters of the motel swimming pool. The cold made me gasp in surprise and I inhaled a boatload of overchlorinated water as a result, causing my body to start convulsing as it tried to rid itself of the offending substance.

This was seriously not my morning!

I probably would have spent the next few minutes trying to figure out which way was up—and ended up drowning in the process—if my ass hadn't slammed into the bottom of the swimming pool at that point.

My eyes popped open, dazzling me with an unending field of white, and my brain threw that internal switch that fired up my ghostsight as my body's innate survival instincts kicked in and it searched for a way out of the mess I'd landed it in yet again.

I immediately saw that I wasn't alone there at the bottom of the pool. The ghosts of three teenage girls killed by a serial rapist back in the '70s stared hungrily at me from out of the black, brackish water that surrounded us as my ghostsight painted everything with a patina of death and decay. The girls' long hair floated like halos around their heads, but there was nothing angelic about their smiles of welcome as they drifted toward me.

Choking and gagging, with my thoughts starting to grow hazy as a result of my continuing lack of oxygen, I got my feet under me and pushed, sending my drowning body rocketing upward.

My vision slipped back to normal as I broke the surface of the water, the light blinding me to my surroundings. Still gagging and choking up everything I had swallowed, I had just enough strength left to thrash my way over to the edge of the pool and grab hold so I wouldn't go under again. I was hanging there, hacking up mouthfuls of chlorinated water, trying to catch my breath, and expecting at any moment to feel the cold, hungry grip of the ghosts' hands around my ankles when someone pressed the barrel of a gun against my forehead.

"Don't you fucking move, *cabrón*," said a voice in my ear.

I had absolutely no intention of doing so, but I didn't tell him that. I couldn't; I was still coughing up half of the swimming pool.

I heard hurried footsteps—two, maybe three people, I couldn't be sure—and then the gun was pulled away from my forehead. The voice spoke again. "You two. Get him out of there!"

Rough hands grabbed my arms and hauled me out of the pool. I was still weak from my near-asphyxiation and almost fell when they tried to make me stand; the hands grabbed me again and held on until my feet steadied under me.

"Damn it! The bastard's dripping all over my new shoes," the one on my right said. My brain automatically cataloged what it could from the sound: male, thirty, maybe thirty-five years old, a bit shorter than I was given the way the sound rose to meet me. He was from somewhere back east, like I was. New York. Maybe South Jersey. I wasn't sure. He was a smoker too; the nicotine practically wafted off of him.

"Fuck your shoes; they're ugly anyway."

On my left. A tall female who I guessed had to be built like an ox because she'd lifted me out of the water one-handed. Russian, or at least Eastern European, from the sound of her voice. *Was she the one I'd kicked in the bathroom? Must not have hit her as hard as I thought.*

"Ugly? What the hell do you know about . . ."

Jersey didn't get any further.

"Shut up," said the guy with the gun, and both of them went silent immediately.

Definitely no doubt about who the boss was.

I was getting tired of standing around shivering in the light unable to see the people who'd just livened up my day so nicely. The dead girls were watching us from the middle of the pool, so I reached out and stole the sight from one of them.

There was a moment of dizziness, sharp and intense, and then the taste of bitter ashes flooded my mouth as the world swam back into view in rich, vibrant colors, ten times brighter and more vivid than anything I remembered from the days before I lost my sight.

Oh, the things the dead can see! They see everything, from the fallen angels that swoop over the narrow city streets on ash gray wings to the changelings that walk among us unseen, safe in their human guises. The glamourlike charms that supernatural entities use to conceal themselves from human sight are no match for the eyes of a ghost.

But what has always struck me as the cruelest irony is that despite being unable to feel emotions of their own, ghosts can see them pouring off the living without any difficulty whatsoever. It's like each emotion has its own wavelength, its own unique color, like a beam of light seen through a prism. And it isn't just the living, either. Inanimate objects can give off emotions too. If the object was important enough to its owner, over time it would soak up whatever emotions the living attached to it. A child's teddy bear might glow with the pure white light of unconditional love, while a secret gift from a clandestine lover might shine with scarlet eroticism. The rule of thumb, I'd discovered, was that the more important the object was to its owner, the brighter the glow.

I didn't want them to know I was capable of seeing anything, so I kept my eyes slightly unfocused as I moved my head from side to side, trying to make it look like I was just trying to hear them better. In the process, I got a decent look at all three of them.

The guy on my right didn't look like anything too out of the ordinary, just a wiry fellow of medium height with a crazy shock of orange hair atop his head going in every which direction and the quick, twitchy movements of somebody with a severe case of ADD. He was dressed in a wide-lapelled maroon suit with a perfectly folded pocket square and pair of now-wet leather shoes. The silvery gleam that surrounded him let me know he was one of the Gifted, those humans who have gained the ability to tap into the supernatural essence of the world and use it for their own means, but the weakness of the aura told me he wasn't all that powerful.

The same couldn't be said for his two companions, however. Just one look at either of them was enough to tell me that I'd gone from the frying pan into the fire.

The woman was not the weight-lifting Russian musclehead I'd been expecting, but was instead a complete stunner who practically dripped sexual attraction: long legs wrapped in a pair of skintight leather pants, a beautifully curvaceous body peeking out of a silk blouse, and a head full of long dark hair that fell past her shoulders. There was a gleam in her eyes that promised delights beyond anything you could possibly imagine, and when she licked her lips just so, as she did when I glanced in her direction, the average red-blooded American male would have had more than a little trouble concentrating.

Thankfully I didn't, as my ghostsight allowed me to see past all of that to the true creature behind the disguise she wore. Don't get me wrong, she was still beautiful, but the demonic blood that ran through her veins was easy enough to see when the Veil was stripped away. The sense of hunger, of sheer need, that rolled off of her had my body responding despite the fact that my head was screaming no. She would no doubt provide a night beyond your wildest dreams, but that might just end up being the last one you would enjoy. I didn't need anything that badly, thank you very much.

But as scary as the demon half-breed might have been, she was nothing compared to the leader of the group. If the cold hadn't had me shaking, the sight of him would have done the trick. He was a tall Hispanic man in his midthirties, maybe six foot one or so, with a cleanly shaven head and an angular face that ended in a dark goatee. His eyes, as black as night, stared out from deep sockets that gave his face an almost skeletal appearance.

He had a fur-lined men's coat draped over his shoulders but was otherwise naked from the waist up, displaying the upper body tattoo he was sporting. That tattoo was a riot of shapes and colors and depicted a hellish landscape where demons and devils were tormenting humans in a hundred different ways. The figures in it, human and demon alike, appeared to writhe and move of their own accord if you stared at them for too long. From the waist down he wore black jeans held up by a belt with an oversized silver buckle, and he had leather motorcycle boots on his feet. In his right hand was the pistol that had been pressed against my forehead just moments before.

The gun wasn't what made him scary, though. Call me

crazy, but I was much more frightened by the aura that surrounded him, an aura full of corruption and the shifting faces of the restless dead—each one representing some innocent soul that he'd taken during the practice of his dark arts—than I was by the blue-tinted piece of Detroit steel in his hand. This guy was a serious practitioner, far more powerful than my friend Denise Clearwater or even her former companion Simon Gallagher, the combat mage.

That much power was scary in and of itself. In the hands of someone like this, it was terrifying.

I didn't know who the hell these people were or what they wanted with me, but it didn't take a genius to realize that going anywhere with them was probably not a good idea, so I did the one thing no one ever expects the blind guy to do.

I ran.

I bolted to the right, wanting to get away from Demon Lady as quickly as I could while still staying out of Tattoo's reach. That meant passing a bit closer to Jersey than I wanted, but I dealt with that by knocking him backward as I pushed past. There was a shout of surprise and a splash, which brought a smile to my face, but I was too busy racing for the iron fence surrounding the pool. If I could get over that and into the building beyond, I might stand a chance . . .

I wasn't worried about Tattoo's gun, as strange as that may sound. After all, if they'd come to kill me they could have done it half a dozen times already. The fact that they hadn't spoke volumes. The gun was meant to intimidate me, to force my compliance, and it only had as much power over me as I was willing to give it. Now that I'd shown I wasn't going to be cowed, they'd be forced to try something else.

The crack of the gunshot and the spang of the bullet ricocheting off the fence in front of me told me I had a lot more to be worried about than I'd thought.

So much for that theory.

I caught the fence with both hands and vaulted over it, the perfect picture of grace in motion. Then my wet feet slipped out from under me as I landed on the flagstone walkway on the other side and I stumbled forward, staggering to and fro as I fought to keep my balance. My vision was starting to white out around the edges, the increasing distance between me and the ghost of the dead girl whose sight I borrowed weakening the link between us, and I knew I'd be blind again in another ten feet or so.

Finally catching my balance, I looked up just in time to see the figure of a man looming on my right.

I never even saw the punch coming.

It caught me in the solar plexus, paralyzing my diaphragm and driving all the air from my lungs with one short, sharp blow.

I went down like a side of beef.

A face loomed over me as I lay there trying to suck air into lungs that were suddenly not cooperating.

"Going somewhere, Princess?" he asked.

Apparently I really did suck at math.

There were four of them, not three.

4

I'd gotten a look at my latest assailant before my link with the dead girl dissolved permanently and, to my surprise, he was fully human. Not a trace of Giftedness about him. He had a lean face, hard eyes, and brown hair cropped close in a crew cut that would have done the Marines proud. He was dressed nondescriptly in a dark peacoat thick enough to conceal the weapon I was certain he was carrying, jeans, and hiking boots. He also stank of cigarette smoke.

"All right, up you go." He grabbed my arm in a steely grip and dragged me to my feet. I was still fighting for breath and didn't have any strength left to protest; it was all I could do to stay up as my head spun from the lack of oxygen. By the time my lungs decided to listen to my brain and allow air back into my body again, we had been joined by the others and any chance I might have had to escape passed.

"Lose something, Rivera?" my captor asked. It was said in jest, but there was just enough of a hint of derision in his tone to let me know there was a history between him and the guy he was talking to, who I guessed was Tattoo.

My hunch was right.

"I'd watch your mouth, Grady," Rivera said. "You're a lot more expendable than he is. It's not that hard to replace a thief."

A hand grabbed my face and turned it a few degrees to the left. For a moment I was tempted to steal his sight, just to be a pain in the ass, but something, perhaps a long buried instinct for survival, stayed my hand.

"I don't know if you can see me or not, *cabrón*, but try that shit again I'll put a bullet through the back of your head. No one makes a fool of me, *comprende?*"

I nodded as much as his grip would allow for. I had no doubt that he'd do exactly what he said he would. Apparently Grady thought it was a mistake to fuck around with Rivera too much as well, for he didn't say a word in his own defense.

"Bring him."

Hands grabbed my arms on either side and I was practically lifted off my feet as they hustled me along. I thought about crying out for help but knew the chances of anyone getting involved were practically nonexistent. People didn't take a room in a place like this to poke their noses in other people's business. The exact opposite, in fact. There could be a couple dozen of them standing around watching right at this very moment, but were the cops to show up five minutes from now you could be damned sure that no one would have seen a thing.

They dragged me, dripping wet and wearing only my

boxer shorts, back up to my room and dropped me into the room's only chair. I heard one of them going through the dresser drawers and then a set of fresh clothes, one of only three that I currently owned, hit me in the chest.

"Get dressed," Rivera told me. "We've got someone to go see."

All of my clothing was the same—black t-shirts and jeans bought with a clerk's help at a local surplus store a few days after arriving in L.A.—and so I didn't have to worry that they'd dressed me up to look the fool. Dry boxers and jeans were followed by a long-sleeved shirt to help hide all of my tattoos from prying eyes and then socks and a pair of sturdy, yet comfortable boots.

I was finally getting my breath back, but I hobbled over to the dresser just the same, keeping up the pretense of being cowed by my captors' presence. I could feel them watching me, but I knew they never would have let me get even that far if they hadn't already gone through the dresser while going through my clothes, so I ignored them. I opened the top drawer, felt around until I found my wallet, a pair of sunglasses, and my harmonica, and stuffed them into the front pockets of my jeans. The wallet and sunglasses were just me being practical, but I didn't go anywhere without my harmonica, not if I could help it at any rate.

"You ready now, Princess?" Grady asked.

I ignored him, turning instead to face toward where I thought Rivera was standing.

"What's this about?" I asked. "Where are we going?"

"You'll find out soon enough. Bring him."

Hands grabbed my arms. I tried to shake them off, having recovered enough to be able to walk on my own again, but they were having none of it. Their grip tightened and they pulled me along with them as they headed out the door.

We went down the steps and out into the parking lot. I heard a car's doors being unlocked and opened.

"Get in."

I did as I was told, finding the roof of the car with my hand to keep from banging my head on it as I slid into the backseat. I ended up sandwiched between Demon Lady and Grady, leaving Jersey and Rivera to take the front. The car's engine started up and I cursed beneath my breath at the sound, recognizing the throaty roar.

Rivera was not only kidnapping me, but he was using my own car to do it!

All right, so it wasn't really my car per se, as blind guys don't usually have too much use for hot rods like the one we were riding in. The Charger actually belonged to my friend, Denise Clearwater. I'd taken it the night I'd fled New Orleans. Denise hadn't been in any condition to object, as I'd just plunged a two-thousand-year-old dagger into her heart five minutes before stealing her car, but I'd been telling myself for weeks that she was okay with my taking it despite all that. I believed it too. I'd swapped the Massachusetts license plate for a California one at a truck stop just outside of Palm Springs and had only used the car a few times since arriving in L.A., but I knew it like the back of my hand at this point. This was definitely my car.

Which meant that if, by some slim chance, someone did actually report my being forcibly removed from the premises against my will, the only clue to my kidnappers' identity—the car they took me away in—would simply lead investigators away on a wild goose chase and ultimately get me into more hot water than I was in now.

I had to hand it to Rivera, it was a brilliant move.

I disliked this guy more with every passing minute.

Jersey shot out of the parking lot like a bat out of hell, throwing me hard against Demon Lady beside me in the process. No soft curves for her; she was all sleek muscle under that outfit. Normally I might have enjoyed being so close to such a beautiful woman, but I had about as much interest in tangling with her as I did in jumping naked into a pool of starving piranha. At least with the piranha I had a chance of getting out alive.

I settled into my seat and did my best to ignore Jersey's driving—*What the hell was his name anyway?*—while trying to figure out what was going on.

If Rivera wanted something for himself, if he had some personal interest in me or my abilities, he probably would have mentioned it by this point. Since he hadn't, I had to assume that he was operating on behalf of a third party.

The question was who?

I ruled out the police or other law enforcement agencies pretty quickly. Rivera wasn't the type to work with law enforcement, first of all, and second, if he was after the reward the authorities were offering he could have simply phoned in my location and let the U.S. Marshals break in my door instead of doing it himself. A million dollars was a pretty big incentive, I had to admit, and it was being offered simply for information leading to my arrest and capture; Rivera wouldn't have even needed to get his hands dirty in order to collect it.

After crossing off the authorities and Rivera himself, I was still left with a long list of potential people that might have sent someone after me, from the relatives of the victims Agent Doherty was convinced I had killed and who knew who I was thanks to an overzealous media, to Simon Gallagher and his followers from New Orleans, the very people I had escaped from with my friend Dmitri's help just a few weeks ago. Truth was, it could be any of half a dozen different groups. And those were just the few I knew about!

It was time to try to find some answers.

"Where are you taking me?" I asked.

No response.

I tried again. "What do you want? Where are we going?"

The foursome continued to ignore me, though Grady let out an amused little chuckle at my continued ignorance.

It was the chuckle that tipped me over the edge.

I was less than thrilled at what had happened so far that morning, and the continued silence in response to my questions was increasing my irritation by the minute, but that laugh told me that my apparent helplessness was amusing to Grady. That was simply unacceptable. I had come too far and endured too much to be laughed at by some thug who'd gotten the drop on me when I wasn't looking.

Without stopping to think about the consequences of what I was about to do, I reached out and stole the driver's sight.

5

While we were holed up in the safe house outside of Atlantic City after fleeing Boston, Denise began teaching me how to better understand and control the strange talents I'd gained in the aftermath of the Preacher's ritual to "see the unseen." We worked on improving my ability to use my ghostsight to see into the spiritual realm and on refining my techniques for borrowing the sight from another individual, either living or dead. Where once I'd needed to not only personally know my target but also be in physical contact with them, now I could borrow from acquaintance or stranger alike, provided I was within twenty feet of them.

Mentally reaching into the front seat from where I was sitting was a piece of cake.

As usual, there was that moment of discomfort and then the whiteout in front of my eyes receded and I could see again.

The driver, of course, could not.

He rubbed frantically at his eyes for a moment and when that didn't restore his sight, he panicked.

"I can't see! I can't fucking see!"

Pretty much what I expected.

Jersey's sudden outburst stunned the others into immobility as they tried to figure out just what was happening to him. In the backseat, I secretly watched it all, nearly laughing aloud at the expression on Rivera's face as he tried to puzzle out Jersey's antics.

In his panic, Jersey inadvertently turned the wheel a few degrees to the left. That put us squarely into the other lane of traffic. For a few seconds I was treated to the sight of oncoming headlights flaring in my eyes and then Rivera overcame his paralysis, reached over, and yanked the wheel to the right, shouting in Spanish as he did.

Horns were blaring, Rivera was cursing, and, beside me, Grady added his own voice to the din.

"What the fuck are you doing, Perkins?"

Perkins? The poor bastard.

Unable to see and therefore unaware that Rivera had just saved all of our lives by putting us back in the right lane, Perkins jerked the wheel back in the other direction. The car careened into the other lane again, narrowly missing a family of four in a Honda Civic. I watched their faces flash past through the side window, their mouths open in a silent "Oh" of surprise. Maybe this hadn't been such a bright idea after all.

"What did you do?"

I shifted my gaze at the sound of her voice and found Demon

Lady staring at me. Watching her expression change as she realized that I was watching her in return—and not just blindly looking in her direction—was even more amusing than all the chaos going on around me, and I couldn't hold back a little chuckle of my own.

Another long horn blast, a thundering crunch as we clipped the car next to us, and then Rivera was shouting for someone to "Get Perkins's fucking hands off the wheel!" and the woman had no choice but to respond.

As the two men in front continued to jerk the wheel back and forth in a furious tug of war, Demon Lady leaned forward over the front seat, grabbed Perkins by each wrist, and yanked his hands upward until he sat there looking like someone holding their hands up in the middle of a robbery.

With Demon Lady and Rivera, the two most powerful individuals in the car, otherwise occupied, I made my move.

Demon Lady's comment to me must have just registered in Grady's mind for he was turning toward me with a look of surprised concern on his face as I brought my arm up across my chest and then violently reversed it, driving the point of my elbow right into his solar plexus in a bid for payback that had me grinning like a lunatic.

My strike hit home like a sledgehammer, driving the air out of his lungs, and leaving him gasping like a fish out of water.

As he struggled to take in a breath, I leaned in close to be sure that he would hear me over all the shouting.

"Fuck you, *Princess*," I said.

Then I reached for the door handle.

I'm not really sure what I thought I was going to do at that point, to be honest. In his panic Perkins had mashed the pedal to the floor and the car was barreling along like a bat out of hell. It had stopped swerving violently back and forth now that Rivera had sole control over the wheel, but diving out at that speed definitely wouldn't have been good for my overall health, not to mention my tender flesh.

Maybe I had some vague idea of pushing Grady out the open door and following him out afterward, hoping he might cushion my fall, but as it turned out I never got the chance to make good on my move. Rivera must have finally understood that I was the source of all the commotion, for as my hand found the door handle he let go of the steering wheel, reached over the seat, and grabbed my shoulder. His fingers found the nerve cluster just beneath my collar bone and dug in, hard.

The pain was so excruciatingly intense that it was more than my weary body could handle.

Out I went.

><del><

A splash of cold water dashed across my face brought me back to the world sometime later. Still foggy, I lifted my hands, intending to wipe the water from my face, only to hear the unmistakable sound of a gun being cocked just behind my head. I froze, hands in the air, as my memory came flooding back to me.

Whisper's warning.

Rivera and his crew.

The fall from the walkway and the subsequent car ride.

Trouble with a capital *T*.

"Put the gun away, Angel. We're all friends here. Isn't that right, Mr. Hunt?"

The voice was suave, cultured, with only the barest trace of an accent that the speaker had no doubt worked hard to lose. I would have bet that a sighted individual never would have heard it at all. I did, though, and filed the information away just in case it ever became relevant.

This man was not a native.

"Come, come, Hunt. I asked you a question."

Cultured *and* impatient, it seemed.

At this point I didn't have too much to lose, so I ran with the first thing that popped into my head. "If you make a regular habit of kidnapping your friends, then I guess that's what we are. And my name's not Hunt."

Silence fell.

Did I mention yet that my mouth has a tendency to get me into trouble? I mentally reminded myself that I wouldn't feel a thing if Rivera pulled that trigger, but then the silence was broken by a man's hearty laughter and I let out the breath I hadn't realized I'd been holding, hopeful that I might live to see what the next five minutes would bring after all.

"Word on the street is that you have a bit of an acerbic tongue, but I see already that they aren't doing you justice. I think I'm going to like you, Mr. Hunt."

Acerbic? Who was this guy?

"I'm telling you, I'm not Hunt. I don't know who that is. My name is Steve Chambers."

That was the name on the fake driver's license I'd commissioned back in New Jersey, before Dmitri, Denise, and I made our fateful trip to New Orleans.

"Steve Chambers? I don't think so." There was definitely a trace of amusement in his tone as he said, "Jeremiah Hunt. Former professor of languages at Harvard University. Previously married to Anne Cummings, now divorced. One child, Elizabeth, now deceased. Any of this ringing a bell?"

I shook my head. "You got the wrong guy."

My host went on as if he hadn't heard me.

"Arrested by the Boston PD on murder charges. Subsequently escaped custody and murdered a police detective by the name of Stanton. Fled Boston for New Orleans, where you were involved in another shoot-out, this time with the FBI. You are currently also wanted for stabbing a woman in the chest with a knife stolen from the Museum of Natural History in Chicago. Am I missing anything, Mr. Hunt?"

I hadn't killed Stanton, the FBI had been shooting at me, not the other way around, and I'd stabbed Denise in the heart in order to save her life, but, aside from those few minor quibbles, he had it all dead to rights. What I didn't understand was how he knew so much.

Still, I wasn't going to cop to being Hunt. Not yet at least.

I leaned forward in my chair and put as much earnestness into my voice as I could.

"Look, I told you, I'm not Hunt. Check my driver's license, you'll see. Your guys made a mistake. Happens to the best of us. I get it, fine. No harm, no foul. Since I'm blind there's no way for me to identify you, so how about you just let me go and we can forget this ever happened, all right?"

Another moment of silence in which I could feel my host studying me, but I didn't have a clue what he was thinking. I got my answer a moment later when the sound of a dial tone filled the room.

Speaker phone, I thought.

A number was dialed and the line was picked up on the other end after just the first ring.

"Federal Bureau of Investigation," said a spry, female voice.

Uh oh.

"I'd like to speak to Agent Doherty," my host said.

"Just a moment, please."

The receptionist put the call on hold, filling the line with classical music.

I knew Doherty; knew him far too well. He'd been the one to push for my arrest back in Boston, believing I was the killer the press had dubbed the Reaper, guilty of murders in multiple states going back a decade and more. When I'd escaped in the wake of Detective Stanton's death, Doherty tracked me to New Orleans, where our next confrontation ended with him shooting me in the back. I'd escaped only by falling into the nearest canal and finding a drainage pipe to hide in. Even then it had been a close thing, for the blood loss and resulting infection had nearly done the job that the bullet hadn't. If Dmitri hadn't found me when he had, if Denise hadn't been willing to risk her life, her very soul, to save me, I wouldn't be here today.

Doherty was as tenacious as a bloodhound. If he learned I was in L.A., my life would become infinitely more difficult. It seemed it was time to give up the ghost, no pun intended.

I sighed and said, "Fine. I'm Hunt. What do you want?"

The hold music continued for a moment, no doubt to prove just who was in charge around here, and then it was cut off with a click as the call was ended.

"Good of you to come to your senses, Mr. Hunt. I would hate to have to involve the authorities in our business."

Our business? I was liking all this less by the minute.

"You mind telling me who you are and what this is all about?"

He chuckled. "Not at all. My name is Carlos Fuentes."

He paused, as if expecting me to recognize him, but I still didn't have a clue as to who he was. The name was drawing a big fat goose egg for me.

"I am the Magister of Los Angeles."

Ah. Now things were starting to make a little more sense.

If Fuentes was telling the truth, then that meant that I'd come to the attention of just the kind of people I'd been trying to avoid.

Denise taught me that the supernatural community in any given area is ruled by a kind of supernatural lord, or regent, if you will, known as a magister. The magister not only sets the laws within their territory but enforces them as well. Magisters do not have to be human, as I understood things, but those that were human were, more often than not, also highly skilled practitioners of the Art. That was one of the ways that they were able to keep the peace within the bounds of their territories. Imagine Gandalf with all his mystical power as a Mafia don with an army of foot soldiers to do his bidding and you'd have a pretty close approximation of what a human magister is capable of.

Some, like the magister who rules the Boston metropolitan area from his home north of the city in Marblehead, are relatively benign. Denise introduced me to him during my search for Elizabeth, and, while he is incredibly powerful, and quite possibly inhuman to boot, I still felt comfortable in his presence.

Not so with Fuentes. For all his civilized culture and veneer, he definitely gave me the creeps.

Unfortunately for me, when I get nervous, I tend to mouth off.

"Well, bully for you," I said to him then. "Must be nice to be at the top, but what's that got to do with me?"

Fuentes ignored me, which was probably for the best but wasn't a good sign of what was to come. He continued on as if he hadn't heard me.

"For weeks now all anyone can talk about is the blind street exorcist who fought Death to a standstill in what's left of the Big Easy. Who used his trusty little harmonica to send the Grim Reaper's ghostly army back across the Veil to the Other Side like the Pied Piper himself. Everywhere I go the name on everyone's lips is that of Jeremiah Hunt.

"Why is that? I wondered. After all, this is my city, is it not? Shouldn't the only name on everyone's lips be that of Carlos Fuentes?"

His comments were growing decidedly more ominous, so I thought it best that I keep my mouth shut and wait for him to finish.

That didn't mean I had to just sit there and be idle, however.

I was at a distinct disadvantage in not knowing where I was, who I was talking to, or even how many other people might be in the room with us, so I decided to rectify that situation. The easiest way for me to do so was to borrow the eyes of a willing ghost so that I could see my surroundings, including whoever else might be in the room with us, but when I cast about with my senses I didn't discover any ghosts conveniently lingering about.

Disappointing, but not surprising given that the crew he'd sent to pick me up had included a very talented human sorcerer, never mind a demon half-breed. I had no doubt that Fuentes could rid himself of any haunts that might be lingering about if he so desired and he apparently had.

Calling my two favorite ghosts, Whisper and Scream, to help me out was another option, but I shot that one down almost before the thought had fully formed in my head. I needed to speak in order to summon Whisper and I doubted my host would take kindly to my interrupting him so rudely. On top of that, something told me I didn't want Whisper, ghost or not, anywhere near a man like Fuentes.

With my two preferred methods now out of the running, I could either steal the sight from one of the two men I was certain were in the room with me—Fuentes and Rivera—or I could go for what was behind door number three and use my ghostsight.

Not being the suicidal sort, I opted for the latter.

Most people don't realize it, but the world we live in is made up of two distinct layers, or realms, if you will. First there's the physical realm, that layer of reality that we experience every minute of every day, where everything we see and feel and touch takes place. Superimposed on that, like a double-exposed photograph, is the spiritual realm, which has just as much impact on our lives as the physical one, though most people don't realize it.

Normal human beings, Mundanes as we call them, exist primarily in the physical realm. Supernatural creatures on the other hand, like the Sorrows I'd fought in New Orleans or the ghosts that I interacted with daily, exist primarily in the spiritual realm. The Gifted—those humans who have abilities above and beyond the average person, like Dmitri's shape-shifting or Denise's facility with the Art—can often walk through both worlds at the same time.

When I use my ghostsight, I can still see the real world and everything in it, but it is reduced to a faint gray haze that hangs in the background. Ghosts, demons, and other supernatural creatures that haunt the spiritual realm show up as clear as day, however, and the glimmering luminescent sheen that surrounds them makes them almost impossible to miss.

For all its benefits, I don't utilize my ghostsight all that often. Or at least I try not to, for it has a distinct disadvantage, namely that using it was the equivalent of shouting "Dinner's out—come and get it!" into a room full of starving people. Ghosts and other assorted Preternaturals in the immediate vicinity would become aware of my presence. More than a few of the creatures out there saw any unprotected human wandering the spiritual realm as the equivalent of a midnight snack. I'd learned to take quick little looks beyond the Veil and be content with that.

As Fuentes kept talking, I tripped that mental switch and looked out at the world through eyes that were no longer entirely blind.

The first thing I saw was Fuentes himself. He was standing in front of me, watching me as he talked, and from the subtle change in the expression on his face I was almost certain he knew that I was watching.

The fact that I could see him as clearly as I could told me a lot in and of itself. He wasn't as visible as a ghost or some other supernatural entity might be, but he glowed with power just the same and confirmed my suspicions that he was a practitioner of no little skill. Just as I would suspect a magister to be.

My best guess put him in his midfifties. He had a hard, weather-beaten face that reminded me of Al Pacino, or maybe Ian McShane, and a full head of wavy hair that was swept over his skull and worn long in back. A well-trimmed beard completed the look. Fuentes was dressed casually in a loose-fitting sports coat tossed over a jersey and jeans, and he wore an ankh on a chain about his neck.

I'd expected the room around us to appear faint and insubstantial, as much of the physical world appears when viewed through the prism of my special sight, but the walls were far more "present" than I anticipated. That told me that we weren't chatting in an ordinary room, and when I looked over Fuentes's shoulder and focused my attention on the wall behind him, I could see the sigils and markings glowing faintly deep within.

Denise taught me about protection wards too, and now I understood why there weren't any ghosts nearby: the room had been effectively walled off from everything but the most powerful sorcerers and demons.

Perhaps even those as well.

As Fuentes continued, I dropped my sight, not wanting to chance attracting anything unsavory even with the wards in place. I had enough unsavory things with me already.

"Then come the reports that the man of the hour himself has been seen right here in the city of Los Angeles," Fuentes said. "Walking L.A.'s fair streets, breathing her storied air. A thousand cities in America and you, Mr. Hunt, chose mine."

I was tempted to tell him that it was a decision that I was beginning to deeply regret, but I bit my tongue to keep quiet.

"I don't believe in coincidence," he told me. "Your presence here is more than simple serendipity, and I'd be a fool not to recognize it as such. And let me tell you, I am not a fool."

Of course not. And if I had a nickel for every time a fool . . . Oh, never mind.

"Let me guess," I said to him, taking a wild stab in the dark. "You've got a ghost that you want me to handle."

6

"Yes and no," Fuentes said, and I could imagine him rocking his hand in a comme ci, comme ça movement as he did so. "It is more a function of *might* I rather than *do* I."

I frowned. "I'm sorry, I'm not following you."

Fuentes laughed and behind me Rivera did the same. The fact that I'd all but forgotten he was there somewhere showed how uncomfortable Fuentes was making me.

"No, I suspect that you do not. So let me try and explain."

His voice had taken on a decidedly patronizing tone, and I knew I was finally starting to see his true personality. All this polite banter had just been window dressing; now we were getting to the heart of the situation.

"Los Angeles is *my* town, Mr. Hunt. I control the entire city as well as the surrounding area for a good fifty miles in every direction. Nothing happens here without my knowing about it. No one enters my city without my knowing about it. Within ten minutes of your frenzied arrival my phone was ringing off the hook with people warning me that one of the opposition's heavy hitters had just arrived in my territory and wanting to know just what I intended to do about it."

One of the opposition's heavy hitters?

"You entered my city without permission, which is something I take personal exception to, Mr. Hunt. Now, I'm a reasonable man and I understand circumstances can sometimes prevent us from observing the usual social niceties. I would have been happy to forgive your transgression if you had come to me shortly after arrival and asked for forgiveness. A small bit of remuneration for the trouble you caused, a bit of personal groveling to show you understood just who is in charge in this fair city, and I would have been content.

"But you didn't do that, did you, Mr. Hunt?"

Math might not be a strong suit of mine, but I understood the art of language rather well and easily spied the trap Fuentes was clearly hoping I'd fall into with such a remark. Saying anything in my own defense was the equivalent of admitting that his recitation of the events in question was an accurate one, thereby making me liable through my own words for whatever judgment he was working his way toward.

There would be no admission of guilt from this ex-Harvard prof; I kept my mouth shut.

"So here's the deal I'm offering, Mr. Hunt. In exchange for my considerable mercy on this issue, you will remain in Los Angeles as part of my staff until I say otherwise. When I have need of your particular services, which I am certain I will at some point in the near future, you will provide those services without question or argument."

He paused and I spoke into the gap. "And then I'm done? We're square?"

"Square? What a curious notion. Of course we're not square. You will simply be free to do as you wish, aside from leaving the city, until I have need of your particular talents again. Should you prove both useful and ambitious, you can rise toward the top of my organization, just as Mr. Rivera there has done."

Yeah, that was just the future I was hoping for too.

"And if I choose not to accept your offer?"

Fuentes let out an exaggerated sigh. "Then I would have no choice but to make a particular phone call that would have rather unpleasant consequences for you."

It took all of my effort not to laugh in his face. Compared to the things that I had come up against over the last few months—Eldredge, the fetch, the Angeu—Fuentes barely measured on my personal bugaboo scale. If he thought I was going to give up my freedom, and my chance to see Denise and Dmitri again, because he was demanding that I do so, he was delusional.

"Looks like you'll be making another long-distance call then. And so soon too."

Rivera rapped me on the back of the head with the gun barrel again in response to my sarcasm, but it was going to take a lot more than that to curtail my snark.

Unfortunately for me, Fuentes had done his homework.

I heard a phone being dialed on speaker, but this time a male voice answered.

"Yeah?"

Fuentes didn't bother identifying himself, just barked out a single command.

"Report."

"The subject was moved to a private nursing facility four days ago. She continues to recover, albeit slowly. Something to do with an infection, most likely carried on the blade of the knife with which she was stabbed. There is some concern about her emotional state, but that is taking a backseat to the physical issues at the moment."

My blood ran cold at the word *she* and by the time the speaker had finished, I knew just who they were talking about.

Denise.

"And the shifter?" Fuentes asked.

I could feel his gaze upon me as he waited for the answer.

"Hasn't left her side since she arrived here."

"You have reasonable access?"

"Of course."

"Good," Fuentes replied, and I could hear the cruel anticipation in his voice as he followed that with, "Please terminate both subjects."

Terminate.

The word seemed to reverberate around and around inside my skull for what felt like an eternity. *Terminate. Terminate. Terminate . . .*

I had no idea if Fuentes had a man in New Orleans or not. Nor did I have any way of figuring that out in the next few seconds. For all I knew the guy on the other end of the line could really just be in the next room, coached with what to say when the time came.

But that was just the thing.

I didn't *know.*

Which was why where I thought he was really didn't matter; I had no choice but to comply with what Fuentes wanted. I couldn't risk it; if there was even a possibility that some asshole with a rifle was sitting outside her hospital ward waiting for an order like the one that had just been given . . .

I couldn't do it.

I *couldn't* take that chance.

"Yes, sir," said the voice on the phone. "Terminate order rece . . ."

"Wait!" I cried, and then without waiting for a response, I said, "I'll do it. You win."

"Sir?" asked the killer. "Is someone there with you, sir?"

Fuentes ignored the question. "I'm rescinding that order for now, Jackson. Stay with her and keep me apprised of any changes."

"Understood, sir," said the other man, and then they hung up.

Leaving me all but a slave to whatever it was that Fuentes wanted from me.

This was really turning out not to be my day.

7

Fuentes had my balls in a vise. He knew it and I knew it, so when he told Rivera that I was going to be staying there on the property with them and to find me a room, I didn't protest.

I wasn't going to find a way out of this mess by trying to avoid it. Instead, I intended to embrace it to the fullest, so when the opportunity came along to take care of this son-of-a-bitch without the chance of there being repercussions against Denise and Dmitri, I'd be ready to take it.

Having gotten what he'd wanted, Fuentes dismissed us. I fumbled my way out of the study behind Rivera. He couldn't be bothered to help lead me to the door and, truth be told, I wouldn't have accepted his help even if it had been offered, so it took me a few moments of trial and error before I managed it.

Rivera led me out of the room and, to my surprise, out of the house. We followed a path around to one side of the building to where, about a hundred yards later, we came to a stop. I heard a key being pushed into a lock and then the sound of a door opening.

"After you," Rivera said. "Watch yourself, there's one step before the door."

I followed his instructions and entered what I later learned was one in a series of little bungalow-like guest houses. As I stepped inside, I felt the door pulled closed behind me and heard the snick of the key in the lock.

The bastard locked me in!

In truth, I couldn't say I was surprised. I clearly wasn't here of my own accord and no matter how much it appeared that I was sufficiently cowed to do their bidding, that didn't mean I wasn't plotting escape or how I could throw a wrench into what was increasingly appearing to be a well-oiled machine. If they were betting that my actions in the car ride or at the motel, or even my demeanor at our little tête-à-tête, was typical of my behavior, they would be correct in that assumption.

Fuentes and, by extension, Rivera were apparently smart enough to realize that and weren't taking any chances with me at the moment.

The shades had been drawn over the windows in the front room, which was the first thing I had to be happy about in the past few hours. It is an interesting side effect of the ritual that I underwent to "see the unseen" during the search for my daughter that I can actually see better in complete darkness than most people can in broad daylight. I can no longer see colors—everything comes out in a thousand varying shades of gray—but at least I can see. The minute you put me in the light, however, everything goes dark. Direct sunlight is the equivalent of a complete whiteout for me; I can't even see the outline of my hand if I hold it directly in front of my face. All I see is white.

Electrical lights are almost as bad, though the use of a pair of strong UV sunglasses lets me see the vague shapes and outlines of things around me. Details are lost, of course; I wouldn't know the face of my own mother from that of a stranger, even up close, but I can tell the difference between a horse and a house.

Enough to make my way about with the help of a cane, at least. If I have to have light, then candlelight is best. The weaker the better.

The guest house wasn't all that big. Three rooms, really: a combination living area–kitchen–dining room that you stepped into as soon as you entered, followed by a bathroom with a toilet, sink, and shower stall, and then a bedroom at the back. The entire structure couldn't have been more than twenty, maybe twenty-five feet in length, and about twelve feet wide. In the bedroom I found a single bed, a chair to sit in, and a television cabinet, that was all. I walked across the room and discovered that the cabinet doubled as a dresser, for there were three drawers of men's clothing inside. The clothes smelled musty and didn't appear to have been moved in some time, as there was a fine layer of dust over all of them. Seeing them there made me wonder about their owner and what might have happened to him. My mind started coming up with all sorts of possibilities, none of them pleasant.

I walked over to the bed and sat down, trying to figure out what to do next.

Nothing all that enlightening occurred to me.

After a few minutes of enduring the silence, I decided it

might be a good idea if I had some company. I raised my face to the ceiling and extended my arms out to either side, palms up. Closing my eyes, I called out softly.

"Come to me, Whisper. Come to me."

I had a lot of questions I wanted answers to. Questions about what it was that Fuentes really wanted and just how far he would go to get it. Questions about what kind of threat he was to Denise and what she might do to protect herself from any retaliation that Fuentes might try to send her way.

And last but certainly not forgotten, a bit more clarity on just what the hell she'd been talking about that morning.

Who was coming? And when?

I repeated my request out into the ether, over and over again, until the room was suddenly filled with the sense that I was no longer alone.

In the darkness I turned to my left, expecting to see a cute dark-haired girl that reminded me so much of my daughter, only to discover that I was nose to nose with a big, hulking brute with a scarred face.

Scream.

His real name was Thomas Matthews, but I called him Scream because that's what he made you want to do: scream. Just looking at him could bring out that feeling in you. Imagine a face that is all harsh planes and sharp angles. Now, hollow out the cheeks and sink the eyes deep into their sockets. Add the gaping hole of a gunshot wound above the left eye and a shock of white hair atop the head and you'll have a close approximation of what Scream looks like to me when he graces me with his presence.

If Whisper was my angel, then Scream was my devil incarnate, all rage and mayhem bound up in human form. He was a giant of a man, even in death, towering over everything at just a hair above seven feet. His fists were like sledgehammers, his legs as thick as oaks, and he had the disposition of a junkyard bulldog that had been kicked one too many times and who now intends to take the leg off the next person that comes too close.

Scream has his own unique way of letting you know he is present, filling the space around him with a sense of fear, doubt, and apprehension that follows him like a cloud. Being in his general vicinity makes most people uncomfortable; being right beside him can make you literally sick with fear. I've never experienced it for myself, being one of the few who seem to be utterly immune, but I've been told that it is like living through all of your very worst fears at exactly the same moment, all the things that haunt your psyche in the deepest dark of the dead of night, the things that no matter how hard you try you can never seem to get away from.

The idea of introducing him to Fuentes made me smile.

It also made me wonder why he was here. I'd been calling Whisper, not Scream.

During the days that he'd been alive, Scream had been an auto mechanic in greater Chicago. He'd been found dead in his shop one night, a victim of an apparent robbery that occurred several months after his daughter, Abigail, had disappeared. The case was still officially open, with no suspects and with less than a snowball's chance in hell of ever getting solved the conventional way. But I knew the truth. Scream had been killed by Eldredge's doppelganger when he'd discovered the fetch's involvement in a string of murders spanning multiple states and more than a decade of time.

The very same murders, in fact, that the FBI had been try-ing to pin on me for several months now.

Whisper had shown up for the first time just a few days after I'd lost the ability to see in the sunlight. I still don't know what it was that had called her to me that first time, but I sus-pect I'll be forever grateful that she came in response to that call. She had been invaluable in helping me learn what had hap-pened to my daughter, Elizabeth. Her father, Scream, had joined us a few days later, and they'd been by my side ever since, through thick and thin.

Along the way the ghosts and I had discovered that we were bound together. When I need to, I can borrow Whisper's sight or Scream's strength. If my need is great enough, I can even borrow both at the same time. But, like my ghostsight, I don't use that ability too often. Linking with one of them leaves me exhausted. Linking with both usually ends with me lying un-conscious on the floor.

I wondered what Scream was doing here.

There was only one way to find out, I supposed.

"Hello, Thomas," I said.

Scream didn't reply, just stared at me with his usual dour expression.

I'll admit it, I was disappointed. Discovering Whisper could talk had gotten me hopeful that maybe Scream could do the same. In a way, he and I have far more in common than Whisper and I do. If there was ghost out there that I should understand and have an affinity for, it was Scream. We'd both lost our daughters to the machinations of the same evil sor-cerer and its murderous imp. We'd both pursued them to the ends of the earth—and in Scream's case, beyond into death—in order to seek justice for our loved ones. We'd both faced our failures, each in our own ways due to our unique circumstances, and striven to go on despite them.

"Not going to talk to me, huh?" I asked gently, not really expecting a reply, just talking to hear myself at that point.

Scream didn't say anything, but he did point solemnly over my shoulder.

I turned to face the door just in time to hear a key slide into the lock outside. I managed to look away and cover my eyes just in time.

The door opened, flooding the room with light from the hallway outside.

"What are you doing in the dark?" Grady asked, and then, right on the heels of that, "Are you alone?"

I tried to look innocent, not an easy feat I know, as I said, "Am I alone? Are you kidding me? Of course I'm alone."

"Then who the hell were you talking to just now?"

I shrugged, studiously ignoring Scream though I could still feel him standing there watching us.

I was waiting for Scream to start doing his thing, waiting for Grady to start feeling uncomfortable, but after a few minutes it was obvious that, like me, Grady didn't seem affected by his presence at all.

I was still pondering just why that was when Grady walked over and said, "Here." I felt him push a paper bag into my hands. The smell of food wafted out of it, and I realized that it had been some time since I'd eaten anything.

"Nothing special, a burger and fries, but I thought you might be hungry," he said.

I honestly didn't know what to say. Was this the same asshole who'd knocked me on my ass earlier?

Apparently, he wasn't finished.

"Rivera says that we're going to be working together for a time, so I figured it might be best if we called a truce."

I gave it a moment's consideration and then stuck out my hand.

"Sure. Truce."

We shook on it.

He turned and head for the door. "We have to hurry or we'll be late."

"Late for what?"

"Your first briefing as part of the crew."

I pulled my sunglasses out of my pocket and slipped them on my face. I moved cautiously because I didn't know the area yet, but it seemed to me that we retraced our steps and returned to the main building through the same door we'd exited from earlier. Instead of going to Fuentes's study, however, Grady explained that we would be meeting in a conference room on the second floor instead.

A glance behind and a quick switch to my ghostsight showed me that Scream was still with us; he'd dropped his corporeal form and was drifting along behind us on the other side of the Veil, there if I needed him but much less likely to be seen by any of Fuentes's human retainers this way. It was nice to know that I wasn't completely alone.

As we walked, Grady explained that the mansion we were in had once belonged to a famous silent movie director who had committed suicide when his star had decided to make the move to doing talkies in the late 1920s. Subsequent owners had continued to add to the initial structure, until they had the sprawling edifice Fuentes called home.

The place was enormous; I counted fifteen rooms alone

between the front door and the conference room and that was just on this floor alone. Fuentes could have housed a small army here, and I wondered if he wasn't doing that very thing. It would have been interesting to wander around for a while and see what I could see, especially when those who saw me would think I was blind, but there would be time enough for that later, I guessed. Right now I wanted to understand just what the hell it was that Fuentes expected me to do for him.

We arrived at the conference room to find it deserted, which gave us a chance to dim the lights a bit to accommodate me and to take our seats at the far end of the table where I could watch the door as the others came in.

It didn't take them long.

Demon Lady was first.

"Ilyana Verikoff," Grady told me in a low voice, providing the final name I'd been missing. To the unaided eye, Ilyana looked like a beautiful human woman in her mid to late twenties, but I knew demon blood ran through her veins and suspected that she was considerably older than she looked.

Like a few hundred years older.

She paused as she came in the door, her gaze falling first directly on me and then on something just over my shoulder. I knew Scream was standing there—I could feel his presence—but I didn't give any indication that I was aware of him in any way. When I didn't acknowledge her scrutiny of Scream or of myself, she let the matter drop without saying anything.

Score one for the good guys.

Perkins came in after Ilyana. Thanks to Grady I learned that his full name was Maximillian but that he preferred to be called Perkins or Max. I thought him to be a bit younger than

Rivera and Grady when they surprised me at the hotel, but now he looked to be easily older than both.

"Perkins is a human dowsing rod," Grady explained.

"A dowsing rod?"

Perkins overheard us and nodded that mop of red hair in our direction. "If you want something found, I'm your guy. That's how we found you, after all." He cackled and I had the distinct impression as he did so that somewhere along the way Perkins had gotten a few of his wires crossed. Maybe it was a result of his unique ability or maybe his ability was a result of his crossed wires, it was hard to tell and frankly, not all that important.

Interestingly, Perkins didn't seem to notice Scream in the way that Ilyana had, but of the three of them he was the one who seemed the most affected. He kept glancing over his shoulder as if afraid that someone was stalking him, and his twitches seemed to be more pronounced than earlier. Twice he stood to leave the room, as if under some kind of unspoken compulsion to get away from the place, only to sit back down again not quite understanding what had happened.

If those around me hadn't been so damned dangerous, I might have found it amusing.

So, demon, dowsing rod, ghost whisperer, and thief. An interesting combination, if I must say so myself. When you added Rivera's sorcery, you had a potent little group and one ripe for causing any manner of mischief.

"So did you do it?"

I turned to find Ilyana watching me, a look of challenge on her face.

"Do what?" I asked.

"Why, kill all those people, of course."

Her English was excellent, even with the slight accent.

Before I had a chance to answer, Rivera stuck his head in the room and said, "Come on. Time to go."

No one seemed surprised by the fact that we were already leaving before the meeting had even officially begun. No one except me, that is.

We quickly moved through the house, passing other groups of people engaged in other tasks, each of which gave us a wide berth the moment they caught sight of either Ilyana or Rivera. By the time we reached the ground floor there was a medium-sized cargo van waiting for us in front of the building.

It was only then that I realized the day had literally disappeared; the sun seemed to have set over an hour ago. I had either been unconscious for longer than I thought or I spent more time in that room alone than I realized.

Rivera climbed behind the wheel, Ilyana took shotgun and the rest of us climbed into the back. Within minutes we were driving away from the complex and headed into the heart of Los Angeles.

8

Of all the places I might have considered as a possible destination for our little outing, a church was not one of them.

Nor was it just any old church, for that matter. No, the Cathedral of Our Lady of the Angels was the largest Roman Catholic church in the entire city, as well as the official seat of the Archdiocese of Los Angeles. It had been designed to serve as both an emotional and physical representation of the might and power of the Vatican.

And we were here to break in.

At least, that was my guess. I couldn't imagine any other reason that a group like this would be visiting a church in the dead of night.

Rivera pulled to the curb while we were still a few hundred

yards away, but even I could see the outline of the twelve-story structure looming out of the night in the distance.

"Talk to me, Max," Rivera said.

The red-haired man leaned forward between the seats, gazing out at the building ahead of us. I could no longer see his face from where I sat, but I could imagine him licking his lips in anticipation of the challenge ahead of us.

"The Cathedral of Our Lady of the Angels," he said, with just the slightest hint of admiration in his tone. "Built in the late nineties. Meant to replace the Cathedral of Saint Vibiana as the older church had suffered extensive damage in the Northridge earthquake. The cathedral itself can hold three thousand people in a single seating. It is three hundred and thirty-three feet long, which is exactly one foot longer than St. Patrick's Cathedral in New York, and cost roughly $190 million by the time construction was finished in 2002."

I noticed Rivera shifting impatiently in the front seat. Max must have noticed as well, for he suddenly dropped the tour guide presentation and got right to the point.

"The relics of St. Vibiana were moved from the glass case above the altar in the old cathedral and reinterred in a marble casket in the mausoleum beneath the new building."

Rivera glanced back at him. "And you're certain what we are looking for is in there?"

Max nodded. "As best I can be, from this distance. Get me closer and I'll be able to take a better reading."

It wasn't the definitive response Rivera had been looking for, and he glared at the older man for a long moment as if that might change the answer. Max, however, stood his ground and gazed right back at him, seemingly unruffled by Rivera's unspoken threats. My respect for him went up a notch; Rivera was one scary dude and probably wouldn't take kindly to being led in the wrong direction, but what was Max going to do? Lie to him?

Not bloody likely. Not if he wanted to live afterward.

In the end, though, it was Rivera who looked away first.

After watching the building again for a few more minutes in silence, he asked, "Security?"

"Private firm paid for by the Vatican. Most nights it's just six men on a rotating foot patrol, ex-cops and former military personnel for the most part, but occasionally they're bolstered by a squad of Templars out of the local commandery."

Templars? As in Knights Templar?

I glanced over at Ilyana and mouthed the word *Templars* in her direction, but she just grinned that stupid "Wouldn't you like to know?" grin back at me and refused to say a word.

Bitch.

As Rivera pulled away from the curb, Max sat back in his seat. I tugged on his sleeve.

"Who the hell is St. Vibiana?" I whispered. I'll be the first to admit that I'd let my Catholic faith lapse years ago, but I didn't remember hearing that name in any of my catechism classes as a youth.

I felt him lean in close.

"Patron saint of Nobodies," he said.

I had the distinct sense he wasn't joking.

Leave it to the Catholic Church to cover all the bases.

Rivera drove past the building and around the corner to a maze of side streets. He made several turns and then pulled the van over at the edge of a local park.

"Everybody out."

Grady and Max produced small penlights and flipped them

on. Rivera then led us through the park and into a small copse of trees. It was even darker beneath the boughs, making it easier for me to see than it was for the others, and I found myself walking just behind Rivera as we neared the edge of the trees.

Ahead of us was the rear of the church.

He waited for the others to catch up and then checked his watch. Looking at Grady, he said, "The patrol comes by again in two and a half minutes. We need to be inside by then."

Grady grinned. "No problem."

Without another word he turned and dashed off across the lawn, headed for the rear of the church. The rest of us followed as quickly as we could.

As we drew closer I could see Grady crouched in front of a single door, using a set of picks to try to open the lock. He was working entirely by feel, his head turned away so he wouldn't be distracted by what he was seeing. His focus was total and he didn't even bother to glance up as the rest of us reached the door and gathered around him.

In the distance, I saw the gleam of a flashlight in the hands of the guard as he made his way toward us.

"Patrol's coming," I whispered, not wanting to distract Grady but knowing the rest of us were going to have to make a decision about what to do if he failed to get the door open in time.

Grady cursed quietly under his breath and redoubled his efforts.

The patrol drew closer, near enough that I could see the guard was carrying a firearm in addition to the flashlight.

"Come on, come on!" Rivera whispered.

Grady glanced at him, annoyed, and then gave his picks a quick little twist.

The door slid open without a sound.

We were in!

We piled through the entrance and pushed the door shut just as the flashlight outside slid across where we'd been standing moments before.

I held my breath, fully expecting the guard to notice something amiss and waiting for the hue and cry to go up at the discovery, but the night remained quiet and after a moment the patrol moved on as well.

I wasn't the only one to let out a deep breath of air.

The team worked like a well-oiled unit, and it was clear they had done this sort of thing together before. They waited for Perkins to get his bearings and then we headed in his wake. With the lights off inside the church it was like broad daylight for me, so I slipped the sunglasses off my face and put them away in my pocket as we moved into the sanctuary proper.

The church was gorgeous, if you were into that sort of thing. Intricately carved wooden statues, gilded trimmings, a gold-flecked railing surrounding the altar; the parish certainly had money to burn, it seemed. Flashlights were flipped on. Like a bloodhound on the scent, Max led us past the altar to a section of the rear wall that looked like one large wooden panel to me. He stared at it for a moment and then reached out and pressed a section of the decorative trim.

Nothing happened.

Perkins frowned, cocked his head to one side, and let his eyes glaze over.

The rest of us waited as patiently as we could.

A moment passed.

Then two.

Grady cleared his throat just as Perkins came back to himself.

"Of course," he said softly, then reached out and pushed the trim directly opposite where he'd tried before.

A six-foot section of the wall popped open to our left.

Behind it was a passage leading downward, beneath the altar.

Perkins smiled.

"After you," he said.

9

The stairs were narrow, so we went down them in single file. Max led the way and Ilyana brought up the rear, with the rest of us scattered haphazardly between them. I had Rivera in front of me, where I could keep an eye on him, and Grady at my back.

"What are we doing here, anyway?" I asked in a whisper just loud enough for either of them to hear me.

Neither of them said anything in response.

Apparently it was "Keep Hunt in the Dark" day.

Fine. So be it.

We continued downward and I counted thirty-nine steps before we reached the bottom. That put us about fifty feet below ground, and we all felt the cooler temperatures as soon as we stepped off the stairs.

The room spread out ahead of us and it was immediately obvious that we were in the church crypt; grottos had been carved into the walls and ossuaries of different shapes, sizes, and colors could be seen in many of them. There were dozens of sarcophagus-like tombs littering the floor as well.

Max headed out into the cavern, searching for what it was we had come there to find.

I tried again. "It might be helpful for me to know what we're supposed to be looking for."

Grady glanced in my direction and shrugged, as if to say it was out of his hands. The others simply ignored me, moving off in different directions as Perkins had, trying to cover as much ground as possible.

Okay, guess I'll have to figure it out on my own, I thought.

With this many tombs in here, I knew there'd be more than a soul or two hanging about, so I triggered my ghost-sight, thinking maybe I could learn something that way.

For a moment I couldn't believe what I was seeing.

The crypt was littered with ghosts.

I lost count after the first few dozen and simply stood there and stared for a moment. There were a lot of them, yes, but that wasn't what had me standing there in dumbfounded amazement; it was the fact that every single one of them was staring at one particular corner of the room. I turned in place, looking about, and it didn't matter which direction I faced, the end result was always the same; the dead were all looking in that direction.

Almost like statues, frozen in place.

What the hell?

I began to thread my way through the tombs, headed for the one on the far side of the room that had captured the attention of all of the ghosts. I'd never seen them act this way, and I have to admit I was growing more curious by the minute.

As I drew closer, I began to see that this particular sarcophagus was different from the others. Most had flat- or rounded-top stones, but this one had a full-sized figure of a man carved into its face. Most were of dark gray or brown stone; this one was fashioned of white marble with veins of rose running through it. Perhaps most significantly, all of the others were crammed into small plots, causing some of the large ones to overlap the smaller, yet this particular tomb was set aside from all the rest in a double-sized plot all its own.

I slipped between the other tombs and the ghosts themselves until I stood right next to the object of their obsession and looked down at what had captured their attention.

The figure on the lid of the sarcophagus was that of a knight, complete with chain armor, sword, and shield!

I stared at it for a long moment, nonplussed.

What the hell was a knight doing on the lid of a stone coffin built in the mid-1990s?

It was something I would expect to see on the tomb of a wealthy merchant or lord from the middle ages. Certainly not anything from the modern era.

Feeling a bit uncomfortable, I looked up and discovered that all of the ghosts had stopped staring at the coffin and were now staring at me.

The hair on the back of my neck stood at attention.

This was getting weirder by the minute.

I reached down and touched the sarcophagus.

Maybe in the back of my mind I was trying to prove it was real, I don't know. But the minute I laid my hand on that tomb all hell broke loose.

Literally.

The ground beneath my feet suddenly shook and the space next to the sarcophagus split open, vomiting forth a massive spectre.

Spirits come in a variety of types and sizes. At the bottom of the food chain are the haunts, spectral presences that are little more than whispers in the dark. You can sense their presence, but they don't have any kind of physical form. Next are your standard apparitions, ghostly presences that repeat the same motions over and over again, like memories caught in an endlessly repeating loop. A step above them are your actual ghosts, spiritual presences that are bound to our plane for one reason or another, unable or perhaps unwilling to move on. They're about as aware of us as we are of them and delight in showing themselves to us whenever they can.

Spectres, on the other hand, are ghosts that have gone in- sane and seek only to annoy, and sometimes to harm, the liv- ing. They are one of the few types of haunts, like their cousins the poltergeists, that can impact the physical world, and more than one ghost hunter has wound up on the other side of the Veil when they've tangled with a spectre that was more pow- erful than they expected.

This one had molded its body to resemble the knight lying atop the sarcophagus cover, and in its hands it held a sword and shield, both of which would most likely be as effective as their physical counterparts. It soared into the air above its tomb and hung there for a moment, eyeing those in the room with crazed hunger and a thirst for the living.

For a moment I thought about not doing anything.

The spectre was a hungry one and it would no doubt at- tack the strongest member of the party first. That would put

Rivera squarely in the spectre's crosshairs, and even I had to admit there was something altogether fitting about that.

But as much as I might like to see that happen, I couldn't let it. I'd learned through hard-won experience that a spectre absorbed the energy and power of its victims. If it defeated a sorcerer like Rivera, it would only get that much stronger and have more power to attack the rest of us. It had to be taken out cleanly or things were going to get worse.

The others were looking in my direction now as the spectre above me roared out a challenge. Rivera yelled something in reply, but I couldn't understand what he said, lost as it was in the echo of the spectre's cry.

I frantically dug out my harmonica and prepared to do battle.

There is a theory in certain circles that ghosts feed off the emotions of the living, that by doing so they can regain, at least for a little while, some of what they have left behind. I don't know if that's true or not. What I do know is that they react to my music like it's a drug of some kind, a balm to the soul that helps them ease the pain they're feeling at being stranded between this world and the next. It's commonly recognized that music can tame even the most wild of beasts, but it is less widely known that it also has the same power over ghosts. Find the right tune and, like the Pied Piper with the children of Hamlin, you can lead a ghost anywhere. Like a junkie that refuses to give up his fix, some ghosts will sit there for hours listening to me play, until they have exhausted all of the energy it takes for them to manifest and they fade away into nothingness.

I didn't think I could do that with a spectre as powerful as this one, but at least I might be able to hold it still long enough for the others to take some action against it.

I would normally spend a few moments listening to the sounds of the world around me, trying to get a feel for the place, to sink into the moment in such a way that the music just seemed to flow from it all. That was one of the tricks Denise Clearwater had taught me, and when I used it I always found it much easier to do what needed to be done.

This time around, I didn't have time for any of that. As the spectre swooped down toward me, I jammed my harp into my mouth and blew.

10

The spectre let out a bloodthirsty shriek of outrage and dove toward me, its body morphing as it came. Its hands grew larger and more elongated, its fingers turning into nasty-looking claws designed to rend and tear, eager for my flesh, while its mouth filled with multiple rows of teeth that looked razor sharp. The front half of its body began to grow more solid as it concentrated its energy there, leaving the rear half to trail off into thin wisps of ectoplasmic material that flickered behind it like a roaring flame.

I cut loose with an old blues riff on my harp—an odd, syncopated little bit designed to disrupt and distract the spectre, to snare it in a web of unexpected notes and rhythms—but I might as well have been whistling Dixie for all the good it did me.

The spectre closed a third of the distance between us in an eye blink, flickering and reappearing like images from a stop-motion film flashed upon a screen, moving closer with each new appearance.

It looked at me, its eyes burning with unholy rage, and shrieked in fury before vanishing again.

I slid from the blues to a folk tune I'd heard in my youth, a gay little affair that skipped along with its own unique beat, but that had no effect on the creature either. By now it had closed two thirds of the distance between us and I had one last shot to get it right . . .

I closed my eyes, reached for the song in my heart . . . and wailed out something that sounded to me like a cat being strangled inside a set of bagpipes.

The spectre flashed into view, right on top of me, and opened its mouth wide, displaying all those rows of glistening sharp teeth.

But this time I'd hit the mark and the spectre was a split second too late. My music had it and wouldn't let go.

The spectre hung there, its face inches from my own, its body flaring out behind it as if blown by a great wind. It shrieked repeatedly at me, trying to break my concentration, for doing so would leave it free to gnaw my face off.

I, understandably, was doing my best not to let that happen.

The music flowed out of me, the notes binding the spectre in midair as effectively as leg irons and chains once bound prisoners. As long as I continued to play, the spectre was forced to listen and, in listening, was trapped by the flow of the music around it.

I could hear the others moving about, but I couldn't see

what they were doing and didn't dare turn around to find out. I could feel the spectre pushing back against the hold my music had upon it and I knew that it wouldn't take much for it to tear itself free should I falter on even the slightest note. This close, there was no way I'd be able to regain the proper melody before it would be upon me, and once that happened it was all over but the dying.

Someone stepped in close behind me. The way my skin pimpled in gooseflesh at the other's proximity made me think it was Ilyana.

I kept playing, trying not to think about how I was now sandwiched between two creatures that would just as soon devour me as give me the time of day, and was shifting into a new refrain when a set of long-nailed fingers began playing with the hair at the nape of my neck.

What the hell?

I tried to shake her off by hunching my shoulders and moving my head slightly, but without success. I wouldn't have minded freeing the spectre to dine on the others, but the fact that I'd be the first snack on the menu kept me from indulging my more ruthless daydreams.

The spectre seemed to inch forward slightly—or was that my imagination? I wasn't certain. I tried to banish Ilyana from my mind and concentrate.

Why weren't the rest of them doing something?

Ilyana dragged a single fingernail down the back of my neck and then took her hand away.

Finally! Maybe now I'll . . .

A hand reached out and grabbed my ass.

That did it. The harp came away from my lips in startled

surprise, the song faltered, and the spectre surged forward past the invisible bonds of my rapidly fading music with a triumphant shriek.

I was done for; I knew it as surely as I knew my own name.

But at the last second I was shoved aside, clearing the way for Ilyana to step into the space I'd been standing in a microsecond before.

I hit the ground hard, the wind knocked briefly out of me, but my instincts for self-preservation were so finely honed that I was turning to look back where I'd been standing in an effort to keep my eyes on the spectre. I was just in time to watch Ilyana's jaw come unhinged somehow and her face stretch impossibly wide as she sucked that spectre right into her mouth and down her throat.

Her neck bulged and her eyes flared red as the spectre seemed to get stuck about halfway down her throat, but she gulped a couple of times, working her throat muscles in conjunction with some help from her fingers, and the last little bits of spectral energy disappeared in a flash.

For a moment she stood there, her head tipped back, an expression on her face so close to sexual satisfaction that I would have sworn that's what it was if I hadn't just seen her swallow a spectre whole, and then she looked over at me with heavily lidded eyes and licked her lips.

"Ummmm," she said. "Tasty."

Behind me, Rivera laughed.

I was so going to kill all of them as soon as I got the chance.

With the spectre defeated, I expected the others to resume their search, but apparently there was no longer any need. Rivera and Grady moved directly to the sarcophagus from which the spectre had erupted, indicating by default that it had been the one they'd been searching for all along.

Grady took a pair of pry bars out of the canvas duffel he was carrying and handed one to Rivera. They positioned themselves along the same side of the sarcophagus, one at either end, and then wedged the tips of their pry bars into the crack where the lid met the side of the stone coffin. Each squatted down to get one shoulder under his pry bar, and then on the count of three they stood up straight, forcing the bars up with them as they went. There was a sharp crack as the seal holding the lid in place was broken and the heavy stone slab slid a few inches in the opposite direction. They repositioned the pry bars, this time using the edge of the sarcophagus as a brace, and repeated the process. The lid slid over to the edge with a grinding sound and tipped over the other side, slamming to the ground with a loud crash.

Wordlessly, the rest of us gathered round and looked inside.

The physical world appeared faint through the lens of my ghostsight, but it was enough. The body in the coffin had clearly been there for a long time. The desiccated flesh was stretched tight over bones clad in linen burial robes of a type I'd never seen before. If it hadn't been for the wide shoulders and substantial pelvic area of the skeleton, I might have assumed it was a woman buried there, given the robes.

The corpse's hands were crossed over the hilt of a sword that rested on its chest, the blade extending downward toward his feet. I was certainly no expert on edged weaponry, but it looked like an English long sword to me, given the length and narrowness of the blade. There was a word inscribed on the blade, but there was too much dust for me to read it.

"Get rid of that," Rivera said and Grady reached in, grabbed the front of the corpse's burial garment, and heaved the corpse out of the coffin, dumping it unceremoniously to the side. The sword popped free and clattered across the stone floor.

I bent to retrieve it, but caught the look Rivera flashed in my direction and decided perhaps that wouldn't be the best idea after all. I stood up slowly, holding my hands up to show I hadn't meant to try any funny business.

Perhaps recognizing that I needed something to do, Rivera said, "You're on overwatch. Make sure nothing else, human or otherwise, tries to sneak up on us while we're doing this."

"Doing what?" I wanted to ask, but I let it go, knowing they weren't going to give me an answer. I'd learn more just by watching.

Ilyana reached into the coffin and picked something up. I didn't realize what it was until she started tossing it back and forth from one hand to the other. The eye sockets seemed to stare at me in silent accusation as the skull bounced from palm to palm.

I looked up, caught her watching me with that sly little gaze of hers, and in my mind's eye I watched again as her jaw came unhinged and she swallowed a rampaging spectre like it was a piece of Halloween candy. I shuddered and turned away, doing my best to ignore Ilyana's little bark of amusement as I did so.

My ghostsight let me see that we were truly alone for the first time since we'd arrived; the horde of ghosts that had been watching us appeared to have fled. For once I wasn't afraid to keep my ghostsight activated; anything that came looking for trouble would find Ilyana waiting instead. Given what she'd done with the spectre, I didn't think she'd have much difficulty handling anything short of a major demon or two.

Even then, I might have bet on her.

The ghosts that had been watching us prior to the spectre's arrival had vanished and there didn't seem to be anything else down here with us, supernatural or otherwise, leaving me with little to watch on "overwatch" other than my companions.

After removing the body and dumping it to one side, Rivera and Grady began methodically going over the interior of the stone coffin, inch by inch. They ran their hands across the stone, knocked on it with their knuckles, tried to push and pull in various place, all without success. Whatever they were looking for, it just didn't seem to be there.

At last, frustrated, Rivera called Perkins over.

"Where is it?" the mage asked, his accent more prominent when he was irritated.

Perkins smiled and held out a hand, palm up.

"Twenty bucks, wasn't it?"

Rivera didn't say anything, and after a moment or two of continued silence, Perkins's smile slowly faded and his hand fell back to his side. Without even bothering to look in that direction, Perkins pointed over his shoulder at the body dumped so carelessly on the floor just a few moments before.

"The sword."

Grady frowned. "You have got to be kidding me."

"Do I look like I'm kidding?" Perkins asked.

"Yes," Grady snapped back, as he walked over to the remains of the coffin's former tenant. "You always look like you're kidding, which is why I'm always calling you a big joke. See how that works?"

Perkins gave him the finger but didn't say anything.

One thing was for sure: there certainly wasn't any love lost between any of my companions. I filed that little fact away with the others I'd picked up over the last day or two. Who knew when something I'd picked up along the way might come in handy?

Grady kicked the bones out of the way, picked up the sword, and carried it back to the others. Perkins reached for it, but Rivera took it from Grady instead.

With Ilyana and me looking on from a distance, Rivera carefully examined the sword. His attention quickly settled on the hilt of the weapon and, more specifically, on the crossguard itself.

As he focused on it, so did I. When seen through the unique filter of my ghostsight, it was less a piece of metal and more a twisting, turning length of living darkness.

I was utterly unsurprised to see the vulpine smile that crossed his face when he gave the crossguard a quick yank and it came free in his hands.

11

The next couple of days passed without incident. Fuentes was so completely confident that his threat against my friends would keep me docile and obedient that I was free to come and go at will as long as I left word where I would be and a cell number at which I could be reached. When I admitted to Fuentes that I didn't even own a cell phone, he had one of his men get me one.

The thing was, I didn't really *have* anywhere to go. The few items I considered my possessions had been picked up from the motel and delivered to Fuentes's compound while we had been at the church. I returned from our "mission" to find my things in a brown paper bag in the middle of my bed. A note inside the bag informed me that the bill at the motel had been settled.

With the motel bill taken care of, I lost just about my only excuse to be out anyway. Living as a fugitive with the FBI on my trail made me naturally wary of being seen in public. The average person on the street might go unnoticed, but a blind guy with a cane always draws someone's attention. The quirks of my condition make it easier for me to slip out at night, but even that was problematic; people tend to remember the guy wearing sunglasses after dark.

In the end, though, the thing that kept me hanging around with little to do was the simple fact that Fuentes was right. I wouldn't do anything to put my friends in danger. I might be a total jerk to most people—I'm well aware that I'm generally what those with sunnier dispositions like to call abrasive—but I will literally go to hell and back to help those who have earned my trust and compassion. Fuentes's threat against my friends might not be real, but I couldn't take the chance that it wasn't. Which, when considered dispassionately, was the real beauty of the trap Fuentes had sprung. My conscience would keep me in line far more effectively than anything Fuentes's people, including Rivera, might do.

I spent the time hanging around the estate, getting to know some of the staff and trying to learn more about Grady, Perkins, and the others. The latter was difficult; while the staff was more than happy to talk about themselves, they were far more reluctant to talk about those they considered to be "Señor Fuentes's friends," and they clammed up tight if I pressed them for more information. I knew I should be thankful—as one of those so-called "friends" myself, their code of silence kept my identity and location secret from anyone who might come asking after me as well—but it was frustrating just the same. I had pretty much given up hope of discovering anything when an unexpected source all but dropped into my lap.

I was in the basement pool room, shooting a game of nineball by myself in the dark, when the door opened suddenly behind me, spilling light into the room and chasing my sight away with it.

I stood up from over the table and turned toward the door. I could sense someone there, even if I couldn't see them. "Hello?"

"I'm sorry," said a voice that I recognized as Perkins's. "I didn't know anyone was in here."

I shrugged. "No problem."

I could practically hear the gears turning in his head as he took in the pool cue in my hand and the balls scattered around the tabletop.

"You're . . . playing pool?" he finally asked.

"No, tiddly-winks," I almost said, but managed to bite my tongue just before the words left my mouth. Compared to the way the rest of those in our little group treated me, Perkins was being downright friendly. If I was going to survive this mess, I needed a lot more information about what was going on than I had right now and the only way I was going to get it was to get someone to talk to me. Perkins seemed genuinely curious about my condition and it made sense to play along, to see what he might give in return. So instead of giving him grief with a smart-ass remark and driving him off, I answered with a simple yes instead.

"But . . . I thought you were blind."

"I am."

"So how . . ."

I held a finger over my lips and whispered, "Shhh. Ancient Chinese secret."

The silence that followed told me he'd missed the joke entirely.

"Oh for heaven's sake, Perkins, lighten up. It's no secret, I was just kidding. Come in and sit down. I'll tell you if you really want to know."

I didn't think he was going to do it, but his curiosity must have gotten the better of him for he hesitated only a moment before doing as I'd asked. He closed the door behind him, and my eyesight returned at the same moment the darkness did.

I glanced at the table, called out a combo, and sank the shot without much effort. College had been expensive, and I'd hustled a lot of pool in my younger days to help pay the bills. Once learned, some skills just don't ever leave you. I could throw a mean game of darts too.

My prowess at nine-ball was lost on my audience though; I might be able to see in the dark, but that didn't mean he could. With a sigh I put the cue down on the table and said, "Light switch is there by your left hand . . ."

It took a moment of fumbling for him to find it and by then I had my sunglasses on, covering my eyes. The glasses weren't strong enough to preserve my vision once the lights came back on, but they weren't for me anyway. I'd learned long ago that the milky whiteness of my eyeballs and the scar tissue that surrounded them made a lot of people uncomfortable, and I didn't want to chase Perkins away before we had the chance to talk.

I pulled a stool out from under the bar that ran the length of the wall next to the pool table and settled onto it. A moment later I heard him do the same.

I knew I was going to have to give some in order to get some, so I figured it was time to lay some cards on the table and see what happened.

"I know it's hard to believe, but once upon a time I was a professor at Harvard University . . ."

I gave him the abbreviated version, hitting only the highlights and ignoring the long, deep valleys between. My daughter's disappearance. The botched police investigation that followed. My own, increasingly desperate, attempts to figure out what had happened to Elizabeth, followed by my long fall from grace. The loss of my job. The loss of my wife. And finally that fateful meeting with the Preacher in the park.

"The ritual was supposed to let me see the unseen, which, from my perspective, meant my missing daughter, but apparently I didn't read the fine print well enough," I said with a bitter little laugh. Even after all this time, I was still angry at myself for not thinking through the bargain that had been placed in front of me. I'd read *Faust*; I knew a devil's deal when I saw one. And yet when the devil in question, the Preacher, had offered another deal in New Orleans, I'd jumped at that one too.

Apparently I'm not as smart as I think I am.

"The ritual stole my normal sight and replaced it with the ability to see the true face of things, from the ghosts that drift among us to the darker, hungrier things that move in the shadows. And just to be certain that I wouldn't miss out on any of the horrors lurking out there, it gave me the ability to see in the dark as clearly as most people see in the light."

Perkins hadn't said a word since I'd started my little soliloquy, and since I couldn't see the expression on his face, I had no idea what he was thinking. Still, I'd come this far and there was little to be gained by stopping now.

"So how'd you get mixed up in all this?" I asked. I thought it was a fairly innocuous question, more of an icebreaker kind of thing than anything else, but I felt his tension level shoot up just the same.

"What do you mean 'all this'?" he asked.

I knew I wouldn't get anywhere by playing coy, so I just decided to lay it out there. "You know what I mean," I told him. "All this—Fuentes and Rivera and what's-her-name, you know, Demon Lady?"

I thought I heard him choke on that last one, but pretended not to notice as I continued.

"I'm sorry, but you don't strike me as a hard-liner like any of the others. Even Grady is in a class above you when it comes to old-fashioned grit and meanness. He fits in with the rest of them; you don't. So what's your story? How'd you end up here? With them?"

He was quiet for such a long time that I thought he wasn't going to answer me, but eventually he spoke up.

"I wasn't always this way," he began, and I knew by his tone that he was talking about his ability to pinpoint an object with just his thoughts. "Had a normal childhood. Or at least as normal a childhood as one can have when you're dirt poor and living on the wrong side of the tracks in Bentonville, Nebraska."

Nebraska? Ugh.

"We didn't have much, so I started working at fourteen and didn't stop until the accident when I was twenty-five."

He went quiet again, so after a few minutes, I prompted him.

"The accident?"

"It was winter. I was late coming home from work one night and my truck broke down on Route 23. I was a good five, six miles from home if I stuck to the road and went the long way round, but only a mile, maybe a mile and a half if I cut across the fields. I knew going that way meant I had to cross the ass-end of Lake Jessup, but it had been below freezing for so many days that I didn't think it would be a problem."

He sighed. "Shows what I know. I was almost to the other side when I felt the ice beneath my feet start to crack. I knew I was in trouble—I still had a good fifteen, maybe twenty feet to go—but I gave it my best anyway, scrambling for the bank as fast as I could go. Almost made it, but almost wasn't good enough. My feet were still kicking when I slid beneath the water.

"Next thing I knew I was waking up in a hospital bed somewhere in Lincoln, which was more than a hundred miles from where I'd gone under the ice. Folks there told me I'd been in a coma for six months. A miracle, they called it."

From the tone of his voice, he thought it was anything but.

"It wasn't long after that when I started getting the feelings, that sense where something was. I'd be in a room with a bunch of people and one of them would say something about an item they'd misplaced. Just like that," he snapped his fingers to show what he meant, "I'd know where it was. If I'd never met that person before or had never been to their house, I could still describe exactly where the item was.

"I was this human dowsing rod. Ask me where something was, picture that something in your head, and I could find it for you.

"Didn't matter what it was. Misplaced cell phone. Missing jewelry. Well water in the backyard. The family heirloom you'd tucked away for safekeeping and then promptly forgotten what you'd done with it.

"I was scared at first, not sure how to handle things, but eventually I came to see that I had a gift, a gift that could be used to help people. Namely, me.

"So I went to Vegas."

I knew what he was going to say at that point—the details might differ a bit, but the essential story was going to be the same, I just knew it—but I kept my mouth shut and let him talk. He was on a roll, after all.

"I thought I'd go in, make a killing, and get out again. All I had to do was 'find' the winning hand. But that turned out to be a lot harder than it looked. You can't find the winning hand in a room full of card players with multiple games going on. The same held true of the baccarat and roulette and poker. There were just too many games, too many distractions. I'd pick a winning hand only to find I was at the wrong table. Or I'd find the right number, but it would be the wrong color. It seemed I couldn't work with more than one variable at a time."

Talk about frustrating, I thought.

"Furious, angry with myself that I had this supposedly amazing power and couldn't even use it to help myself, I left the casino, caught the first bus I came to, and ended up in L.A.

"I saw a sign in the bus station for the local horse track and figured what the hell. I only had a few bucks left in my pocket; I was going to be out on the street the next day anyway, so why not give it one last shot?"

He fell silent for a minute, and then, "Did you know they bring the horses out before the race to this little grassy section on the side of the track?"

I didn't and told him so.

"Yeah, they do. Like five minutes before the race starts the jockeys lead the horses out of the stables and over to this grassy area where they stand around for a few minutes, waiting to be let onto the track. With the right kind of ticket you can go down there and get a good look at the horses, right up close, ya know? That's all it took. My hands started tingling and I knew right away which horse was going to win. I went up to the window and, with something like ten seconds to spare, I bet everything I had on that horse.

"Turns out he was the long shot and paid 30 to 1. I waited a few races and then did it again. By the time I left the track that day, I had ten thousand dollars in my pocket and a smile on my face as wide as a Buick."

Being able to pick the winning horse every time? That was a far more useful skill than the one I'd been blessed with.

Perkins didn't think so.

"I got greedy. Won too many races."

I could see where this was going. "Which brought you to the attention of track security."

"Track security?" He laughed. "Hardly. Even if they'd been on to me, which they weren't, they wouldn't have been able to figure out how I was doing it."

That left only one option.

"It brought you to Fuentes's attention."

"Exactly. Turns out he owned the track and offered me a deal. Come work for him or pay back all the money I'd 'stolen' by using my powers to win the races."

Sounded familiar. "Why didn't you just pay it back?"

I could almost hear him shrug. "Couldn't. I'd already spent most of it."

Even knowing I'd been shanghaied in similar fashion, I still felt bad for the guy.

"I'm not the only one, you know," he said.

"Only one what?"

"Tricked into working for Fuentes. Rumor is that Grady and Verikoff had to face choices of their own."

Now that was interesting.

"How do you know?"

Before he had a chance to answer, the door behind him opened and Grady's voice filled the room.

"Let's go, ladies. We've got a job to do."

12

We piled into the Charger just as we had the other night, except this time it was Rivera behind the wheel instead of Perkins. Grady rode shotgun while I was sandwiched between Ilyana and Perkins in the backseat.

No sooner had I sat down than Grady leaned over the front seat and handed me a pair of sunglasses. I tried to give them back, saying, "Thanks but I already have a pair."

He, however, refused to take them.

"I know you do, Princess, but trust me, you want these. Just put them on over your others."

Over the other pair? For all I knew he was trying to help me win the worst-dressed award for the evening, but something in the tone of his voice made me decide to trust him. Heaven only knows why. I opened up the earpieces and slipped the glasses on over the pair I was already wearing, just as he'd suggested. To my surprise, the outer pair fit quite neatly over the inner pair and even had extensions on the sides of each lens to cover my peripheral vision.

With the glasses on, I cautiously opened my eyes.

Instead of being drowned in a sea of white, I could see!

Not well, and certainly not with any detail, but the combination of the two pairs of sunglasses allowed me to see the sketchy shapes of the things around me, similar to the way in which I can see the real world, like a faint negative of the spirit one I can see while using my ghostsight.

My surprise must have shown on my face for I heard Grady grunt with satisfaction.

From the seat beside me, Perkins asked, "What are they, Grady?"

"Prescription sunglasses made especially for glaucoma patients. Extreme UV protection and some of the darkest polarization you can find. I thought Hunt might be a bit more useful if he had some idea of what was going on."

Amen to that, I thought.

We drove for about a half hour and then left the smoothness of the highway behind, exchanging it for the rugged bumps and potholes that dotted the back road we'd turned onto like lumps on a measles patient. Fifteen minutes later we slowed to a stop. Grady got out of the car and disappeared from view ahead of us.

"What's going on?" I asked, not really expecting a response.

To my surprise, Verikoff answered.

"There's a chain blocking the way. Grady is dealing with it."

It didn't take him long; just a few moments later the door

reopened and he slipped back inside. "'Bout a hundred yards up on the right," he said.

Rivera drove us forward, the tires crunching over dirt and gravel, and then he brought the car to a stop. The engine idled for a moment and then stopped.

We'd reached our destination.

As we all got out of the car, Rivera said something beneath his breath in his native tongue. I'll be the first to admit my Spanish isn't all that great, but it sounded to me like he said *"Madre de Dios, protégenos y sálvanos,"* which roughly translates into English as, "Mother of God, protect and save us."

From what? I wondered.

That's when I felt them.

Ghosts surrounded us, their attention like a physical weight on my neck and shoulders, heavier than anything I'd ever experienced before. Curious, I took my sunglasses off, both pairs, and slipped them into my pocket before I mentally reached into the back of my head and flipped the switch that activated my ghostsight.

What I saw made me gasp in surprise.

The car was parked at the end of a long drive. Ahead of us was a massive Spanish-style villa that sprawled across the land on which it had been built, like a fat spider sitting patiently in its web, waiting for its prey to wander into its trap. The house had been the victim of a fire at some point in the past; one wing was partially collapsed, the brick and tile twisted and warped by the heat of the flames and still covered with the soot that the fire had left behind. No effort had been made to repair the damage; judging from the look of things, that side of the house had been open to the elements for some time, perhaps even since the immediate aftermath of the blaze.

It did not feel empty, however. Abandoned, yes, maybe even forgotten, but not empty. Something lurked there, behind the darkened windows and closed doors, something dark and malevolent that suffused the entire structure with a miasma so thick that it felt as if the house was going to reach out and drag you down into its depths before you had the good sense to turn and run.

But as uncomfortable and strange as the house appeared, it was the presence of the ghosts that surrounded it that made me stiffen in surprise. Not since the Angeu had amassed his army of wraiths on the outskirts of New Orleans to invade the world of the living had I seen this many ghosts assembled in one place. They surrounded the house, staring in our direction, their attention concentrated on us with the kind of unblinking focus that only the dead can manage.

For a moment I was struck with such an overwhelming sense of hatred and malice that I literally staggered beneath the weight of it, my knees buckling, and only my grip on the frame of the open car door kept me from collapsing to the ground. Then, just as quickly as it had come, that psychic assault dissipated as the ghosts turned their attention away from us and focused once more upon the house that they had no doubt been watching prior to our arrival.

"You all right?" Perkins asked at my elbow, and it took me a moment to find my voice.

"Yeah. What is this place?"

"Lovely, isn't it? Once upon a time, it was the home of man named Glenn Wagner. Perhaps you've heard of him?"

Who hadn't? Wagner was perhaps the most notorious mass murderer since Jeffrey Dahmer in the late '80s. Selecting his victims from the film that was brought in to be developed at the local photo processing store where he worked, Wagner had murdered twenty-nine men, women, and children before he was caught eight years ago. The first attempt to convict him for the crimes ended in a mistrial when a member of the jury slipped out of the hotel where they were being sequestered to give an exclusive interview to a local reporter. Despite the fact that the rate of acquittals rises precipitously for second trials, Wagner was still convicted of twenty-three of the twenty-nine murders for which he was charged. He'd been sent to Sing Sing to serve a 165-year sentence with no chance of parole, only to be beaten to death by a fellow inmate a year later when Wagner had refused to pass the salt during the evening meal.

The investigation, trial, and subsequent murder of the murderer himself had been national news for months on end. There probably wasn't an adult over the age of twenty-one in this country who hadn't heard of Glenn Wagner, myself included.

"Yeah, I've heard of him," I said dryly. Then, "What the hell are we doing here?"

I could almost hear Perkins shrug as he said, "Looking for another piece of the Key, would be my guess, though you'd have to ask Rivera to be sure."

"The Key?" I asked. I had no idea what Perkins was talking about. *What key?*

The answer to my question, however, would have to wait. Verikoff appeared at my elbow, interrupting my exchange with Perkins.

"Stay close once we're inside," she told me. "If you wander off I can't protect you."

"Protect me from what?" I wanted to know, but she walked off without answering, following Grady and Rivera as they headed toward the front door. The ghosts parted before them, but only Verikoff seemed to know they were there. While the others walked blithely forward, oblivious, she turned and snarled at the closest bunch of spirits, causing them to pull back enough to give Rivera and his party room to pass.

"Don't know about you, but I'm not staying out here alone," Perkins said to me and hurried to catch up with the others, leaving me standing there next to the car on my own.

"You have got to be freakin' kidding me," I muttered, as I did the same.

The lodestone around my neck generally worked to keep ghosts at bay, but I still shoved my hand in my pocket and kept it wrapped around my harmonica as I passed through the throng, ready to pull it out and play at the first sign the spirits were getting restless. To my surprise, however, the ghosts left us alone, and soon we were all standing in front of the door, waiting, as Rivera reached out and tried the handle.

The door swung open with a loud creak.

I chuckled. I couldn't help it; it was such a horror-film cliché that it struck me as wildly funny.

Apparently no one else shared my sense of humor.

Verikoff leaned in close, near enough that I could feel her breath hot in my ear. "Personally, I don't care what happens to you, but Fuentes seems to think you'll be useful, so shut up, follow orders, and maybe you'll get out of this alive."

As pep talks go, it totally sucked, but I managed to stuff my quirky sense of humor back down into the back of my brain and focus on what was ahead of us.

We stepped through the door and entered the house.

I imagine there wasn't much for the others to see, just an empty foyer devoid of furniture. With no living relatives to claim Wagner's belongings, the state had confiscated everything he had owned. I suspected that had more to do with not wanting pieces of his furniture to start showing up on eBay than any real need on the part of the state, but the end result was the same: Wagner's prior home was nothing more than an empty shell.

To me, however, the place was far from empty. Ghostsight allows me to see the true nature of things, and the inside of Wagner's home was certainly no exception. What appeared to be an empty foyer in the real world was draped in thick cobwebs of horror, desperation, and decay. The emotions hung about the place, pulsing with intensity, no doubt fed by the presence of the ghosts hanging around outside, full of regret and hot with the need for vengeance and justification. My skin crawled at the sight of all that pain and fear given material form and I did my best not to let anything touch my flesh.

As we moved farther into the house, I expected the ghosts to crowd in behind us, but, to my surprise, they remained outside the building entirely.

Now it didn't take much mental effort to realize that the ghosts were most likely the spirits of those whom Wagner had murdered. Similarly, it wasn't hard to figure out that the state had missed quite a few of his victims, dozens, in fact, if the first conclusion was correct and each and every ghost represented one of those murdered victims. Ghosts often congregate at physical locations that were particularly important to them during their lifetimes; the house in which they were murdered would certainly qualify. But I'd never known them to avoid entering such a place. If anything, they'd be more apt to be found there than anywhere else.

So what was going on here?

These thoughts were still on my mind as Rivera turned to Perkins and said, "Find him."

13

Perkins stepped forward and stood in the center of the room. Letting his arms hang loosely at his sides, he bowed his head and began to breathe slowly and deeply. Through the lens of my ghostsight, I could see his hands begin to glow, faintly at first and then with greater intensity until a pale blue light surrounded them completely.

With his eyes still closed, Perkins lifted his head and brought his hands up in front of him. The energy wafted out from his fingertips and drifted through the air like the tendrils of some alien creature, seeking, searching, looking for whatever it was that he needed to find. I watched those questing tendrils of power lazily stream outward and begin sliding across the walls, floor, and ceiling around us as if they had minds of their own, poking and prodding every little nook and cranny they discovered along the way.

Ilyana turned her head to watch as one of them drifted past where she stood and I knew that she, too, could see them. I suspected Rivera could as well, but he was watching the room around us, his body tight with tension, as if he were waiting for something to explode out of the walls around us and attack. It was a far cry from the cavalier attitude he'd had in the necropolis beneath the church the other night, and I wondered what he knew about this place that had him so on edge.

Just then the energy snapped back into Perkins's body, rocking him on his feet and pulling my attention away from our glorious leader. As Perkins opened his eyes, I saw with my ghostsight that they were full of fear. Whatever it was that he had seen through the guise of his power, it wasn't all sunshine and roses.

"The basement," he said quietly. "He's in the basement."

Rivera nodded, turned and headed for the kitchen and, presumably, the door to the lower level at the back of that room.

I stepped over to Perkins, asked if he was all right, noting as I did that the energy that had surrounded him just seconds before had all but vanished. Only the faintest aura still remained, surrounding his fingers like a halo. I could see his hands were shaking, and when he looked at me I knew the trembling was from fear rather than exertion.

"It's really him, Hunt. That evil son-of-a-bitch isn't dead at all. He's right here, waiting for us."

"Who? Who's waiting for us?"

But Perkins just shook his head and hurried to catch up with the others.

I was liking this little excursion less and less by the minute.

By the time I caught up with the others they were gathered in front of an open door on the far side of the kitchen, staring at the stairs leading downward into darkness.

Rivera cast an impatient glance my way but didn't say anything. Instead, he raised a hand and said a few words in what sounded like Latin. A red globe of sorcerous energy about the size of a basketball sprang to life in his hand. With another whispered phrase, this time in a language I didn't recognize, he sent it drifting down the stairs ahead of us, lighting the way.

My head was starting to pound from using my ghostsight and I was beginning to grow concerned about just what its use might attract in this place, so, reluctantly, I let it go. In the presence of that light coming from Rivera's sorcery, I expected to find myself lost in my own personal whiteout, but to my surprise that didn't happen. In fact, the light didn't bother me at all; I could see just as well as if I'd been standing in complete darkness.

I was still pondering the ramifications of this when we reached the bottom of the stairs. With a flick of his wrist, Rivera sent the ball of energy drifting toward the ceiling to hover over the center of the room, casting its light about the space around us and revealing that we stood in an unfinished basement. Cement floors and walls greeted us, with the exception of a gaping hole in the floor in the far corner of the room.

Rivera glanced at Perkins, who inclined his head toward the hole.

Beside me, Grady reached beneath his shirt and removed a large, semiautomatic pistol from where he'd been carrying it at the small of his back. He released and reseated the magazine, more likely out of nervousness than any real need to do such a thing, and then chambered a round.

The click of the slide was loud in the empty room.

Ilyana was making her own preparations as well. Hers were more subtle though; I didn't notice anything outright, but when I looked in her direction she seemed more predatory than she had moments before. Her head seemed to jut forward farther on her neck, like a bird of prey's, and for just an instant I thought I saw blackened, tattered wings spread out behind her like a bat's. She licked her lips and looked around, focusing on the hole that I'd seen when we'd first descended the stairs.

We moved in that direction.

As we drew closer I could see faded outlines of human forms drawn on the floor and back wall near the excavated area in white police tape. I remembered the corpses that had been found stacked in the basement of the Wagner house in the early days of the investigation, and how several dozen more had been found buried in a mass grave in the basement of his home. I was looking at that very burial site now, and the realization sent chills of horror creeping up my spine.

As they approached the hole, Rivera and Grady moved to either side, letting Ilyana approach from the center. I moved to join them, but Perkins reached out and grabbed my arm, stopping me.

"You don't want any of that. Trust me," he whispered.

"Any of what?"

I just wanted someone to explain what the heck we were doing there and what we hoped to gain in the process.

Grady had his gun out and pointed at the hole. Sparks of arcane power were dancing around Rivera's hands as he held them up before him, combat-style, ready for use at the slightest notice. Only Ilyana approached the hole without obvious caution, striding right up to the edge and looking down into its depths.

"It's empty," she said. "Nothing but dirt."

Rivera and Grady stepped forward and peered over the edge themselves, relaxing only after they'd seen for themselves that Ilyana was right. I took that as the cue for Perkins and myself to do the same.

The hole in the ground was rectangular and roughly fifteen, maybe eighteen feet deep. It looked like it had been excavated some time ago; the earth along the sides was dried and cracked, though it was hard to tell that at first under the globe's red light.

"So where is he?" Rivera asked.

I didn't hear Perkins's reply; my attention was caught by the smell of freshly turned earth that was wafting out of the pit.

That's not right, I thought. *Dried earth that hasn't been turned in months shouldn't smell like that.*

I triggered my ghostsight . . . and was nearly knocked off my feet from the flood of hatred shooting up from the depths of that hole, like a river of emotion thundering over the spot where I stood, bashing and battering me in its current. I held my ground and peered through the emotion, trying to see where it was coming from.

There was a shape down there, just beneath the surface of the earth.

A human shape . . .

"Guys, you might want to take a look . . ."

That was as far as I got.

Something exploded out of the earth at the bottom of the pit and launched itself upward, soaring up toward the ceiling.

Instinct screamed in the back of my mind, and I threw myself out of the way, so the claws that were supposed to tear my face off barely managed to nick my shirt instead. I hit the floor hard, my back slamming into the cold concrete, but that didn't stop me from crab-walking backward in an effort to put as much distance between myself and the thing that had just tried to kill me as possible.

Which was why I was in a perfect position to see the whatever-it-was resolve itself into the image of a man, hovering just beneath the ceiling and staring down at us all with an expression of savage hunger and delight.

He was a Caucasian man in his midthirties, with eyes as black as coal surrounding pinpoints of red staring out of a lean, hard face missing its nose. In its place was a rotting hole, as if some savage animal had torn the appendage away and the wound had been left to fester on its own. He was dressed in the tattered remains of an orange prison uniform sans shoes. Even with the change in his appearance, he was still recognizable.

Wagner.

What the fuck?

I lay on the ground, stunned by what I was seeing. It hadn't been that long ago that I'd seen another creature like this one in the swamps of New Orleans, a creature named Blackburn that had taken a memory in exchange for information. I had thought him to be unique, and yet here I was looking at another of his kind, if you could call it that. If he had chosen that moment to attack I would have been a goner; my brain just couldn't wrap itself around what it was seeing.

Grady, however, didn't have that problem. He brought his

gun up in the fastest draw I've ever seen, pulling the trigger and firing twice in the space of what felt like only the briefest second.

Unfortunately, he might as well have been throwing rocks.

Wagner jinked to one side, letting the bullets zip past him without even sparing them a glance. I remembered how Blackburn had seemed to cross the floor at Pointe du Lac in the blink of an eye and shuddered at the speed of these creatures.

All Grady had managed to do was catch Wagner's attention.

"I'm going to enjoy feasting on you," the fiend said in a voice as cold as winter and then dove forward with hands and claws extended.

Grady didn't bother firing again; he just stood there, unmoving.

I opened my mouth to scream his name, knowing even as I did so that at the speed Wagner was moving he was going to be on top of Grady before I had the chance to get the sound out of my mouth, but I had forgotten that we weren't the only two people in the room.

A blur of motion that I barely identified as Ilyana shot across the room and intercepted Wagner before he could reach Grady, slamming into him and sending him pinwheeling backward to crash into the wall behind him.

The blow would have been enough to shake most preternaturals, never mind a normal man, but Wagner barely seemed to notice it. He came surging back across the space that was separating him from Ilyana with a roar, his claws a blur as he slashed at her with unbelievable speed.

To my surprise she blocked every strike and even managed to land a few of her own in between. After a few minutes of that, Wagner attempted to back off and Ilyana let him. The two of them hung there, ten feet off the ground, waiting to see what the other would do.

Rivera's voice rang out.

"We're here for the Key and that's all. Give it to us and we'll leave you in peace."

Wagner laughed and there was nothing human in the sound.

"I'm not a fool, Rivera."

They knew each other?

"Even if I were to turn over the Key, you wouldn't leave me alone. I know it and you do too. You may be content to be Fuentes's lapdog but I am not."

The last word was barely out of Wagner's mouth when he made his move. Rather than rushing Ilyana a second time or having a go at Rivera, Wagner flung himself upward, straight at the ceiling above his head, no doubt in a bid to try to crash through it and escape through the structure above. It wasn't a bad plan, as plans go; if he made it into the open air, for all I knew he might have been able to get away.

Rivera had apparently been waiting for Wagner to make just such an attempt, for even as the other man shot toward the ceiling, the sorcerer unleashed the power that he'd been holding ready in his bare hands. Black flames shot forth from his palms in a thick stream and washed across Wagner's lower body as if flung from some kind of arcane flamethrower. I could feel the heat from where I was standing and assumed that was the end of Wagner, but once again my expectations fell far short of reality.

The would-be fugitive screamed in agony, but he didn't let the flames or his own pain slow him down. He crashed into and then through the ceiling above our heads, sending pieces of wood, insulation, and floor tile from the room above raining down toward us as he disappeared from view.

I was still staring at the hole in the ceiling that Wagner had disappeared through, amazed that he hadn't been burnt to a cinder, when Rivera ordered Ilyana to go after him.

"And when I catch him?" she asked.

Not if, when.

"He's all yours," Rivera replied.

Ilyana took off in pursuit.

Rivera watched her go and then turned to where Grady, Perkins, and I stood waiting.

"The Key is here somewhere," he told us. "Find it."

14

In the end, it really didn't take us very long to do as he'd asked. Perkins's gift told us that what we were looking for was at the bottom of the hole from which Wagner had emerged, and once we knew that it didn't take us very long to find the safe that was buried there. Rivera used his sorcery to lift the safe out of the hole and set it down on the floor, after which Grady went to work with his own unique set of skills.

He had the safe open inside of ten minutes.

Along with a fair amount of cash, the safe also contained several unmarked DVDs and a small velvet bag.

Inside the bag was another piece of metal similar to the one we'd removed from the crypt beneath the church several days before.

Grady tossed the bag to Rivera and then began taking stacks of money wrapped in rubber bands out of the safe and stuffing them into his pockets.

Seeing me watching him, he grabbed a stack and tossed it in my direction, saying, "You want it, you can have it. I doubt Wagner's going to need it anymore."

But I didn't want it; didn't want anything to do with it, in fact, and I let it fall to the floor in front of me without making any attempt to catch it.

"Suit yourself," Grady said.

He took several stacks for himself and handed roughly the same amount to Perkins, who shot me a guilty look as he took it but stuffed it in his pockets just the same.

The light above our heads started to dim and Rivera hurried us along. I glanced upward, past the drifting ball of arcane energy to the hole through which Ilyana and Wagner had disappeared.

"What about Ilyana?" I asked.

"What about her?"

Rivera's reply was said over his shoulder as he headed for the stairs back to the ground floor. Perkins and Grady were already ahead of him, so I hustled to catch up.

"She's not back yet. Should we be worried?"

"About what?"

I could hear how ridiculous my question sounded and decided I'd quit while I was ahead. No sense making them think I was an even bigger fool than they already did.

She was a half-breed demon. What was there to be worried about?
What indeed.

We walked through the house and then back outside to

the car. I was reaching for the door handle when something about the size of a bowling ball bounced off the door beside me, startling me. I think I let out a little yelp of surprise.

When I looked down and saw the severed head of Glenn Wagner staring back at me from the dirt at my feet, I reacted without thinking, kicking it away from me like a soccer ball. I may have let out another yelp, this one much louder.

Ilyana thought this was hysterical. She came walking out of the darkness surrounding us, wiping her bloody hands on an orange scrap of cloth and laughing long and hard at my reaction.

"You should have seen your face," she said, amidst gales of laughter.

And to think I'd been worried about her safety.

I did my best to ignore the laughter of the others around me as I slipped my sunglasses back over my eyes and climbed into the car for the drive back to the estate.

>+−<

There are distinct advantages to being able to walk about in the dark and still be able to see. For one thing, you don't have to turn on any lights when you get up in the middle of the night to use the restroom. For another, you can spy fairly effectively on anyone you want, say, your boss, without them realizing that you are there. As I was doing now.

The fear and resulting adrenaline rush I'd experienced earlier had turned into hunger pangs hours later, and I'd come into the main house to grab something from the refrigerator to eat as a late night snack. In doing so I noticed a light coming from a room at the end of the hall, a room I knew to be Fuentes's study. The light was spilling through the partially open door and I could hear two voices coming out of it as well, but I was too far away to hear what was being said or who it was that was doing the talking.

The safe move would have been to pretend I hadn't heard anything, turn away, and continue on my way to the kitchen but I've never been known to play it safe anyway. As quietly as I could, I crept down the darkened hallway toward the partially open door.

The voices grew clear and I could hear fairly well by the time I settled into a crouch less than a yard away from the entrance, my back to one wall.

"Well?" a voice I recognized as Fuentes's asked. "Do you have it?"

There was a clank, as if a piece of metal had been tossed onto the desk lightly. "You were right; Wagner was using the place as his new lair."

Fuentes laughed. "What did I tell you? Nosferatu are always so predictable."

Nosferatu? I'd heard the word before—it was the name of the creature in the very first vampire film by F. W. Murnau, never mind the name of the film itself. But I never imagined the things were real. *How much did Murnau really know?* I wondered.

". . . any more. I let Verikoff sate her needs on him when he refused to cooperate."

I'd missed Rivera's opening, but it wasn't hard to put two and two together to know they were still talking about Wagner.

"And good riddance, too," Fuentes replied. "Any other trouble?"

"None. Though I have to admit that I'm surprised by some of Hunt's abilities. He knew where Wagner was hiding before the rest of us did, for instance."

"Don't underestimate him, Rivera. He's like a rat; he'll fight if you back him into a corner."

Rivera said something that I didn't catch and both men laughed heartily.

Laugh away, assholes, I thought. *We'll see who laughs last.*

I wasn't sure what Fuentes was up to or why he wanted this key he was looking for, but one thing was certain. I was going to rain on their parade as soon as the opportunity presented itself. Once I knew that my friends were safe, I was determined to fuck up Fuentes's world so badly that he and Rivera were going to wish that they'd left me alone in that crappy little motel room to mind my own business.

"And the third piece?" Rivera asked.

"Either Durante gave it to that pissy little sycophant of his or else it is hidden somewhere in the house in the canyon. I want you to go to the house with the entire crew tomorrow night and see what you can find. If it's not there, I want you to find that whiny bastard."

Noise from the other end of the hallway told me someone was on their way. As quietly as I could I stood up, crossed the hall, and slipped inside the bathroom I knew was there. I left the door open the barest crack so that I could hear what was going on in the hallway, and stood with my back to it. If I had to, I could always lock the door, pretend to use the bathroom, and then try to bluff my way through with some story about needing to speak to Mr. Fuentes if someone was waiting for me when I emerged.

Lights went on in the hallway outside the door and I froze,

squeezing my eyes shut against the light. I hadn't thought I'd need them, so I left the sunglasses Grady had given me back in my room; they would have proved rather helpful right about now, I knew. Holding my breath, I waited for whoever it was to go away.

Footsteps approached.

I tensed, one hand curling into a fist.

Even Rivera and Fuentes had fallen silent.

Any second now . . .

The door directly to the left of the bathroom opened and someone began muttering beneath their breath in Spanish. I almost gasped in relief; it was just the maid, returning laundry to the linen closet next door. From the sound of it she was none too happy about the way the day shift had stacked the sheets, either.

I stood there, listening as she closed the closet and walked off down the hall, still talking to herself. It was only when the lights went off that I let go of the breath I'd been holding and relaxed.

I gave it another minute or two, then cautiously opened the door and looked out.

The hallway was empty.

I found I could hear Fuentes and Rivera just fine from the bathroom where I was standing, however, so I decided to stay where I was in order to decrease the chance of being discovered while I continued my clandestine activities.

The two men had moved on to a different topic, it seemed. It sounded like they were discussing . . . a war in L.A.?

"Once we have downtown, Metro South and Southwest should fall fairly easily. We can form a staging area in Inglewood and use that to take control of Westchester, Marina del Rey, and Venice."

"What about Papa Toulese?"

Fuentes laughed. "He won't even know what hit him. The forces we'll have at our disposal will easily defeat the Loa supporting him. Without them, his riders will be nothing more than tired horses. We'll eat them for breakfast!"

Rivera asked a question, but it was too low for me to hear.

Fuentes's answer, on the other hand, came through loud and clear. "We'll use the Key to open another gate in Malibu. From there, we can close on Drake and his people from two sides, with you leading the main force moving north through Santa Monica and I'll put Verikoff in charge of the greener troops coming through the gate. She can march down through Topanga and catch Drake between your two forces."

"Flank him. Catch him in a pincher movement. Hell, charge him head on. Drake is not likely to surrender no matter what," Rivera said.

"Fine," was Fuentes's immediate answer. "Let him fall with his troops, then. I don't care; I'm going to have to execute him anyway if he lives. We can't have two claims for the throne, after all.

Flanking maneuvers? Pinching movements? Battalions of troops?

I had no idea what they were talking about, but one thing was for certain; it didn't sound good for L.A. one way or another.

And all of it, apparently, revolved around this Key Fuentes was searching for.

Find that, I thought, *and you'll have the upper hand. It might be the one thing that can get Fuentes off of Denise's and Dmitri's backs.*

The two of them were still talking, but I was getting the sense that I was pushing my luck and decided to get while the getting was good. I'd learned a lot, even if I couldn't make sense of it all yet. That would come with time, I knew. Right now, all I needed was a direction to work in and that I'd found.

Find the Key, I told myself, as I slipped down the hallway and headed back to my bungalow.

Find the Key and control the game.

15

The next day Fuentes put me to work on one of his crews, hauling construction supplies from one job site to the next. For hours I hefted bags of concrete and stacks of lumber, loading them onto trucks at one location and then unloading them all over again at the next. It was grunt work and didn't require much thought, but it had been a long time since I had worked that hard and it took it out of me.

By the time we returned to the estate in the late afternoon, I was exhausted. Once in my bungalow, I quickly showered to rid myself of all the concrete dust that had accumulated during the day and then dried off. I was going to slip into my spare clothes but found that they were still drying from being washed the night before. Deciding that sleep took precedence over getting my clothing dried, I slipped into bed naked and was asleep in seconds.

Ilyana woke me a short time later with several quick little slaps on the cheek.

"Ow!" I said, as I was startled into wakefulness to find her sitting on the edge of my bed in the dark. "What are you doing? That hurt!"

For a moment her eyes flashed red with anger and then she relaxed and her expression became decidedly more . . . hungry. She reached out and gently placed her hand against my still stinging cheek, matching it against the red mark that was no doubt emblazoned there.

"Awwww, do you want me to kiss it and make it better?" she asked, in a voice that might have been meant to be seductive but was far from it.

In fact, upon hearing it, my testicles retreated in much the same way they would if I decided to go skinny-dipping in a glacial lake in mid-February.

In Norway.

Conscious of her nearness and my nakedness, I quickly changed the subject.

"How did you get in here?" I asked, pulling the sheets up closer to my neck.

"You invited me," came the reply. "I couldn't have come in otherwise."

No, I didn't. I distinctly would have remembered that. I was equally certain that she wasn't telling the truth about needing to be invited, either. I wasn't an expert on preternaturals, by any stretch of the imagination, and my lessons with Denise had been cut off far more abruptly than I had hoped, but I had the feeling that Ilyana could go anywhere and everywhere she wanted to, regardless of whether she'd been invited or not. Granted, the supernatural elements of the world often acted in less than logical ways, but I didn't think this was one of those times. She'd entered Wagner's former home without difficulty, hadn't she?

Sitting in the dark, naked, with a half-breed demon nearby who seemed to have an unhealthy interest in me, sexually or otherwise, just didn't seem to be the right time to argue, however. So instead, I asked another question.

"Why are you here?"

I almost said, "What do you want?" but decided at the last second that the answer to that question might get me into more trouble than it was worth.

"Why am I here?" she repeated. "Perhaps I just wanted to see you."

Right. Like the lion playing with the gazelle before it eats it for lunch.

I shook my head, wondered if she could see it in the darkness, and then decided that yeah, she probably could.

"Seriously, why are you here?"

Ilyana got up from the bed so abruptly that I thought she was going to lose it, but all she did was toss my clothes at me from the small dresser.

"We've got another job to do, let's go."

I caught my clothes, reached for the blankets, and stopped.

"Um . . . would you mind?" I asked.

Ilyana looked at me.

"Mind what?" she asked.

"Turning around so I can get dressed."

"Why?"

I stared at her. "Why what?"

"Why do you want me to turn around?"

This was getting ridiculous. I didn't know if she truly didn't understand a concept like common courtesy or the need to not embarrass ourselves or if she was just playing with me.

Deciding that I wouldn't give her the satisfaction of making me uncomfortable, I threw off the sheets, got out of bed, and proceeded to get dressed right there in front of her. Her gaze roamed over my body as I did so, taking in the tattoos and the scars, but she didn't say anything about either while she waited for me to finish.

It was only when I was completely dressed and headed out the door that she said, "I think I like you better the other way."

I pretended not to hear her. The last thing I needed was a sexual relationship with a half-human, half-demon hybrid that ate spectres for breakfast and tossed the heads of vampires around like baseballs.

Rivera was waiting for us by the car when we came out the front door. Seconds later Perkins and Grady joined us as well.

"Hail, hail the gang's all here," I said, trying to lighten the mood, but no one laughed.

I could tell this was going to be another fun outing.

We all piled into the car and got on our way.

>+<

The house was high in the Hollywood Hills and sat behind an eight-foot security wall of brick and stone. At first I thought we'd have to scale the walls, but I was thinking far too literally. The entrance had one of those keypads on a little stand near the gate; those with the right access key could flash the card in front of the pad and, when it was properly read and authorized, simply wait for the gate to be opened automatically. Rivera drove up, rolled down the window, and placed his hand flat against the pad.

There was a bright flash, a smell like scorched ozone, and then the gate began to roll slowly open.

As we drove through, I glanced back at the keypad. There wasn't much left of it beyond a smoking, twisted hunk of metal.

The house sat at the end of the long, sloping drive. There was a garage to the right whose door must have been linked to the gate, for it was almost finished rising as we pulled into view. Rivera ignored the garage, however, choosing to park out in front of the main entrance.

We'd been on two of these little excursions so far and each time we'd encountered something that wasn't all that happy with our general presence, from the spectre in the church crypt to the presence of the Nosferatu in the basement of the murder house. All of us, except perhaps Ilyana, were a bit tense as a result as we got out of the car and headed for the front door.

Grady tried the handle and found the door locked. Without a word he pulled a set of lock picks out of his inner coat pocket and got to work. It took him less than a minute to breach the door and another ninety seconds to bypass the alarm system from the control pad just inside the entryway.

A minute and a half to defeat a state-of-the-art security system? The owner, this Durante guy Fuentes was talking about the other night I suspected, should have saved his money and just bought a dog.

We all knew the drill by now so Rivera didn't even have to say anything once we were inside. Perkins stepped to the middle of the foyer as we all gave him room to work. He bent to the task with the attention and energy he'd used the time before, but after several minutes of him turning in place and staring blankly at the walls, it was clear something was wrong.

"Today would be nice, Perkins," Grady said.

Perkins frowned without opening his eyes and tried again.

After a few minutes of us standing around in silence, he said, "There's something blocking . . ."

Rivera didn't hesitate. "Take a look, Hunt."

Right.

I slipped my sunglasses off my face and triggered my ghostsight.

Technically speaking, I could have left the sunglasses on; they don't really interfere with my view when I am looking at the world in this particular fashion. Sometimes, though, you need to act in ways that make sense to you rather than in ways that make you question the whole basis of your reality. It made sense to me to take off my sunglasses so that's what I did.

There were no ghosts here, or, at least, none that I could see at that moment, but there was definitely some magick being utilized. The walls of the room were covered in a shimmering silver glow and everywhere I looked I saw the same thing.

"Try it again," I told Perkins and this time I watched as he did so. Just as he had in the murder house, he called forth these twisting, turning tendrils of energy and sent them out questing for the object he was looking for. I wondered if he even knew this was how his power worked, then I decided that it didn't matter. One way or another he managed to find what he was looking for and that was the important thing.

Except here, every time the tendrils tried to reach beyond this room into the next, the silver glow pushed them back and didn't allow them any further activity. It was like seeing a bolt of electricity grounded, its energy stolen.

"He's right," I said to Rivera. "There some kind of mystical energy field surrounding the entire room and keeping Perkins from finding whatever it is he's looking for."

"So let's try the next room," Grady said and began moving in that direction, but I stopped him.

"I'm afraid it's there as well. As far as I can tell, it's in every room. Maybe even covering the entire building."

Rivera closed his eyes, extended his hands on either side of him. He must have discovered the same thing I did, for he cursed several times under his breath as he examined this room and the next.

When he came back he said, "All right, we're going to have to do this the old-fashioned way. The entire building seems to have been warded, so we're going to have to split up and search the place manually. If you find anything unusual, let either Verikoff or myself know. Questions?"

He looked at me as he said it, but I didn't respond. They had yet to answer any of the questions I needed answered, so I didn't see any point in asking any more. I knew we were looking for another piece of the "Key," whatever that might actually be, and guessed that it probably resembled the other two we had already collected. I'd wander around, preferably away from the others, and look for it even as I was doing my best to learn as much about the individual who owned the place as possible.

Both Fuentes and Rivera had mentioned someone by the name of Durante, and I was willing to bet that this had been his home. If that was the case, then perhaps some incriminating information about Durante's rivals, namely Fuentes, might be stashed somewhere on the premises. If I could find that, I'd be in a much better position to demand my release and an end to any pending threats against my friends.

We split up, each of us going in a different direction. The house was more a mansion than a home, with three floors and multiple wings, so there was plenty of space for each of us to individually investigate.

Rivera sent me up to the second level, near the back of the house, where I found a variety of bedrooms. Probably figured I'd get in the least amount of trouble back there. I refrained from turning on any lights and left the curtains drawn where I found them that way, wanting to protect my ability to see. If I found a room where the curtains were open, I pulled them shut. After coming across a couple of similar-looking rooms it became clear that these were, in all likelihood, guest rooms. Some looked recently cleaned, others not to have even been opened in the last several months.

One in particular, however, turned out to be fairly interesting.

Unlike the others, this one looked to have been used more recently. In fact, it appeared to be used on a regular basis, if the men's clothing in the closet and dresser was any indication. The styles were all recent and there was even a dry cleaning tag from two weeks ago sitting atop the dresser.

But what interested me the most were the framed photographs hanging on the wall, as well as the three standing on the nightstand.

I couldn't see what was in any of them. It is a strange quirk of my condition that photographs always appear as blank images to me unless I am viewing them through someone else's sight. It could be one of the living or it could be one of the dead; it didn't matter. All that mattered was that I was seeing them through eyes that weren't my own.

The person who had stayed in this room had been close to the owner, whose name I suspected of being Durante. I didn't know what had happened to Durante or why he wasn't here now, but if I could find someone who had been close to him in the past then I might learn some of those answers. And those answers would, no doubt, lead me to an understanding of just what Fuentes and Rivera were trying to accomplish by taking control of this key.

In order to view the pictures, I was going to need some help.

I stood up and moved to the center of the room. I raised my face to the ceiling and extended my arms out to either side, palms up. Closing my eyes, I called out softly.

"Come to me, Whisper. Come to me."

As I called her name, I pictured her doing what I wanted, having learned over time that a bit of positive reinforcement went a long way to helping the summons to be successful.

I repeated my request, over and over again, until I felt a hand slip into mine and knew that I was no longer alone.

16

"Lend me your eyes," I asked her. I kept my voice low, not wanting any of the others to know I had company.

There was a moment of dizziness and then the taste of bitter ashes flooded my mouth and I could see again.

As was my habit, I looked down to check on her, noting for what seemed the thousandth time the vacant way that her eyes wandered thanks to my commandeering her vision. As always, I was struck by her resemblance to my dead daughter, Elizabeth. She had the same dark hair, the same bright eyes. Even that impish little grin Elizabeth used to wear. I would be forever thankful to Whisper for the role she had played in helping my daughter find her final rest, and the similarities between the two were a constant reminder of all that had happened between us.

Satisfied that all was as it should be, I turned my attention to the photographs. They were of a variety of scenes and locations, but the same two men appeared in every single one of them.

The first was an energetic-looking Italian in his late thirties with dark hair and a wide smile. He was actually the focus of many of the photos and it was clear that he was some sort of public figure, appearing at a variety of what looked to be media or charity events. In more than half the photos he was shaking someone's hand and smiling at the camera.

Given what I'd heard about him so far, I guessed that this was Durante.

It was the second man, however, that I was more interested in. Fuentes had mentioned Durante's aide, and I assumed that the blond-haired, blue-eyed man that appeared in the backdrop of many of the shots was that person. He was tall and thinner than Durante, with a snappier and less conservative style of dress. One might even say flamboyant. He seemed to have his gaze focused on Durante in nearly every picture.

As I glanced over the collection, I noticed a photo standing off by itself on the edge of the nightstand. Walking over, I saw that it showed the two men standing together on the deck of a sailboat, drinks in hands, arms on each other's shoulders. It could just have been a photo of two friends having a good time, but something about the way they were standing together made me think that perhaps there had been something more between them. It would also explain why Fuentes thought the man might have the Key.

I decided then and there that I'd find him first.

I slipped the photo out of its frame and folded it in half before stashing it in my pocket. I was about to contain my search when I heard it.

Screaming.

It was a long, horrid wail that rose in pitch and volume, the kind of thing you might expect to hear in a medieval torture chamber, not in a well-to-do mansion in the Hollywood Hills.

At least, not usually.

Shouts erupted over the screaming. I thought I recognized Rivera's voice and possibly Ilyana's too.

It seemed my companions were in trouble.

I could have left them to whatever disaster they'd stumbled into this time, but my conscience wouldn't let me. Perkins was just as much a prisoner of Fuentes's ambition as I was and there were some indications that Grady and Ilyana might fall into that category as well. If any of that were true, if they had been forced to work for Fuentes in the same manner I had, I couldn't just leave them to their fate.

I turned to Whisper. "I still need your help," I told her. I wasn't going to be of use to anyone if I couldn't see what was going on, so I needed Whisper to stay with me and allow me to keep borrowing her vision. Thankfully she seemed to understand, for she nodded and gripped my hand tighter, silently signaling for me to lead the way. I smiled, wondered how I'd ended up with such a loyal little girl as one of my closest friends, and took off down the hall, following the sound of the screams.

The cries grew more distinct as I got closer, and I realized that my initial impressions had been correct. Something was happening to Perkins and the others were doing what they could to help him, though it didn't sound like they were having much success. As I rounded a corner and skidded to a stop at the entrance to the room in which they stood, I discovered why.

The room where the action was happening was a study, if the three-story-high collection of books and artifacts could be called that without it seeming a bit ridiculous. Shelves lined the walls from floor to ceiling, filled with books of all shapes and sizes. Ladders stood against the shelving on either side of the room, designed to provide access to the higher levels. A large cherrywood desk stood off to one side of the room, leather chairs and a couch nearby. It wasn't hard to imagine Durante at work in this place; it had a distinctly masculine feel to the room.

Of course, the pitched battle going on in the middle of the room tended to distract one from design evaluations.

Perkins hung ten feet off the floor, skewered through the stomach with what appeared to be the two-handed sword taken from the suit of armor standing just inside the doorway to my left. He was obviously still alive, for he was howling in pain, his hands wrapped around the blade of the weapon at the point just before it disappeared into his gut.

Rivera and Ilyana stood on the floor in front of and below him, doing what they could to keep the cascade of objects, from books to chairs to decorative marble busts, from striking him as they were repeatedly flung in his direction. They were getting about ninety percent of what was being thrown at him, but every time an item got through Perkins would howl in agony again. Grady apparently was already down for the count; I could see him lying on the floor a few yards away, unconscious, half buried beneath the twin to the couch that stood in front of the desk on the far side of the room.

What I couldn't see was whatever it was that was pressing the attack in the first place. Aside from us, the room appeared to be empty.

Poltergeist, I thought.

Had to be a powerful one too. Knocking over coffee cups or the occasional book was more in line with what the average poltergeist could accomplish. When you got into moving furniture and sending deadly weapons soaring through the air with pinpoint accuracy, you were well beyond the normal.

I was reaching into my pocket for my harmonica when the suit of armor standing next to me swung its armored gauntlet outward and smashed me in the face.

Pain exploded through my skull and my link with Whisper was broken. The bastard had gotten me good; blood was running down my face and the back of my throat. I was pretty sure my nose was broken and worried that my cheekbone might have suffered the same fate. As I tried to analyze the extent of the damage, I realized as well that I was sprawled on the floor, no doubt having fallen there in the wake of the blow without even knowing I had.

The clank of a steel gauntleted foot warned me.

Unable to see anything thanks to the loss of my link with Whisper and the electric lights the others had turned on in the room, I simply threw myself to the side, hoping to avoid whatever was coming. I felt something go whistling by my head, scant inches away, and then I was climbing to my feet and triggering my ghostsight so that I'd be able to see.

The poltergeist stood on the desk I'd noted earlier, hands out and mouth open in a silent scream of rage. He appeared as he must have at the moment of his death and, despite all the damage done to him, I was still able to recognize him as the man in the photographs from the bedroom, Durante.

They'd worked him over before killing him; that much was obvious. Deep, savage cuts crisscrossed his face, the wounds gaping open by a quarter inch or more, and his left ear was missing entirely. When he raised his hands to send another barrage in our direction, I could see that he was missing several fingers.

Even as I watched, Ilyana launched herself toward the ghost, perhaps to try and devour it as she'd done with the spectre that first night we'd gone on a mission like this, but she didn't even make it halfway across the room before Durante waved his hand and sent her flying back the way she had come. Ilyana tumbled end over end and then slammed into the wall with enough force to spill several shelves of books down to the floor.

As she staggered to her feet, he waved a three-fingered hand at a leather reading chair in the corner and sent it flying across the room to smash her back down again.

In facing down the half-breed, Durante had forgotten about the sorcerer. No longer hampered by the need to keep objects from striking Perkins now that Durante had focused his attention on Ilyana and me, Rivera conjured up a blast of arcane energy that he sent soaring across the room at the ghost.

I watched the literal ball of power splash across the ghost's form and thought, "That's it; game over."

But I was wrong.

Durante shook off the strike the way a prizefighter shrugs off a punch in the first round of a title match. He looked over at us both, grinned, and sent the entire contents of the shelves behind him hurling in Rivera's direction.

Books rained around him as he hit the floor and tried to protect himself. The rain became a flood became a veritable tide as he was buried under the onslaught.

The ghost turned and screamed in rage in my direction.

We were in serious trouble.

I was mentally screaming for help, sending out a summons

to Scream with as much force as I could muster, even as I pulled my harmonica out of my pocket and brought it to my lips. I opened my mouth, intending to send out a tune that would hold the poltergeist in place, only to have two steel arms wrap themselves around the middle of my chest and squeeze.

The air left my lungs in a sudden rush, leaving me nothing to power my instrument, never mind breathe on my own. I could feel the world around me starting to fade out as I fought for the air I needed to survive, and if it hadn't been for Scream's timely arrival I probably wouldn't have made it.

Scream entered the room like a runaway freight train, bursting through a wall and charging across the floor to slam into the other ghost with all the precision of a carpet-bombing campaign. The two of them were hurled backward and disappeared on the other side of the desk.

I brought my harmonica to my lips, ready to play but afraid to cause any harm to Scream if he was still holding on to Durante. I couldn't see either of them, and needed line of sight to make the banishing work, so I climbed to my feet and forced myself to head in that direction.

I'd barely taken three steps before Durante rose slowly up from the other side of the desk, hovering in midair and staring at me.

Of Scream there was no sign.

Uh oh, I thought.

I began to play just as the ghost flung itself toward me.

The music surged through the room, a complicated melody that dipped and swirled and spun like a living thing.

The ghost flew into the force of it and slowed, but it wasn't enough to stop him. He kept coming.

I played harder, louder, varying the key in an attempt to

find just the right refrain as the ghost flew directly at me, to no avail. Just as he reached out to seize me in his spectral grasp, I reached for one final minor key change . . .

Durante's ghost crashed into me, sending darkness washing over me like the tide.

>—◄

When I came to the others were crouched around me, concern on at least one of their faces.

"What happened?" I asked. All I could remember were those final seconds as Durante reached for me . . .

"You did it," Grady told me, as he helped me sit up. He had a lump on the side of his head that no doubt matched the swelling of my nose, but at least we were both alive. Ilyana and Rivera looked battered and bruised, but otherwise okay.

"Perkins?" I asked, remembering the sight of him skewered to the wall.

Grady shook his head. "He didn't make it."

That was that. None of us had the strength or the desire to continue searching after that. Rivera was all set to go, but Grady and I refused to leave Perkins behind. They had already used the ladders to climb up, remove the sword, and lower his body to the ground, so all we had to do was transport it to the car. We wrapped him in a tablecloth we found in a nearby closet and then, with Ilyana's help, carried him out to the Charger. Rivera's lack of involvement, his downright refusal to help, in fact, convinced me that Perkins was right. The only one of us actively cooperating with Fuentes was Rivera; the rest of us were here against our will. I filed that away for future reference, as I might be able to use it if and when the opportunity presented itself. With allies on the inside, I might just be able to find a way to get us all out of this mess once and for all.

But that would have to wait until later. For now, we needed to go home and rest. Fuentes wasn't going to give up until he had the Key and neither was I.

Though he didn't know that yet.

Back at the estate, Grady took control of Perkins's body and I headed for my bungalow without a backward glance. Once inside I checked to be sure I still had the picture I'd taken from the bedroom of Durante's mansion; I did. I stashed it inside my shoe, thinking it would be the last place someone would look once I was dressed in the morning, and then went into the bathroom to review the damage.

My face was swollen, yes, but thankfully my nose wasn't broken. I took a long, hot shower, letting the water soak into my muscles, hoping to ease the stiffness before it set in too deeply, and then sat in the front room for a while, thinking. I'd learned quite a bit in the last twenty-four hours, but I was still a long way from going to the head of the class. Some important elements were still outside my reach.

What, exactly, was the Key? What did it do? Why was Fuentes willing to kill for it? Were these others willing to die to keep it from his hands?

Exhaustion finally won out over the adrenaline rush of the earlier combat and I headed off to bed, suddenly desperate for sleep.

17

The chill woke me from a deep sleep.

I sat up in bed, confused. It had been a balmy seventy degrees when I'd gone to bed and I'd left the window open to try and catch a little bit of the night air. Now it felt like I'd been dropped into the middle of the Arctic in nothing but my boxer shorts; goose bumps had broken out all over my flesh and my teeth were on the verge of chattering.

As the fog of sleep cleared from my head, I began to put two and two together. I'd felt cold like this before and I didn't like what it heralded, didn't like it at all. I got out of bed, pulled my jeans on over my bare legs, and then hunted around until I found my shirt. With my arms wrapped around my chest, I went in search of my visitor.

I found him in the front room, standing by the window looking out into the darkness. The moon had not yet risen and the lights in the room were off, allowing me to see without difficulty. Not that he would have been hard to find; cold air seemed to pour off of him like the winter wind.

He was dressed as he'd been the last time I'd seen him, in black pants and a black frock coat over a simple white, button-down shirt. A wide-brimmed hat, like that worn by a traveling preacher from the Old West, rested atop his head, hiding all but a few wispy strands of white hair that hung down past his collar in back. He stood with his back to me, his hands slipped into the shallow pockets on the front of his vest.

As I entered the room, he turned staring at me with those empty eye sockets that were a strange and eerie counterpart to my own.

"I'm surprised, Hunt," he said, in that cold, sterile voice of his. "I never would have figured you for a Hollywood kind of guy."

"Yeah, well, I chose L.A. just so I could disappoint you. Don't you feel special now?"

My nerves were on edge, my heart pounding in my chest. The Preacher had made no overt threat toward me on either of the two occasions when I'd encountered him previously, but just being in his presence unnerved me. I felt like the gazelle at the watering hole nervously eyeing the crocodile on the opposite bank. At any moment it might slip into the water . . .

He pretended not to hear me as he went on. "And the company you're keeping these days? Carlos Fuentes? Really, Hunt, what are you thinking?"

I ground my teeth together in an effort not to respond to

his jibes. I'd been shanghaied into service, but I'd be damned if I was going to tell him that. Something told me that admitting weakness once too often in front of him might make him turn on me, like the crocodile on that gazelle, and I had no intention of being either his lunch or dinner if I could help it.

"What do you want?" I asked.

His smile grew wider. "Why, I've come to collect, of course."

Just like that I was back in the Harvard Playhouse with my wife, Anne, in the early years of our marriage, back before Elizabeth had disappeared, before it all went to hell. We'd gone out to see *Peter Pan*, but at the last minute Anne had changed her mind, had decided that the crowd waiting in front of the playhouse was too big, too noisy, and she'd dragged me down the street to a smaller venue. They were putting on a production of *Faust* that night, and Anne had rolled her eyes spookily and demanded that I take her. In those days I still did whatever my wife asked, and so fifteen minutes later we were staring up at the stage, enrapt, as the Devil arrived to claim his due. The smile on that long-ago actor's face matched perfectly the one on the Preacher's now.

I shook off the feeling. I didn't know who or what the Preacher actually was—devil, demon, or something worse—but I'd made no bargain as demanding as Faust's.

All I had done was promise to carry out a task for him.

How hard could that be?

I squared my shoulders and shook off the chill. "All right, a deal's a deal," I told him. "What is it you want me to do?"

The Preacher watched me closely as he said, "I want you to deliver all three pieces of the Clavis Sclerata to me."

Whatever I'd been expecting, it was not that. I tried to

ignore the kicked-in-the-nuts feeling that washed over me at the sound of that name and did my best to keep my expression the same as I said, "The what?"

The Preacher cocked his head sideways slightly and said in a voice heavy with anticipation, "Are you refusing to carry out the task?"

I was about to deliver one of my trademark wiseass replies but the words froze halfway to my lips. Something about his sudden stillness and the peculiar way he asked the question, emphasizing certain words over others, put the hair up on the back of my neck.

Careful, Hunt, I thought. *Almost stepped in it that time.*

"Um . . . I am NOT refusing the task. I am simply asking for more information."

"You know quite well what I'm asking for, Hunt. You can't play games with me. Get me the Key. If you do not, I will hunt you to the ends of the earth to claim what is mine."

Without another word he stepped to the door, opened it, and walked into the darkness outside. By the time I crossed the room he was already out of sight, though where he had gone or how he had done it I didn't know. No one should be able to move that fast.

No one.

It was only when I was back inside, locking the door behind me, that I paused to wonder how the Preacher had gotten inside in the first place. The front door had been locked; I'd made sure of it before going to sleep. A quick check of the windows showed that all of those were sealed too. About the only thing that was out of place was the mirror in the front room; it hung slightly askew from its usual position.

You're in California, I reminded myself. Tremors happen all the time. A minor one shifted the position of the mirror, no doubt.

But even as I headed back to bed, my mind kept returning to that same image over and over again.

The mirror, hanging on the wall, slightly askew.

18

Fuentes didn't have anything on deck for us the next day, so I used the morning to do a little legwork of my own. I had one of the estate staff drop me off at a local movie theater, ostensibly to see a show, but really just to provide an excuse for being out for the morning. I bought a ticket to the latest Hollywood blockbuster starring Denzel Washington, just in case someone asked for proof, and then found my way to the nearest bus stop with the help of some random strangers.

The bus took me the rest of the way downtown to my true destination, the main branch of the Los Angeles Public Library system.

I needed to understand more about the situation into which I'd gotten myself. Fuentes and the Preacher were both after the same artifact, the Clavis Scelerata, or the Key of Wickedness, whatever the hell that was, and I was expected to help both of them get their hands on it. It was not a comfortable place to be. I didn't know why they wanted it or what, exactly, they intended to do with it once they had it. And that was just one aspect of this entire mess. Without thinking about it too much I knew that this was just one small piece of whatever was going on. I had a few pieces of the puzzle, but only a few, and even when taken together they weren't enough to allow me to understand exactly what was going on. Like a shadow glimpsed beneath the surface of the water, dark and indistinct, I had the sense of something larger and more dangerous looming in the background but that was all. Without more information, I was completely at the mercy of those running the show. I was hoping the library might hold some of the answers I needed.

I doubted I'd find much on the Key, but I wasn't here for that anyway. There was more than one way to skin a cat, and I intended to attack the problem from the other direction and see what I could find on this Durante character and his mysterious companion.

Short of breaking into the library in the dead of night to be able to read the material in complete darkness, there was no way for me to do the research myself. I was going to need some help. I knew I could simply ask the librarian for assistance, but something told me not to go that route. It would be too easy for anyone following in my footsteps to track them down and, given the nature of what I was involved in, would more than likely put them in danger. No, I needed something a bit more circumspect.

After asking one of my fellow passengers for directions, I got off the bus, unfolded my cane, and made my way down the street to the drugstore on the corner. Once inside I asked a clerk to help me find a package of Sominex, the over-the-counter sleep aid. I had a choice of original or maximum strength, so I chose the latter and then had the clerk add two bottles of Coke to the list.

Once outside the store, I tore open the package of Sominex and took out three of the tablets. I stuffed the rest of the box into my pocket and then opened one of the bottles of Coke, dropped the tablets inside and waited for them to dissolve before closing the bottle again.

Now armed with my secret weapon, I went in search of my assistant for the morning.

In Boston, where I had lived for many years, there were always a few homeless people hanging around outside the public library. This was for a variety of reasons, not the least of which was the fact that the library provided access to a rest-room and the ability to sit in a comfortable chair and while away the hours of the day in relative peace. If the homeless person didn't smell too bad and didn't disturb the other patrons, most of the librarians I'd known over the years had been gra-cious enough to leave them alone. I was hoping the same would be true here in L.A.

"Spare some change?" a male voice asked as I made my way up the stairs toward the front entrance.

I stopped and turned to face the spot where the sound had come from. "Maybe. Can you read?"

"Course I can read. Do I look stupid?"

I chose not to make the obvious reply and answered instead, "Maybe we can help each other then. I'll give you twenty bucks if you come inside and help me find the information I need."

"Give me the money first and then I'll help."

I laughed. "Now it's my turn to ask if I look stupid. I'll give you the twenty when I'm done with my research. Shouldn't take more than an hour. What do you say?"

Ten minutes later we were settled at a table as close to the library's public computers as I could get without sitting at a terminal of my own. That would come later; first, I needed to get my helper into the right frame of mind, so to speak.

His name, as it turned out, was Mike. I sent him off to gather the last several issues of the *Financial Times* and was sitting there enjoying my Coke when he returned. I offered him the other bottle, the one doctored with Sominex, and smiled in satisfaction as I heard him take a long gulp. He sat down in the chair next to mine and asked what to do with the magazine. I directed him to take out the newest edition and read me the table of contents. I indicated three articles I wanted to hear and asked him to start reading those articles aloud to me. He continued to sip at his Coke as he read and it wasn't long before the combination of dull reading material and the hefty dose of Sominex began to take an effect. As Mike continued to read aloud, he started to yawn every few paragraphs. His reading pace slowed, his words became slurred and, after a few more minutes, he stopped altogether. When the sound of his snoring reached me, I knew he was out.

That was exactly what I'd been waiting for.

Bracing myself for the pain, I reached out and stole his sight.

Pain flared through my head, but it wasn't as bad as it had been in days past. All the practice over the last few months had made the transition easier, and the sandpaper-on-the-back-of-my-eyeballs feeling faded pretty quickly this time. In less than a minute I was looking out at the world through borrowed eyes.

The library swam into view around me, muted and faded, like something left too long in the summer sun, but visible nonetheless. I wasn't concerned; that's how the world typically appeared when seen through the eyes of a Mundane. My helper was pretty much as I'd pictured him: a thin, middle-aged white guy in cast-off clothing that was desperately in need of a good scrubbing. He needed one too, truth be told. The brilliant white of his sneakers caught my eyes and made me wonder where he had gotten them. Never mind how he managed to keep them so clean.

I got up, moved over to the nearest computer terminal, and took a seat. I fired up the browser, navigated to Google's home page, and began looking for information about the men in the photograph. I knew one of them had to be Michael Durante, and it only took a few seconds to confirm that fact by doing an image search on his name. Hundreds of photos of Durante at various media and charity events around the city came up, and it was easy to confirm that Durante was the energetic-looking Italian with his arm around the other man, smiling at the camera, in the photo I'd taken from Durante's study.

I began hunting through the other images, looking for one that also captured the second man in my photograph. He was a much more elusive target, and I spent fifteen minutes going through image after image before I found him in one. Unfortunately, his identity was not noted in the write-up that accompanied the photo.

Turning to a standard Google search, I started hunting

down articles about Michael Durante, hoping to learn more about the man and, in the process, discover the identity of the elusive man in my photo.

MAYORAL CANDIDATE MURDERED was the first link that came up as part of the search results set. Given the conversation I'd overheard between Rivera and Fuentes, never mind the police tape at the mansion the other night, I wasn't surprised. I clicked the link and began reading.

The article was from the *LA Times* and the reporting was pretty straightforward. Michael Durante, entrepreneur, philanthropist, and Los Angeles mayoral candidate had been found tied up and tortured to death in his home in the Hollywood Hills roughly three weeks before I'd arrived in the city.

There's one murder the FBI can't blame me for, I thought.

Durante had been discovered by his maid when she'd come in on a Monday morning for her usual shift. He'd been bound, gagged, and secured to the bed with nylon rope, the kind found in thousands of hardware stores across the country. The article noted that he'd been stabbed to death after being tortured but didn't contain any further details. From my prior experience in working with the police, I knew those details had been deliberately withheld from the article in case a suspect tripped up during an interrogation and said something revealing that he or she couldn't have learned from the local press.

As the front-runner in the mayor's race, Durante had had his fair share of political enemies, it seemed. The article detailed his ongoing dispute with the labor unions as well as his divisive immigration policies. Quotes from unnamed police sources familiar with the investigation stated the attack had most likely been politically motivated and that investigators had several good leads which they were currently following. An arrest was expected soon.

Leaving that article behind, I moved on to several others, including a follow-up written just the week before. All of them pretty much said the same thing: the police hadn't made any significant progress since the initial leads had come in. They had apparently backed off on their promise of a quick arrest and had settled in for the long, slow grind, it seemed.

While hunting through the article on the murder investigation, I stumbled on a link to a gossip site that had done a brief exposé on Durante at the height of his campaign. The article included a photograph supposedly taken aboard a private yacht during a function celebrating the announcement of Durante's candidacy for mayor, and right there in black and white, with his arm around Durante's shoulders, was my mystery man.

The gossip rag identified him as Jack Bergman, Durante's campaign manager and "friend," and went on to note that there might be a little more than a platonic relationship going on between the two men. I didn't care about any of that; what the two of them did between themselves was their business, not mine. All that mattered to me was that I now had a name to go with the face. Given the proliferation of information on the Internet today, a name was often all you needed to be able to track somebody down. I was betting that Bergman might be able to shed some light on whatever it was that had been going on between Durante and Fuentes.

I glanced over at my helper. He had his head on the tabletop, snoring gently. His breathing seemed to be even and regular, which was good; an adverse reaction to Sominex would have scrapped my plans but good.

Satisfied that all was well in dreamland, I turned back to the computer and did another Google search, this time for Jack Bergman.

7,760,000 results.

You have got to be shitting me.

Adding "L.A." to the search dropped the results set down to just over four million hits, but that was still far too large a sample to work with. A quick check of Facebook showed a few thousand results there as well, though that shrank to several hundred when adding L.A. to the mix.

I wasn't worried; my Googlefu was strong. I went back to my search page and added Michael Durante to the string, putting quotes around the names to get the search to focus on the full name rather than the individual words.

That did the trick; eighty-seven results was a far more manageable set of possibilities to work through.

Or so I thought. But half an hour later I was no closer to finding good ole Jack than I'd been when I'd started. The man was Mr. Invisible. No address. No police record. No Facebook or LinkedIn profiles. Just a few casual mentions in articles having to do with Durante and his candidacy but that was all.

Who the hell was this guy? And where did he go?

I sat back and gave it some thought. I could probably find him via his driver's license, but had no way of getting into the department of motor vehicles computer system to carry out a search. Same went for the local utility company. But that did leave me one other avenue.

Property tax records.

As in most major cities, information on property owners and the land they occupied was public record. It only took me a few minutes to find the Web site for the assessor's office of Los Angeles County and from there to look up Jack Bergman.

There were four Jack Bergmans that owned property within the boundaries of Los Angeles County. I was immediately able to eliminate one due to the fact that the record had the man listed as deceased for more than ten years, which left only three to deal with. Two of them had bought property within the last six months, so I crossed them off the list as well. It was a bit arbitrary, I knew, but they just didn't feel right, and I had learned to trust my gut at least a little bit in matters like this.

That left me with only one name.

John A. Bergman at 402 West Cavalier Drive.

It was time to pay Jack a visit.

I gathered my things, tucked the twenty I'd promised my helper into his jacket pocket, and used his sight to help me navigate over to the librarian's desk. With my sunglasses firmly on my face, I explained that I was blind and asked if she would be kind enough to call me a cab.

Ten minutes later I was on the 405 headed toward West Cavalier Drive and what I hoped would be some answers.

>+++<

"You sure this is the place, man?"

I leaned forward so I could hear the cabbie better through the thick plexiglass window that separated us.

"402 West Cavalier Drive?"

"Yeah, yeah. I got the right address an all, I'm jus' asking if you're sure this is where you wanted to go. It's all boarded up and shit."

"Boarded up?"

"Yeah, you know, plywood over the windows and two-by-fours nailed over the doorframe? From all the graffiti it looks like it's been this way for at least a couple of months, maybe more."

Damn. Teach me to listen to my gut.

"I must have the wrong address then. Sorry for the trouble." I told him to take me back to Fuentes's place in the Hollywood Hills, which he was more than happy to do.

"Whatever you say. You're the boss," he said, in that cheery voice of his, and suddenly I wanted to hit him. I settled for leaning back in the seat and fuming.

It had not been a very productive day.

19

The sun was going down by the time I made it back to Fuentes's estate. I had the cabbie drop me off at the main gate and then had a security team member take me back to my bungalow in one of the electric carts kept on hand to make getting around the property easier. I kept the curtains drawn at all times so once inside all I had to do was shut the door behind me to shut out the last of the day's light. Taking off my sunglasses, I let my eyes adjust to the darkness.

Roaming around L.A. all day had left me feeling gritty and hungry. I took care of the latter first, calling a local pizza joint and ordering a large pie with everything on it. Once that was handled, I grabbed a change of clothing from the bedroom and headed for the shower.

I turned the water on and let it heat up for a moment, then

stripped and turned to get into the shower. From the corner of my eye I caught a glimpse of my reflection in the mirror over the sink.

Someone else's face stared back at me.

I spun around, my hands clenched into fists, ready to defend myself as my heart pounded in my chest and adrenaline flooded my system.

My own eyes, wide and frightened, stared back at me from the surface of the mirror.

There was nothing, and no one, else there.

Just my reflection.

"You're seeing things, Hunt," I said aloud, trying to reassure myself, but my voice sounded hollow against the backdrop of the running water.

I could have sworn the face I'd seen hadn't been my own. My years hunting my daughter, Elizabeth, had given me a lean, wiry look, never mind an upper body covered in tattoos. The face I'd seen had been wider, and darker, than my own. I think it was the eyes that caught my attention though; it's hard to miss the pale whiteness of my orbs, but the eyes I had seen had been dark and full of a kind of crackling intensity that had shocked me to the core.

And yet . . . I had to have imagined it.

What else could it have been but that?

Well aware of what stress can do to a person, I shook my head to clear it of the crazy notion and stepped into the shower, convinced the hot water would turn me into a new man.

A shower and some food, that's what you need, Hunt.

A shower and some food.

Half an hour later I knew I'd been right. The shower had washed away the grime of the city streets and half a large pizza supreme had eased the hunger pangs in my gut. I felt good, better than I had in days really, and the nonsense of the face in the mirror seemed to be just that—nonsense and nothing more. A result of poor lighting on a barely glimpsed image and a day spent staring at photographs of Jack Bergman and his employer, Michael Durante, though borrowed eyes.

Shaking my head and laughing at my own absurdity, I grabbed another slice of pizza and sat back, trying to figure out my next step. I needed to find Bergman, if he was still alive, that much was clear. Bergman could explain the relationship between Durante and Fuentes, might even be able to tell me what this mysterious Key was and why Fuentes wanted it so badly.

Right now he was my only link to some badly needed answers, and I had to find him before anyone else did.

Unfortunately, I had no idea where I might find the guy, which made setting up a meeting between us rather difficult.

I was going to need some help.

I might not know where Bergman had gone to ground, but I knew someone who most likely did. All I had to do was ask her.

I stood up and moved to the center of the room. I raised my face to the ceiling and extended my arms out to either side, palms up. Closing my eyes, I called out softly.

"Come to me, Whisper. Come to me."

As I called her name, I pictured her doing what I wanted.

I repeated my request, over and over again, until at last I felt the air pressure in the room change and knew that I was no longer alone.

I opened my eyes, expecting to see Whisper standing nearby, and was surprised to find her standing on the far side of the room, as far away from me as she could get without being in a different room entirely. She was staring at me with an expression that could only be defined as fear.

What the hell?

I hadn't seen Whisper this edgy, not even the night this had all started, when she'd shown up in my motel room with warnings that "he's coming." Rivera and his crew had shown up seconds later, bashing down my door and doing what they could to take me hostage. Only Whisper's warning had allowed me to fight my way clear and get out of the room. Of course I hadn't gotten far, but at this point that was like water under the bridge; nothing to be done about it now. I'd come to the conclusion that the "he" Whisper had been referring to was either Rivera or Fuentes, though I supposed it could refer to someone I had yet to meet.

Now there's a lovely thought.

I shook myself, chasing the negativity away. *Focus, Hunt.*

"I need your help, Whisper," I told her now.

She just kept staring at me with eyes wide open and that uneasy look on her face.

I'd never seen her react to me like this before. The first, faint stirring of irritation passed through me.

"Come here, Whisper. I need you to help me, understand?"

Whisper shook her head.

Somewhere in the back of my mind I processed the fact that she'd actually responded to a specific statement, that she'd shown beyond a reasonable doubt that she recognized what I was saying, and felt a thrill of wonder that the two of us were actually communicating directly. That wonder, however, was quickly replaced with irritation as I realized that she was refusing my request.

My temper flared and I could feel my lips curling into a snarl of anger.

"I said get over here!"

The shout echoed in the confined space of the bungalow, leaving no doubt as to who thought they were in charge of the relationship.

What was wrong with me?

I didn't shout at Whisper. Ever. It was something you just didn't do; I knew that instinctively. Had known it since the day we'd met. And yet here I was, raising my voice.

Expecting Whisper to vanish at the first sign of confrontation, I was surprised when I looked up again to find her still standing there.

Now, however, she wasn't alone.

Where Whisper went, Scream was never far behind.

I should have remembered that too.

Scream stood roughly halfway between Whisper and me. He, too, stared at me, with not a fearful but a disgusted expression on his face.

Being in his general vicinity makes most people uncomfortable; being right beside him could make you literally sick with fear. I had never experienced Scream's aura of terror before—had, in fact, thought I was immune—but as I stood there I was suddenly assaulted with all my worst fears at the same moment. My thoughts were flooded with all the things that haunt my psyche in the deepest dark of the dead of night, the things that no matter how hard I try I can never seem to get away from, and the sensation made me literally take several steps backward, away from my ghostly companions.

If I thought my temper had flared before, it went positively supernova now. I did not like being intimidated, particularly by something as insubstantial as a ghost, and my fury enveloped me with the swiftness of a summer storm rolling in off the plains.

My hand dipped into my pocket and came out again with my harmonica clenched securely in its grip. I'm not sure exactly what I intended to do—control him? banish him?—but thankfully, whatever it was, I didn't get the chance to see it through. As my harp rose to my lips, Whisper and Scream exchanged a glance between them and then vanished as if they had never been there at all.

I stalked around the room, ranting and raving and doing God knows what all; everything was pretty much a blur after that. I know I broke a few dishes and smashed my foot through the coffee table in an effort to release all the anger that had built up inside me during the confrontation. It must have worked, for eventually I wandered into the bedroom, collapsed on the bed, and fell asleep . . .

20

. . . only to find myself behind the wheel of the Charger I don't know how much later. I was parked by the side of the road, staring across the two lanes of traffic at a three-story motel that looked like a thousand others across the city, including the fleabag place I'd been staying in when Rivera and his crew had found me the week before. It was the kind of place you went to when you needed to lie low and didn't want to be found for a while.

I had no idea how I came to be there. I didn't remember getting in the car. I didn't remember driving there, wherever *there* actually was.

Had I been sleepwalking?

I'd heard of people doing crazy things while caught in a fugue state somewhere between sleep and wakefulness, but

I never thought it would happen to me. I knew I was under a lot of stress, but come on! Driving while asleep? This was ridiculous!

I glanced around, noted that it was still dark out.

The clock on the dash said 4:16 a.m., which meant dawn wasn't all that far away. I wasn't sure exactly where I was, but figured I'd have a better chance of getting back to Fuentes if I left now than if I hung around waiting to be trapped by the rising sun.

I shook my head to clear it, put one hand on the wheel and the other on the key, intending to start the engine, when my gaze drifted back to the motel across the street.

A blond-haired man was hurrying along the second-floor crosswalk, a bag of groceries in his hands. I only caught a glimpse of his face, but a glimpse was enough.

It was Jack Bergman.

I was positive of it.

My first instinct was to rush across the street, but I stayed were I was, watching him. From here I had a good view of the entire upper floor of the motel and was able to watch as he stopped at the third door from the end, pulled out a key, and, with a wary glance around him, opened the door and slipped inside.

The fleabag motel. The early morning run for groceries before anyone else was awake. The surreptitious glances around him to be sure no one was watching.

This was a man on the run.

But from who? Fuentes?

Or someone I didn't even know about yet?

Only one way to find out.

I got out of the car, locked it up, and hustled across the street. I figured I had, at best, another half hour of darkness left in which to make my move. After that, it was back to being blind for the day until darkness fell once more.

Hopefully it would be enough time to do what I needed to do.

I had no clue how it had happened, but somehow my sub-conscious mind must have put two and two together and de-duced where Bergman was hiding out. Stranger things had happened, I knew, so I didn't try to analyze it too much as I hurried across the street and into the motel parking lot.

The room he'd rented was the third from the end, which meant the only window was the big plate glass one in front. That was also the only other exit besides the door, as his unit backed up against the one behind him on the other side of the building. Bergman wouldn't be expecting anyone at this hour; hell, he prob-ably wasn't expecting anyone at all. If I could get inside the motel room I was pretty confident that I could get him to listen to me.

Hard and fast, that's the way it needed to be done, I de-cided. Explanations could come after I knew he wasn't going anywhere.

I hurried down the walkway until I reached the room I'd seen him enter. Looking around and not seeing anyone else, I leaned close to the door and listened for a moment.

Nothing.

Hopefully Bergman was alone.

I bent down to where the edge of the building met the sur-face of the walkway and scooped up a little of the dirt and grime that had gathered there with my finger. Adding a bit of spit, I smeared the guck over the outside surface of the peep-hole. Bergman wouldn't be able to see through it now to con-firm I was who I said I was.

Satisfied, I stepped to the side and put my back to the wall next to the door. Reaching out with my left hand, I knocked briskly.

A moment passed, then a voice called out from inside.

"Who's there?"

"Management, sir," I said, in a clear voice. "You dropped this on your way across the parking lot."

I heard the chain come off and the bolt thrown back as Bergman unlocked the door. As soon as it started to open I spun around and slammed all my weight against the door, forcing it open and sending Bergman falling backward to the floor.

Had to give him credit, he rolled over and started scrambling for the bathroom on hands and knees even as the door was swinging shut behind me. I let him go, knowing he wasn't going anywhere once he locked himself inside.

As the click of the lock resonated in my ears, I went around the room, turning off the lights and restoring my ability to see.

I walked over to the bathroom and knocked on the door.

"Hey, Bergman! Come on out of there. All I want to do is talk."

For a long moment there wasn't any response and then a querulous voice said, "You'd better leave. I'm calling the police."

I looked around the motel room, noted the cell phone sitting on the little table next to the bag of groceries he'd just carried in, and grinned.

"That's fine with me," I said. "Call away. We can all have a little chat together. I'm sure they'll be more than happy to come down here, especially when they remember that you're a material witness in the murder investigation of a mayoral candidate and all around superrich dude. This should be fun."

I walked over to the table, turned one of the chairs near it around to face the bathroom door, and settled down to wait.

After a couple minutes of silence, his voice came through the door again.

"Are you still there?"

I nearly laughed. "Yes, I'm still here."

"Who are you? What do you want?"

"My name is Jeremiah and I already told you what I want. I want to talk."

"I don't believe you. You're one of Fuentes's people, aren't you?"

Now that was an interesting leap of logic. I frowned. I thought I was the only one who'd been looking for Bergman, but apparently that wasn't the case. I wondered just what else had been going on behind the scenes that I hadn't been aware of. Did Fuentes have people out looking for Bergman even now? Had I been followed here?

I stepped over to the window and drew the curtain aside a few inches, looking out into the parking lot below. This early in the morning it was deserted; the cars empty and dark.

Relieved, I turned around, only to find Bergman standing in the doorway of the bathroom, the shower rod held over one shoulder like a baseball bat.

"You'd better leave before I hurt you," he said. His voice didn't even shake. Much.

I knew that I wasn't in any danger; even blind I was confident I could take the guy. But I raised my hands anyway, wanting him to understand I really wasn't a threat.

"We both know you're not going to hit me with that thing, so why don't we sit down and talk? That would be much easier on both of us, don't you think?"

Apparently, no, he didn't think so, for he gave a shout and charged right at me!

I waited, timing my move for the moment when he was committed to his own, and as he started to swing the shower rod as if hoping to hit a grand slam with my head as the baseball, I stepped inside the arc of his strike, blocked his forearms with one of my own, and used the other to deliver a sharp blow to his solar plexus.

That was all it took.

Bergman dropped like a stone, fighting to suck air into his temporarily paralyzed lungs.

I kicked the shower rod out of reach, grabbed him by the shoulders, and hefted him up and into the seat I'd vacated earlier.

Then I waited for him to catch his breath.

It took several minutes, and a lot of gasping for air like a fish out of water, but eventually he had control of himself. In between his overeager attempts to get air into his lungs, I tried again.

"Look, Bergman. I told you all I wanted to do was talk and I meant it. Why is that so flipping difficult to understand?"

"Fuentes's people aren't exactly known for their conversational talents."

Touché.

"Well, I'm not one of 'Fuentes's people.' At least, not by choice."

I gave him a quick rundown of how I'd been blackmailed into working for the man and how the last thing I wanted was for Fuentes to come out on top in anything, including his search for Bergman.

"So this isn't some elaborate set-up to get me to tell you what I know, only to have you cut my throat and leave my body in the Dumpster out back?"

I stared at him, surprised at the utter deviousness that would be required to think up such a plan.

"Do I look like the kind of guy who . . ." I started to say and then thought better of it. With my messed up eyes, dyed hair, and esoteric tattoos, yes, I probably *did* look like the kind of guy who would do something like that.

I sighed. Decided I'd had enough.

"All right, forget about it." I pointed at the door. "There's the exit; be my guest."

He looked at me and then at the door. You could practically see the wheels turning in the guy's head. *Is this just trap? Just a way to get my hopes up and then, when I make a break for it, discover he's got half a dozen other thugs with him waiting to make my life miserable?*

I suddenly felt sorry for him. Just what the hell had he been through?

I thought for sure he was going to make a break for it, but it seemed my offer had the opposite effect. For whatever reason, Bergman seemed to relax and settled back in his chair.

"You mind if we turn on some lights?"

"Actually, I do. Sensitive eyes."

He seemed to take that in without too much fuss. "Okay if I smoke then?"

I realized then how odd this must seem to him; me sitting out here in the pitch dark while waiting for him to come out of the bathroom. Even now, with just the thin strip of light spilling out of the bathroom door, everything else was still pretty much lost in the shadows.

I nodded my head. Then, in case he couldn't see me, said, "Be my guest."

He pulled a crumpled pack out of the front pocket of his shirt and shook out a cigarette, which he placed between his lips but didn't light.

"Trying to quit, but not quite there yet," he said, in answer to my unspoken question.

He watched me watching him for a long moment.

"*So, Jeremiah,* if that's even your real name," he said at last. "What is it you want to talk about?"

21

"Durante," I said, without hesitation. "Or, more specifically, his relationship with Fuentes."

I thought getting answers out of him was going to be like pulling teeth, but once he started talking he didn't hold back.

"Relationship? What relationship?" Bergman asked. "The two of them were like gasoline and fire; if you brought them together things were bound to get explosive."

"So they were rivals?"

Bergman shook his head. "It was much worse than that. Calling them archenemies might be closer to the mark."

"Why? What did they have between them?"

"Fuentes was everything that Durante hated: arrogant, self-absorbed, entirely focused on his own wants and needs."

"So what? There are a thousand people like that within

spitting distance of any corner in downtown L.A.," I said. "What caused the animosity between the two of them?"

Bergman shrugged. "Why do any two people hate each other? They just did, that's all."

I could see this was going to get me nowhere fast. It was time to get to the point.

"So it had nothing to do with Durante being a practitioner of the Art."

It was a reasonable guess and I knew I was on target when Bergman tensed.

"I don't know what you're talking about," he said.

I didn't have time to screw around. The sun would be up soon, and I didn't want to get caught in the light. Driving back would be difficult if that happened, even with my two pairs of shades. If I got stuck, my options would be severely limited. Calling for help would no doubt endanger Bergman. Even if I made up some reasonably plausible explanation, word would eventually get back to Fuentes that I had to be "rescued" and he'd start to wonder just what I was doing at a rundown motel like this and he'd send somebody, most likely Rivera, to investigate. Bergman would be a sitting duck. Besides, who would I call anyway? With Perkins dead, I didn't know who I could trust.

My other option would be to call a cab, which would get me back to Fuentes without difficulty but would cause problems of a different sort. I'd have to explain where the car had gone, which in turn would generate questions about what I was doing here, and I'd be right back to where I started.

Neither one would do. I had to get to the point and do it quickly if I hoped to get anything useful out of Bergman.

So instead of arguing with him, I said, "Okay then, let me show you what I mean," and snatched his sight away from him.

The typical few minutes of fear and panic followed until I told him, in a loud and annoyed voice, to be quiet and gave his sight back to him.

A headache came roaring in to replace what I'd just given back, but I figured it was a small price to pay if my little demonstration got Bergman to open up.

Thankfully, my gamble paid off.

"You're one of them," Bergman said, with more than a little hint of wonder in his tone.

I wasn't certain who he meant by "them" but I ran with it anyway.

"Yes, I'm one of 'them' as you so quaintly put it, so how about we drop this dancing about?" A line from an old movie popped into my head and I just went with it. "Help me help you, Bergman. Help me help you and then I'll be out of your hair."

The guy must have been a Tom Cruise fan for, to my surprise, it actually worked.

"All right, fine. Yes, the feud between them probably had more to do with Michael's position as magister than anything else."

"I'm listening."

"It started a few weeks after Michael had announced his run for mayor," he began. "We were at a private function at the 44 when Fuentes and that pet sorcerer of his barged in."

I didn't know what the 44 was, probably a restaurant or nightclub, but it didn't take much thought to determine who Bergman was talking about with his pet sorcerer reference.

"Words were exchanged. I don't remember them exactly, but there were a lot of accusations on Fuentes's part that Michael wasn't fit to be mayor, never mind magister, and that he should simply step down before things got ugly."

"That must have endeared Fuentes to Durante."

Bergman shrugged. "Michael was a good man: calm, reasoned. He tried to talk to Fuentes, but every time he opened his mouth the other man would start ranting and raving again. It was embarrassing, to be blunt. Eventually, Michael had no choice but to toss him out."

I couldn't imagine a purely mundane security team escorting both Fuentes and Rivera from the premises, so there must have been a bit more to those bodyguards than Bergman was letting on, but that was fine. I could read between the lines well enough.

"After that, things quickly deteriorated. Fuentes began actively campaigning against Michael's run for mayor. As a 'leading figure in the Latino community,' Fuentes made public statements against Michael's candidacy, but the real war was going on behind the scenes. Rumors were spread to various tabloid papers. Events picketed and disrupted. Allies were threatened or bought off. By the end, the two of them were ready to tear each other's throats out."

Something just wasn't making sense.

"I thought magisters had the power to determine who takes up the mantle after them," I said. "If Durante hated Fuentes so much, why on earth did he choose him as his successor?"

"That's just it; he didn't!" Bergman said heatedly. "He chose Marcus Worthington! I was there when he did it and even recorded the choice in his personal journal."

I had no idea who Marcus Worthington was, but I wasn't about to let on just how green I was, so I didn't say anything. The fact that Durante had made a written record of his choice was interesting, though. "Do you have that journal with you?"

"It was taken from the house the same night that Michael died."

Of course.

"Marcus had the experience, the vision, and most important to Durante, the moral temperament to fill his shoes as Magister."

"And Fuentes didn't."

"Damn right he didn't! The man's nothing more than a thug."

I couldn't argue with that.

"So what happened?"

Bergman was quiet for a moment and then, "I can't prove it, but I think Fuentes had Durante killed."

No shit, Sherlock, I wanted to say, but I bit my tongue and waited to hear the rest.

"Michael was tied down, tortured with a knife," Bergman said. "The authorities didn't let me in to see him, not even for identification purposes at the morgue, but I had a friend in the medical examiner's office get me enough of the details. Whoever killed him had been looking for information and the only person I know with that kind of interest in Michael was Fuentes.

"When a magister dies without naming a successor, the decision as to who will fill the position is determined by a vote taken by a council of the seniormost practitioners in the region. Fuentes had been working behind the scenes for months apparently, caging favors and storing them up for when the time was right. By the time Michael was found murdered, Fuentes had either obligated or bought off most of the members of that council so that he was the one and only candidate considered."

That sounded like the Fuentes I knew. Wait until the time is right and then bend circumstances to best fit your needs and desires.

"So what's with this Key that Fuentes is after? Why does he want it so badly?"

Bergman shook his head. "I don't know."

I stared at him, not saying anything.

Most people can't stand silence and Bergman was no different. "Really, I don't," he said after only a moment or so.

"Come on, Bergman!" I said sharply. "Do I look stupid? You were Durante's right hand man for how many years? And you don't know anything about the very thing that more than likely got your boss killed?"

My reluctant companion sighed, hesitated, and then said, "Michael only mentioned this 'Key' once and that was on the night he died."

He was quiet for so long after that that I thought he wasn't going to say anything more. When he did, it was in a subdued tone, as if the very memory was painful, and I had no doubt that it was.

"I was at Michael's, waiting for him to return from a meeting with some of his department heads. We were going to go to go out on the boat the next day; we'd both been looking forward to it.

"But he stormed in that night, visibly upset. He told me there was trouble brewing and that it was best that I got out of town for a few days. I didn't want to leave him, especially if something was happening, but he told me it was related to things 'beyond the normal' as he liked to call them and it was best if his enemies couldn't use me as a target.

"When I still refused, he had his bodyguards forcibly

remove me from the house and take me to a hotel in Palm Springs for the night."

I could see where this was going. Without his bodyguards present, Durante had been much more vulnerable than he might otherwise have been. His enemies had gotten to him because he'd been more concerned about Bergman's life than his own.

I could practically taste Bergman's regret. I'd been there, done that, and knew the special kind of hell such regret truly was.

"Before I left, I heard Michael on the phone with someone, ranting that he'd rather burn in hell for eternity than give the Key to Fuentes. That letting him take control of the Key would be a nightmare on earth.

"That was the last time I saw him alive. And the only time I heard him mention a Key. I'm sorry."

"No, I'm sorry," I replied, surprising myself. And I genuinely was. The more I heard about Fuentes, the less I liked. I still didn't know what the Key was or exactly what it did, but it was quickly becoming apparent that it must be an artifact of considerable power if Fuentes was putting this much effort into recovering it.

If that was indeed the case, I had no doubt that Durante had been right—letting Fuentes get his hands on the Key would, indeed, be a nightmare.

"Any idea who he was talking to that evening?" I asked, as gently as I could.

"None. I've been trying to figure that out for weeks now."

And just like that my great lead came to a stuttering halt. If Bergman didn't know what the Key was or where Durante might have hidden it, I was pretty much out of luck.

"So now what?"

"Now I suggest you find a different hiding place. If I was able to track you down, I'm sure those less pleasant than I can do the same."

"But I don't know anything."

I felt bad for the guy. "I know that," I told him, "and you know that, but Fuentes's thugs don't. If I were you I wouldn't take the chance."

I thanked him for his time and headed for the door. Just before I reached it, I turned back to face him.

"One last thing," I said. "Where the hell are we anyway?"

22

Dawn was edging its way over the horizon when I stepped back inside my bungalow. I was exhausted, mentally and physically. Apparently sleepwalking—and sleep-driving—required more than a fair bit of energy. Combine that with the heightened level of tension that seemed to be the norm here at Casa Fuentes and you ended up feeling the way I did now: like I'd been hit by a truck, only to have it back up and run over me a second time.

I walked into the bedroom and collapsed on the bed, still fully clothed.

Sleep must have come instantly, for the next thing I knew Grady was standing over me some indeterminate time later, poking me with the tip of my cane.

"Wake up, Princess. We've got work to do."

I mumbled something about shoving that cane somewhere uncomfortable if he touched me with it again, but apparently my threat wasn't all that convincing for he went right back to jabbing me with it.

"Come on, Hunt." Poke. "Get your ass out of bed." Poke. "Rivera's waiting."

It was the mention of Rivera that got me moving. Even in the short time I'd been here, I'd learned that it was best not to irritate the fiery Latino sorcerer if you could avoid it.

I sat up and looked around. It was dark enough that I could see Grady standing there in the shadows, but he must have left the front door open because I could see a little bit of light leaking in through the doorway behind him.

Shaking my head to clear it, I asked, "What does he want?"

"How the hell should I know?"

Grady folded my cane up and tossed it on the bed beside me. "Get up and ask him yourself," he said, as he turned and left the room.

Always the pleasant one, that was Grady all right.

I took a few minutes to change my clothes and splash some water on my face before making my way outside and over to the main house to look for Rivera.

I found him waiting for me in the foyer, along with Ilyana and Grady. Tension was in the air and I had a hunch I wasn't going to like whatever came next.

Turns out I was right.

We left the house and piled into the Charger. It felt odd to have so much room, and I wondered if anyone else in the car was thinking of Perkins's absence. Not a single word had been spoken about him since Grady had carried off his corpse two nights before. I wondered what had happened to it and then decided that I really didn't want to know. There were just too many things that fed upon the dead; pretending that he'd been given a decent burial or cremation was much better. Who knew? Perhaps he had.

The sky was clear, the sun was shining brightly, and I couldn't see a damn thing, even with both pairs of shades. So instead I sat back and waited to hear what we were up to.

When, after ten minutes, no one volunteered any information to that effect, I leaned forward and said, "So where are we going anyway?"

"To talk to some people," Rivera replied from the front passenger seat. "Keep your mouth shut and your eyes open. We'll do the rest."

I refrained from commenting on the wisdom inherent in telling a blind man to keep his eyes open—Rivera wouldn't appreciate the irony, I knew—and instead concentrated on the implications of what Rivera had just revealed.

Fuentes had obviously expected to find the third and final piece of the Key at Durante's, and our inability to do so—along with what seemed thus far his inability to find Bergman—must have left him scrambling for new options. He was no doubt betting that someone in L.A.'s supernatural community knew where it was and was sending us to shake a few trees and see what fell out. It was a scattershot strategy, at best, and told me what I needed to know about how close Fuentes was to finding the remaining portion of the Key, which was not close at all.

That gave me a little breathing room, it seemed.

Unless, of course, something actually fell out of one of the trees we were being sent to shake.

We got on the highway for a short distance and then left that behind for a variety of back streets, as evidenced by the constant starts and stops we made along the way. Eventually, maybe twenty minutes or so after we'd left Fuentes's, we pulled over and stopped.

"Remember what I said, Hunt," Rivera said, as we got out of the car. "Keep your eyes open for anything like that thing we faced the other night but otherwise let us handle things."

Right.

The scent of beer and stale sweat that met my nostrils the minute we stepped through the door told me we were in a bar. The sudden explosion of movement and a shouted "Get him!," followed by the crash of furniture and several grunts of pain, told me someone, most likely the bartender, had made a bid for freedom and failed.

I didn't think that was going to sit well with Rivera and I was right.

"Just where the *fuck* do you think *you're* going?" Rivera asked.

The reply was too mumbled for me to understand, but the voice was clearly male.

"I don't give a damn what you thought; I've got some questions and you're going to answer them. If you don't, I'll make you wish you'd never been born, understand?"

Another mumbled reply.

There was too much light in the bar for me to see anything. I didn't dare borrow the sight of any of my companions—I'd pushed my luck far enough in that area already—so I cast about looking for a ghost I might entice with my music.

No luck.

The bar was empty of apparitions, though whether that was because it was normally that way or because the ghosts had fled at the first sign of our arrival, I didn't know. Either way the result was the same; I was still unable to see.

"Have you seen this man?" Rivera asked.

"No."

The squeal of pain that erupted thirty seconds later told me that Rivera didn't believe the man's answer.

Perhaps it was better that I couldn't see after all.

"Look again. Are you sure you don't recognize him?"

The response this time was quick and clear. "It's Durante's gopher. That Bergman guy."

I nearly froze at the mention of Bergman's name, and it was only my heightened sense of self-preservation that kept me from doing so. If they knew I'd been out doing research on my own there'd be hell to pay, of that I was certain. I kept a bored look on my face and pretended not to know what was going on around me, all the while listening closely.

"Word is he used to drink here pretty regularly?"

"Yeah. Every Wednesday, like clockwork."

There was no attempt to hold back information now. Whatever Rivera had done to the guy, it had certainly impressed on him the need to cooperate.

"Was he here this week?"

"No."

Another scream, longer this time.

"Whadd'ya do that for?" the man said, after he'd stopped screaming and regained his breath.

"To remind you that I'm not fucking around. I want to know where this guy is."

"I don't know. I swear to you; I don't know."

"Verikoff?"

Ilyana spoke up for the first time since entering the building. "He's telling the truth, I think."

What? She was some kind of human-demon lie detector now? I made a mental note to remind myself to watch what I said in her presence.

"Who'd he come in here with?" Rivera wanted to know.

"Nobody."

"No one? Ever?"

I could hear the frown in Rivera's tone.

Apparently, so could the man he was addressing, for he began pleading with him. "Don't look at me like that. I'm telling you the truth. He always came in alone. I swear, man, I swear. Don't touch me again. Please!"

I started to feel sick to my stomach and turned away, unwilling to listen to any more. I could sense Ilyana's presence nearby, but she didn't say anything as I walked past. The questioning went on for several more minutes, with predictable results. The guy didn't know anything and we left there with our souls a little darker for what we'd done but with no information to show for it.

And so it went, for the rest of the day.

We'd pull up to some location, question whoever we'd come to see, and then move on to the next. From time to time I was able to borrow the sight from a nearby ghost and take a look at those Rivera was bracing for information. They ran the gamut—men and women; Mundane, Gifted, and Preternatural; young, old, and in between. By late afternoon word had apparently spread and many of those we went looking for were not in their usual places. We kept at it though, scouring the streets until well after dark, for Rivera was loath to return to Fuentes without anything new, but eventually we were forced to do just that. Continuing to bang on doors and windows was just going to send those we were looking for deeper into hiding and that was the last thing Rivera wanted.

The ride back was passed in silence and Rivera stalked off before the engine had even finished ticking. As I got out of the car, Grady said, "I could use a drink. Anyone else?"

I was about to decline, not wanting to spend any more time in the company of these sociopaths than I had to, but Ilyana grabbed my arm and answered for us both.

"Make that three," she said.

It seemed I was having that drink after all.

23

We retired to the poolroom where Grady had found me talking with Perkins a few days before. Ilyana led me over to a seat at the bar and climbed onto the stool beside me. Grady must have moved around behind the bar, for I heard glasses being knocked about and then something being poured.

"It isn't the best whiskey Fuentes's money can buy, but I'm sure you'll agree that it's a damn sight better than you're used to drinking, Hunt," Grady said as he clinked a glass down in front of me.

I wrapped my hand around the glass and raised it to my lips, intending to take a drink, but a hand on my arm stopped me.

"Hang on there, Princess. We've got to make a toast first."

"A toast?" I asked. "To what?" It didn't seem like there was all that much to be toasting lately.

But Grady surprised me.

"To Perkins," he said. "May his Gift guide him well in the afterlife."

"To Perkins," Ilyana said.

"To Perkins," I echoed.

Grady was right: Fuentes's whiskey *was* a damn sight better than anything I'd ever had. It burned pleasantly on its way down.

"Hit me again," I said, putting the glass down on the counter, and Grady complied. By the time he and Ilyana began playing pool a few minutes later, my head was just starting to buzz.

Which might explain why I asked my next question.

"So what's Rivera's story? Why's he so gung ho to please Fuentes all the time?"

The clacking of the pool ball stopped and silence fell. It hung there for a long moment, a wet curtain dropped over the festivities. I was about to tell them never mind when Ilyana spoke up.

"Sons typically like to please their fathers, don't they?"

I was in the midst of taking another sip and choked at her reply, spewing that fine whiskey all over the bar in front of me.

"Rivera's his son? Seriously?"

I just couldn't see it. There was no familial resemblance, never mind not a large enough spread in their ages. Unless Fuentes was a lot older than he looked, he would have had to father Rivera in his early teens.

"Well, not by blood," Grady said. "But blood has little to do with it in this situation. Fuentes plucked Rivera out of an orphanage when he was a teenager. Brought him up in his household, treated him as if he were his own child. It was

Fuentes who identified Rivera's particular penchant for the Art, who trained him and set him on the path he's on today. Without Fuentes, I have little doubt that Rivera would either be in jail or dead at this point."

Ilyana cut in, her tone full of disgust. "Rivera is Fuentes's attack dog, and if you find him at your door you'd best run if you get the chance. Quite a few of Fuentes's more vocal opponents disappeared or were killed under mysterious circumstances in the days immediately after he became magister. There are quite a few in the city who believe that last thing those people saw was Rivera darkening their doorway just before the end."

"Why no one has blown him away yet is beyond me," Grady muttered under his breath.

Hearing him, I wondered the same.

"What do they want?"

"Who?" Ilyana asked.

"Fuentes and Rivera. Fuentes is already magister of the city. What more is there?"

Grady laughed, but there was no joy in it. "What do most megalomaniacs want? To rule the world, right?"

I couldn't tell if he was serious or not and that frightened me a little.

Actually, that frightened me a lot.

The conversation moved on from there, but I pretty much stayed out of it as I pondered what I'd learned. It seemed that Fuentes had seized control with Rivera's help, which jibed with the things Bergman had told me previously. I assumed he'd been right—that Fuentes, or rather Rivera on behalf of Fuentes, had murdered Durante in an effort to get the Key and had failed to acquire the Key. Now they were trying to understand just what the former magister had done with the artifact and they were using us to do the dirty work.

That pissed me off, but without a way to get out from under Fuentes's thumb I didn't see what there was that I could do about it. It was extremely frustrating and eventually made my head hurt.

With a little help from that most excellent whiskey, of course.

After a time I bid the others good night and slipped out the door, headed to my bungalow for what I hoped would be restful and much needed sleep.

>++<

I woke up feeling worse than when I'd gone to bed, my muscles aching and my joints stiff and sore. I felt as if I'd put myself through the wringer half a dozen times and hoped that my discomfort wasn't a sign that I was catching the flu. I hated being sick.

I stretched out a leg, trying to relieve a cramp, and my foot brushed up against something soft and warm.

It took my sleep-fogged brain a few seconds to realize it was someone's leg.

I jerked my foot back and then froze, afraid my motion would disturb whoever was in the bed with me. I waited through several long, tense seconds, but the other person didn't stir.

That was when I realized I was naked.

I normally slept in just a pair of boxers, but those were now missing. Even worse, my groin was not only sore, but had that dried-sticky feeling I get when falling asleep before washing up after sex.

What the hell?

My senses were fully awake now. The room was dark and a cautious sniff brought me the musky scent of sex still hanging in the air. It had a peculiar flare to it, though, one that I couldn't identify.

Experimentally, I reached out with my left hand and, even though I was expecting it, nearly recoiled when it came in contact with the smooth, sleekness of a woman's hip.

A woman as naked as I was.

As light as it was, my touch must have awoken my companion, for she shifted position slightly and said sleepily, "I thought you'd had enough."

My heart jackhammered in my chest the way I imagined a mouse's heart might when cornered by a cat. Adrenaline flooded my system as fear hit me like a freight train. I had to physically fight the desire to flee that washed over me in that instant of recognition.

I knew that voice.

Knew that accent.

Ilyana.

24

How in hell's name did I end up in bed with Ilyana?

That was the thought that was spinning around my head like a kid's spinner toy on steroids as I fumbled for an answer to her remark. It hadn't been a question, not exactly, but when a beautiful woman whom you've apparently just had sex with thinks you're asking for more sex, you want to be as careful as possible in turning her down.

Especially when she has demon blood running through her veins.

An image of Ilyana swallowing that spectre whole the other night like an anaconda swallowing a mouse flashed through my mind, and I felt the skin across my body break out in goose bumps as fear seized me in its iron grip.

You had sex with a demon, my mind gibbered at me.

More than once, apparently.

Just what the fuck were you thinking?

I didn't know.

My ability to understand my actions was hampered by the fact that I had no memory of even considering such a thing, never mind carrying it out.

I couldn't explain it and yet here I was.

In the same way that I couldn't recall driving to Bergman's hotel the night before, I didn't remember anything from the moment I went to sleep until the moment I woke up naked in bed. At some point I had left my bungalow and walked to hers. I'd most likely made up some clever witticism to get her to invite me inside and then had apparently somehow maneuvered her into bed for a night of repeated sexual antics.

I didn't remember any of it.

It was like the punch line of a bad joke.

"What's the matter? Cat got your tongue?" she prompted.

"No," I said, surprised at the steadiness of my voice given how surprised and, quite frankly, mortified I was to find myself there. "Just thinking a bit. I'm sorry I woke you."

"Eh, no big deal," she said, "We've got to get up soon anyway or Rivera will come looking for us." She kicked off the covers and stretched languidly.

I couldn't help myself. I turned to watch, taking in the swell of her chest, the sleek curve of her hip, the long smooth muscle of her thigh . . .

Maybe she'd forgotten that I could see perfectly well in the dark, but I didn't think so. She was doing it on purpose to manipulate me, and I found myself wondering just what she wanted. Unfortunately, it was working. I felt my body stirring at the sight and glanced away, unwilling to be drawn into her game now that I was aware of it.

How the hell had I ended up here? I wondered again.

When I didn't respond, Ilyana slipped the sheet back over herself and rolled to face me. She watched me for several minutes, not saying anything, and then asked, "Did you really do it?"

"Do what?"

"Kill that detective in Boston. Scranton, or whatever his name was."

Someone had been checking up on me, it seemed.

"Stanton. His name was Stanton. And no, I didn't kill him."

Her eyes gleamed in the darkness, like a predator's.

"So who did?"

I explained about the fetch, the shape-changing creature that I and several others, including Stanton, had faced off against months before, of how that creature had kidnapped my daughter and been the cause, directly or indirectly, of all that had happened to me before I'd fled Boston for the Big Easy. It was a long convoluted story, but it actually felt good baring my soul; I didn't think I'd ever told it in its entirety to anyone before.

When I finished she was quiet for a moment, then said softly, "You are a good father, Jeremiah."

"Right," I said, my voice dripping with sarcasm. "If I was a good father none of this would have happened in the first place."

"Nyet!" she said sharply, causing me to jump in surprise.

She grabbed my chin in a viselike grip and made sure I was paying attention. "You *are* a good father. Much better than mine, who left me to fend for myself when I became of age. Terrible things happen to those left unprotected where I come from; he knew it, and he left anyway. Look where that got me."

She sighed, then curled her body around mine and laid her head on my chest. Her hair ticked my nose.

It wasn't the kind of behavior you expected from a demon, half-breed or not.

My common sense reminded me that I was lying there with the human equivalent of a barracuda, one that got pissed off rather easily too, but my curiosity pushed the question out of my mouth anyway.

"How did you end up working for Fuentes anyway?"

She stiffened and for a moment I was afraid she was going to do something painful to me, like rip my guts out with her bare hands, but then she settled down and started talking.

"I am not 'working' for him, as you say. I have no choice in the matter."

"How's that?" I asked, even as Fuentes's threats against Dmitri and Denise rang in my memory. Our host certainly had a variety of methods by which to insure our cooperation, and I didn't doubt Ilyana's story would turn out to be more similar to my own than I expected.

"Let's just say that I am not free to make my own choices in the matter. I will do as I am asked."

Though she didn't say it, something about her tone made me think that she'd left the phrase "for the time being" off of the end of her statement.

Since she was in a semitalkative mood, I decided to change the subject.

"So what's this Key we've been hunting for?"

I tried to be casual about it, but Ilyana apparently had

hearing as good as, if not better than, my own and caught the nuances in my tone. She tipped her head up to look at me, knowingly.

"What's the matter, Hunt? Feeling left out?"

Yes, I was, but not for the reason that she thought. "Come on, Ilyana. I live enough of my life in the dark; I don't need to be deliberately put there by those I'm trying to help."

I didn't know if it was my request or if she was just in a talkative mood, but she answered.

"The Clavis Sclerata. Latin for the Key of Wickedness or the Infernal Key."

I was a former professor of ancient languages at Harvard University. I certainly didn't need the translation, but I kept my mouth shut, not wanting to interrupt the flow of information.

"Legend has it that the Key was fashioned by a Jesuit priest named Raphael Xavier Chavez in Lisbon in the late sixteenth century. Father Chavez was a highly placed member of the Inquisition and was tasked by the Holy See with learning as much about their enemy as he possibly could.

"Believing that the best way to obtain information about the Infernal Realm and the creatures that dwelt there was to capture one of its denizens and force the information out of it, Chavez fashioned a key that would serve two purposes: the first was to open one of the Nine Gates that provide access to the Infernal Realm, the second, to summon a lesser demon. Chavez believed the information gained could then be used to better arm the Church against its ancient enemies."

Eight years ago I would have laughed at the very notion of the existence of an Infernal Realm, never mind that it was populated by demonic creatures that threatened the very safety of the world above, but now I knew better. I knew too much now, had seen too much, to ever laugh at anything of that nature again.

If Ilyana said the Key was intended to open a door to hell itself, then I believed her.

"So what happened?" I asked.

She laughed. "As they say, pride goeth before the fall. Chavez told the wrong person about his plans and a group of practitioners hostile to the Church made a predawn raid on the cathedral Chavez was using for his research. They released the demon, which promptly hunted down and slaughtered Chavez for the torture he had inflicted upon it, leaving the infiltrators free to steal the Key and disappear back into the night.

"For hundreds of years the Key was lost to myth and legend. Many believed it didn't exist. But then Fuentes received word from what he called an 'impeccable source' that a man by the name of Michael Durante was the current guardian of the Key."

"The mayoral candidate? The one found murdered a few months ago? That Durante?"

She nodded. "That's the one. Durante was also one of the most skilled practitioners of the Art in all of L.A. That didn't matter to Fuentes, however. He still sent Rivera and me to try and 'persuade' Durante to give up the Key. Durante, of course, laughed in our faces and then threw us out."

I imagined that went over well with Rivera.

"Did Fuentes have anything to do with Durante's death?"

Ilyana just looked at me, not saying anything.

I took that as answer enough.

"What happened to the Key?"

"Fuentes didn't know it at the time, but Durante split it

into three pieces and hid each piece in a different location. We've found two, but there's still one out there somewhere."

I was about to ask what Fuentes intended to do with the Key once he found all of the pieces, but a sharp knock at the door interrupted us.

"Come!" Ilyana called, before I could object.

The door opened and in walked Rivera.

The look of surprise on his face at seeing me in Ilyana's bed might have been priceless, if I wasn't so wrapped up in amazement at the fact that I could see.

Bright sunshine was streaming through the door behind Rivera but I could see!

25

I blinked several times, unable to speak.

Colors jumped out at me, crisp and bright, in a fashion similar to when I was "borrowing" the eyes of a ghost, but different as well. It took me a moment to realize that there was no corresponding splash of emotion to go along with them. Rivera was clearly annoyed at finding me there, but I couldn't see the aura of darkness that should have been shimmering around him as a result of that annoyance.

Had my sight somehow miraculously returned? Had I lost my Gift?

Rivera said something in a language I didn't understand and Ilyana answered him in the same tongue. I barely noticed; I was too wrapped up in what I was seeing. Everything was sharp, vibrant, and clear, and it was that fact that told me this

..sn't my old sight come back to me but something new entirely. It was like going from a color television set circa 1982 to a twenty-first-century high-definition plasma screen. There was just no comparison.

What the hell was going on?

In the back of my head I realized that being able to see was going to be a huge tactical advantage in the days ahead if I was going to wrest the Key from Fuentes's control, so I did everything I could to remain outwardly calm.

Two nights ago I'd somehow managed to find the hiding place of Durante's right-hand man while sleepwalking—a particularly impressive feat given it had required me driving in the dark with no recollection of having done so. Last night I ended up having wild sex with Ilyana and didn't remember even a single minute of it. Now I was able to see in the light as well as, if not better than, I could see in the dark, something that hadn't been a reality for me for years.

I felt like I was standing on the edge of a deep abyss and was afraid to look down for fear it would tip me over the edge.

Rivera said something to me, dragging me back to the present.

"What was that?" I asked.

His look was full of daggers as he said, "Get your clothes on and be out front in five minutes. We have work to do."

With another annoyed glance at Ilyana, he strode out the door and yanked it shut in his wake.

Ilyana sighed and then slipped out of bed. She padded naked on silent feet to the door of the bathroom, glancing back at me coyly from the entrance.

"Want to share the shower?" she asked.

One side of me was saying, "Oh yes" while the other was

screaming like the knights in that Monty Python clip, "Run away! Run away!"

I chose the safer alternative.

I looked down beside the bed, searching for my clothes. When I didn't see them anywhere, I asked Ilyana.

"What clothes?" she replied.

"The ones I was wearing when I came here last night."

She laughed and it was a surprisingly engaging sound. Gone was the hint of cruelty that so often characterized her reaction to the world around her; this was just pure amusement.

I liked it.

I didn't, however, like her reply.

"You weren't wearing any."

"Excuse me?"

She stood in the doorway, making no move to cover up her more than attractive form and said with no little amusement, "You weren't wearing any. You showed up at my door wrapped in a sheet with nothing on underneath it."

I felt my mouth drop open in shock.

I'd wandered over here, naked, wrapped in a sheet?

She laughed again and then stepped into the bathroom. From around the corner I heard her say, "You'd better go put on some clothes. You don't want to keep Rivera waiting."

I found the sheet she was talking about, wrapped it around myself, and headed back to my bungalow, ignoring the knowing looks from the gaggle of housekeepers I passed on the walkway in the process.

If I hadn't been so worried that I was losing my mind, I might have even found the situation comical.

>+—+<

"Where to?" Grady asked, from behind the wheel of the Charger ten minutes later.

Rivera handed him a slip of paper, but didn't say anything more. He sat in the front passenger seat, brooding, and I wondered how much of that was in response to his discovery of Ilyana and me together in her bungalow.

After Rivera had intruded on us, I'd gone back to my own bungalow and quickly showered and dressed. Knowing I was going to be out in the sun, and needing to keep up appearances, I looked for my sunglasses. I thought I'd placed both pairs—my own and the dark-tinted pair Grady had gotten for me with the side pieces—on the nightstand by the bed, but I found only the latter. I didn't have time to do a broader search, so I just grabbed the pair that was there and hustled out to the car.

It was still midmorning, so the sun was high and bright, even from behind the glasses, and I kept waiting for my vision to fail, for the curtain of white that I'd lived with for so many years now to descend over everything around me, but that didn't happen and eventually I stopped worrying about it and just went with the flow. We kept to the highway for about half an hour and then left that behind, making our way down a variety of side streets that looked vaguely familiar.

Thirty-five minutes after leaving Fuentes's property we pulled into the parking lot of a very familiar-looking motel and I started to get nervous.

Grady parked directly in front of the office. Rivera and Ilyana went in to speak to the manager while Grady and I waited outside the car. I kept my head down, not wanting to give away the fact that I'd been here before, but inside I was screaming. I hoped like hell that Bergman had taken my advice and gotten out of there or things were going to get ugly very quickly.

If Bergman was captured, I didn't know what I was going to do.

Rivera came out of the manager's office just a few moments later, Ilyana in his wake. He pointed to the second floor, said, "Room 239," and then strode in that direction.

Taking the same stairs that I used less than forty-eight hours before, we climbed to the second floor and approached the door. As Rivera moved forward, he made a complicated gesture with his hand and then flicked it in the direction of the door, which blew it inward. Without hesitation he stepped in after it.

We followed.

I knew the minute we stepped inside that the room was empty and I breathed a quick sigh of relief. Finding Bergman here would have been a bit awkward, to say the least.

There was a duffel bag on the bed with some clothing piled beside it. It looked as if he'd been interrupted while packing his things and had left in a hurry as a result, which might mean he wasn't all that far ahead of us.

Rivera must have come to the same conclusion. As he stepped over to examine the items in the duffel, he sent Grady to do a quick perimeter check, just in case Bergman was still in sight.

Bergman didn't seem the type to leave his things behind and that had me a little concerned. I glanced around, looking for some clue as to where he might have gone.

The place didn't look any different than it had when I'd been here last, with the exception of the pizza box on the table across from the bed.

Next to the pizza box was a pair of sunglasses.

My sunglasses.

My heart nearly stopped.

If Rivera recognized them I was up shit's creek without a boat, never mind a paddle.

I had to get those glasses.

The question was how?

The motel room was so small that any motion I made in the direction of the table would easily have been seen and would no doubt draw Rivera's attention. All he'd have to do would be to look past me to see the sunglasses. They weren't all that unusual a pair, not like the ones I was currently wearing, but he was a pretty astute guy and might put two and two together anyway. Especially if he asked me to produce my own for comparison.

All this went through my mind in the few seconds it took for him to poke through the clothes surrounding Bergman's duffel. He threw the shirt he had in his hands down in disgust and turned toward the table . . .

"Did you check the bathroom window?" I asked suddenly, stepping forward so as to block his view of the items on the tabletop. "That's how I got away from you, if you remember . . ."

Whatever Rivera was about to say was lost when Grady burst through the door. "South side," he gasped out, pointing. "Black SUV. Two others with him."

Rivera took off like a shot, Ilyana at his heels. Grady caught his breath for a second, then joined them.

I made to follow, glancing over at the table as I did.

The sunglasses were gone.

The only other person who'd been in the room was Ilyana, which meant she must have noticed my interest in them and scooped them up when I wasn't looking. I'd been so busy watching Rivera that I hadn't realized I was being watched in turn.

I didn't know whether to be relieved or worried even more than I was before.

Because I was blind, no one expected me to be able to keep up when they went charging off like that, so I used that to my advantage, stepping out of the room and following the walkway around to the south side of the building where I would have a good view of what was happening.

I was just in time to see the others dash into the street as a black SUV roared around the corner at the far end. There had to be a hundred yards between them, but that didn't stop Rivera from giving it his best shot, sending an honest-to-goodness fireball streaking down the street after them.

For a second I thought he might actually get lucky and clip the rear end of the vehicle, but just as it seemed like the ball was going to slam into the rear half of the vehicle, blue green lightning arced out of the SUV and intercepted the fireball, forcing it to detonate in a blinding flash of light.

Unharmed, the SUV roared out of sight.

I stared after it.

Not only had that lightning flash been familiar, but just before the SUV pulled out of sight, I thought I'd seen Dmitri's face staring back at me from out of the passenger's seat.

Things were getting stranger by the minute.

26

I pretended to feel my way downstairs and reached the car in time to witness the end of an argument between Rivera and Grady. Rivera was furious, blaming Grady for not having engaged those who'd spirited Bergman away the minute he'd first laid eyes on them. Grady, in turn, argued that there was nothing he could have done; he was, after all, just a human thief, as Rivera was always fond of reminding him. Ilyana had to step between them to keep them from coming to blows. I was thankful for the disruption, knowing that it would distract Rivera from thoughts of the sunglasses, if he'd seen them at all.

Ilyana took over the driving duties, leaving Grady to ride in back with me and be available to answer Rivera's questions. Most of them revolved around the two individuals who'd accompanied Bergman. Grady claimed not to have gotten the best look at them and could only describe them as being a "large man" and a "dark-haired woman," neither of whom he recognized. After pressing him on the topic for several minutes and not getting any more detailed answers, Rivera gave up in frustration.

It seemed clear that Rivera thought Grady was lying, but then again, maybe I was seeing it that way because I was convinced he was lying too. Grady had been much closer than I had been; if I'd managed to get a decent look at the face of the man in the passenger seat of the truck, he should have been able to as well. All of which raised an interesting question— what did Grady have to gain by lying to Rivera?

I didn't have a clue.

After playing mental tug-of-war with that one for a while, my thoughts turned to questioning whether it had actually been Dmitri I had seen or if it was just wishful thinking on my part. Denise and Dmitri were my closest friends. Hell, they were my only friends. They had stuck with me through thick and thin in Boston. I had done the same in return when Denise's obligations drew us to New Orleans. That was what friends did for one another; they watched each other's backs.

If the two of them were here, that meant that they couldn't still be under the thumb of Fuentes's man in the Big Easy, and I could breathe a sigh of relief that my actions wouldn't get them hurt. My choices would be back to being my own, which was how I certainly preferred them to be. No more indentured servitude, no more questionable ethics or blatant law-breaking. Never mind that I'd be free to get the hell out of Dodge and leave Fuentes and his cronies in the dust behind me.

I'd still have to deal with the Preacher, sure, but that was a risk that, right about now, I'd be willing to take.

If only it were that easy, I thought. No matter how many times I went back over what I'd seen earlier, I still couldn't quite convince myself that I was right, that it *had* been Dmitri I'd seen. And without that certainty, I wasn't going anywhere.

Fuentes was out when we returned, so we were spared the ass-chewing I was certain we would receive for failing to grab Bergman when we had the chance. Rivera sent Ilyana and Grady off on separate errands, leaving me to fend for myself for the afternoon. I headed into the kitchen, had one of the housekeepers whip me up a couple of sandwiches and get me a bottle of beer, and then retired to my bungalow to do some thinking.

As evening drew near I began to grow uncomfortable. The events of the last two nights had been unusual, even for me, and I was searching for explanations that made sense, any kind of sense. I supposed it was possible that my subconscious mind might have added up several separate and seemingly unrelated pieces of information and then parsed that combination of data into a logical guess for where Bergman was hiding, but it seemed unlikely as I didn't know the city very well and certainly wasn't familiar enough with it to pick that hotel out of hundreds of others. And I suppose it was possible for me to have driven most of the way there just fine, but then gotten distracted at the end of the trip and forgotten how I'd arrived there.

Possible, but highly unlikely.

The same was true for my dalliance with Ilyana. Yes, she was beautiful, with a body that would make even the most jaded player sit up and take notice, but I also had a rather healthy fear of the inhuman side of her heritage and couldn't imagine making a pass at her, never mind showing up at her door naked beneath a bedsheet. I didn't have that much to drink!

Maybe it was stress, I thought. *Stress can do crazy things to a person.*

No, there was something stranger going on here, and it was my inability to put my finger on it that was making me uneasy. I'd spent considerable time that afternoon thinking it all through and the only common denominator that I could come up with was that both incidents had begun when I'd been asleep.

Ergo, as evening drew closer, I decided that I wasn't going to do so.

Sleep, that is.

At about five o'clock I went over to the main house and raided the kitchen, bringing back a dozen Red Bulls and a jar of instant coffee to use in the coffeemaker back in the bungalow. I hadn't heard from nor seen any of the others since the events of that afternoon, which was just fine with me. I planned to watch movies and drink caffeine all night long, hoping that by breaking the pattern I wouldn't have to deal with these crazy nighttime activities again that evening.

Sometimes my naïveté surprises even me.

By ten o'clock I'd polished off four of the Red Bulls and half a dozen cups of coffee. I was so hopped up on caffeine that my stomach churned incessantly and I was having a hard time sitting still. After rewinding the movie I was watching three different times because I couldn't focus long enough to know what was going on, I decided that maybe a change of scenery might be in order.

Ten minutes later I was behind the wheel of the Charger, cruising through the Hollywood Hills with the windows down, enjoying the crisp, cool air blowing in my face.

I drove through the Hills, cruised down to Universal City and out to Toluca Lake, then back around Griffith Park by way of the I-5 freeway. I cut back west via Los Feliz Boulevard, headed for the 101.

That's when I felt it.

The faint stirring of something *other* in the back of my mind.

At first I ignored it, thinking it was just fatigue playing tricks on me or maybe the beginnings of a headache. But the feeling began to grow stronger and I started having a hard time focusing on what I was doing. My thoughts were scattered, and entwined within them were fleeting images of things that I was certain I'd never seen before. People and places and things that just shouldn't be, things that made me shudder and shake in my boots.

I shook my head, trying to clear it, and nearly ran off the road as my hands jerked the wheel to the right.

That's when I knew I was in serious trouble.

I hadn't turned the wheel.

I was dead certain of it.

An ice pick began poking about in my brain, sending spikes of blinding pain jabbing through my system and making me jerk about like a puppet on a string.

I'm not alone in here, I thought.

That's when the attack intensified. Whatever it was inside my head with me began to force its will upon me, trying to take control. I watched as one of my hands let go of the wheel, seemingly of its own accord, and jabbed the button on the radio. Loud, blaring music filled the car as my hand turned up the volume even as I struggled to force it back to the steering wheel. The spikes of pain in my head grew more frequent, the music blared in my ears, and my hands began jerking about as my control of the situation slipped away.

Darkness began to pool at the edges of my vision as I felt my personality forced into the back of my mind and glimpsed another, stronger entity settle into its place.

I remember thinking, *Damn, he's pissed!* as my consciousness seemed to fray like an old sheet flapping in hurricane-force winds, and I slipped down into darkness, screaming in vain against the power that had taken control of my body.

27

. . . I surged up from a prone position with the remains of a scream fading from my lips. It was like turning on a light: one minute I was lost and drifting, the next fully aware and in control of my body again.

I had no idea how much time had passed.

Or where I even was.

All I knew was that something *other* had taken control of me, had made me dance and sing and prance about like a puppet on a string, all while I was trapped unaware in the back of my mind.

It was absolutely terrifying.

Adrenaline flooded my system, a belated response to the threat my mind was just now beginning to understand. My instincts were telling me that I had two choices—fight or flight—

but neither was really possible. I couldn't fight something I couldn't see. And I couldn't run away from something that I was carrying around in my own head. The paradox threatened to overload my synapses and panic loomed, a dark wave rising high above my head, ready to drown me in its depths.

As I fought to keep control, I glanced down at myself, only to discover that my hands, arms, and chest were covered in drying blood!

I scrambled to my feet, frantically patting myself down, convinced the blood would turn out to be mine despite the fact that I wasn't feeling any pain.

Thankfully, it wasn't.

Just whose it was remained to be seen, but I'd deal with that when the time came.

My frantic self-examination had left my fingers and palms covered in warm, sticky blood that had the feel of drying glue, so I glanced about, looking for a place to wash it off.

I was standing in a kitchen, one I didn't recognize. Dark wood cabinets. Stainless steel appliances. Marble countertops. An island, with a sink, stood in the center of the room, and I went directly to it, nudging the faucet on with my elbow and rinsing my hands beneath the stream with a near compulsive fervor until they were free of blood.

As I turned away from the sink, hands cold and dripping, I realized that the thing in my head, whatever it might be, was allowing me to see through its eyes again. Everything had that crisp, hyper-real tinge to it, which was fine when you were looking at countertops but decidedly unsettling when looking at what seemed like gallons of blood drying on your clothing.

Afraid of what I would find, I went in search of the owner of that blood.

I'd left a faint trail of blood drops behind me when I'd entered the kitchen who knew how many hours earlier. It was dried now, but still clearly discernible for what it was, and I followed it out of the kitchen and down the hall to what had once been a bedroom but which was now nothing more than an abattoir.

The blood splashed on the front of my shirt was nothing compared to the amount that had been spilled from the body of the man on the bed in front of me. The entire bed seemed to be bathed in crimson, and its thick coppery scent filled the air, forcing me to bury my nose in the crook of my arm to keep from vomiting.

The trail of blood on the floor was thicker here than in the kitchen, and I followed it right up to the side of the bed.

The victim was spread-eagle across the bed, his arms and legs tied in such a way that they stretched him in opposite directions. His position reminded me of the position of the figure in Leonardo da Vinci's *Vitruvian Man*.

Unlike Leonardo's creation, however, the man on the bed had been mercilessly tortured.

Due to his nakedness, it was easy for me to see the dozens of cuts that had been carved into his flesh: on his chest, shoulders, stomach, arms, legs, even the bottoms of his feet. The blood that had spilled from his wounds had splashed the wall behind him and had pooled beneath his frame before running down the sides of the bed.

In addition to the knife wounds, he'd also been beaten, his face so swollen and misshapen that at first I didn't recognize him. But after staring at his face for several long moments the pieces of the puzzle finally came together and I knew.

The man on the bed was Sean Grady.

I recoiled.

Good God! Had I done this?

The blood on my clothes and hands would suggest that I had, but I didn't understand why. What had I been looking for? What had I wanted from him?

Or rather, what had the thing inside my head wanted?

Grady hadn't been the most sterling of characters, but he certainly hadn't deserved this. No one deserved this.

The killer had left a calling card as well; he'd used Grady's blood to write "I'm coming for you . . ." in large letters on the wall above the headboard.

I turned away, my thoughts awhirl as I tried to figure out what to do next, and that's when it hit me. Something Bergman said when we'd been talking the other night.

He'd been tied down, tortured with a knife . . .

The words were still ringing in my ears when I turned to look at Grady again.

Tied down, tortured with a knife . . .

I was starting to suspect I knew just who it was that was riding around with me inside my head.

But I would have to deal with him later. Right now I was standing in an active murder scene with enough blood on my clothes to land me in prison for the rest of my life. I had to do what I could to make it seem as if I'd never been here. Then, once I'd taken care of that, I had to get out of this apartment and back to Fuentes's property without anyone getting a look at me.

No small task, I assure you.

Back in Boston I'd worked as a freelance consultant to the Boston Police Department, more specifically homicide detective Miles Stanton. He'd call me in when things got a little unusual, so I'd been to my fair share of crime scenes. One thing I learned was that there was no way to eliminate all of the evidence of my presence there. There were just too many variables in play: trace evidence like hair and fiber samples, fingerprints, and DNA identification. You couldn't hide the fact that someone had been there; hell, the body alone would accomplish that all on its own. But you could hide that it had been you, specifically, that had been present, provided you had a little bit of luck on your side.

I was horrified about what had happened to Grady, but I knew I hadn't done it, not consciously or willingly anyway, and I wasn't going to take the rap for it if I could help it. I was already being hunted for murders I hadn't committed; it seemed somehow fair, given the circumstances, that I keep them from hunting me for the one I had.

The vast majority of law enforcement officials were good, honest people trying to do a difficult job in less than ideal conditions. Just like anyone else, they sometimes made mistakes. I needed to confuse the evidentiary picture enough that it would appear that mistakes had been made, even when the reality was quite different.

And who knew, maybe one of the investigators would make a mistake when processing the scene, increasing my chances of staying out of the suspect limelight.

I still had no idea whose property this was—Grady's or someone else's. If it was the latter, they could come home at any moment, so I worked as quickly and efficiently as possible, my heart pounding like a gong inside my chest the entire time.

Back in the kitchen, I found the paper towel roll and tore off a couple of sheets. Using those as makeshift gloves, I opened up the cabinet under the sink and hunted around until I found what I wanted, a bottle of household bleach. Taking the bleach back into the bedroom, I went hunting for the other item I needed, a vacuum cleaner. I was starting to think that Grady— or whoever actually owned the place—used a cleaning service that brought in their own equipment, but then I found a decade-old upright hidden away at the back of a hall closet.

I crossed my fingers and checked the bag . . .

It was full!

Armed with everything I needed, I headed back to the bedroom.

Being careful not to step in the rapidly cooling blood, I picked up the bleach in my paper-towel-covered hand, twisted off the cap, and then poured the entire bottle over Grady's corpse, moving my arm up and down his form in order to spread the liquid out as much as possible. My biggest concern was DNA evidence. I knew the bleach wouldn't destroy it, but, if given long enough, it would degrade any DNA samples enough that they couldn't be used to make a definitive match. The sharp, pungent smell of the bleach mixed with the metallic scent of spilled blood had me fighting to keep from vomiting.

Three more minutes, I told myself, *that's all I need, three more minutes.*

I tossed the plastic jug of bleach aside and picked up the vacuum bag. Snatching a pen off the nightstand, I poked a hole in the bag and then did the same thing with its contents that I had done with the bleach, namely dump it on Grady. Dirt, dust, lint, thread, fingernail clippings, you name it—it all ended up on the corpse, adding to the trace evidence the investigators would have to deal with. I was hoping there had been a lot of visitors to the apartment in the days prior to the last time it had been vacuumed, each new person adding exponentially to the workload of the forensics team.

As I tossed the bag away, I was struck with the unmistakable feeling of being watched from behind.

I spun around, bringing my arms up just in case I needed to defend myself.

As I did so I could see a figure behind me doing the same and I knew in that moment that there was no way of escaping this confrontation. Whoever it was had no doubt seen me and could now tie me to the murder; I was going to have to be certain that newcomer couldn't tell anyone what he or she had seen.

My body kicked itself into fight mode right about the same moment I completed my turn and came face to face with my attacker . . .

. . . who looked just like me!

For a second I thought the doppelganger nightmare had returned, that the fetch that Denise, Dmitri, and I had slain months before in Boston had somehow survived and had returned to make my life hell, but the true explanation was much simpler than that.

I was looking at a mirror.

I'd been so focused on the body on the bed that I hadn't noticed the wide, rectangular mirror on the wall behind the dresser. The threatening figure was nothing more than my own reflection.

Relief swept over me, but it was fleeting. The scare reinforced my awareness that time was at a premium and the longer I was here the more chance there was of someone discovering me standing over the corpse.

It was time to go.

Too bad it wasn't that easy. I couldn't just walk out of the building with Grady's blood all over me. The first person who got a good look would run off screaming and before long I'd be right back where I'd been before, running from the police and hoping they didn't start shooting.

I used the paper towels to protect myself from leaving fingerprints as I started going through the dresser drawers, looking for something to cover myself up. Grady was a bit bulkier than I was, so a sweatshirt or even an oversized t-shirt would do the trick nicely, provided it was a dark color; black would be ideal, but blue, green, or brown would work nicely as well.

The first shirt I came to was a black Grateful Dead concert tee. Even I didn't think the irony was funny, and my humor is blacker than most. Still, it was the right size and I pulled it on, being careful to keep the front of the shirt away from my body as I pulled it down. The shirt was even large enough to cover most of the bloodstain on the front of my jeans.

With any luck, this might actually work.

I had one last thing to do before I left.

I went into the kitchen and looked around until I found a dishrag. Towel in hand, I went back through the rooms I'd been in, seeking out the places I was certain I had touched after regaining consciousness and making some educated guesses on others as I went. Each location was wiped down with the towel in an effort to eliminate any fingerprints I might have left behind. It wasn't perfect, but it would have to do.

When I was finished, I went to the front door, listened, and then, not hearing anything, quietly turned the knob and peeked out into the hallway.

It was empty.

Keeping my head down, I stepped out into the hallway, pulled the door shut behind me, and headed for the stairs at the far end. I could practically feel the building security cameras pointed at the back of my head all the way down the hall.

I heard the elevator ding as I pulled open the door to the stairwell, but then I was inside and headed downward. The three-foot-high twenty-four on the wall next to me told me that I had a long way to go, but the chances of running into anyone on the stairs were drastically reduced compared to the chance of doing the same on the elevator.

Ten minutes later I stepped out the emergency entrance, wandered around to the front, and slipped into the first taxi in line.

My heart was still pounding as we drove away into the night.

28

I had the cabbie drop me off down the street from the property and walked the rest of the way, slipping through the trees until I reached the back wall and then going over the top to keep from being seen by the guards at the gate.

Once on the property, I kept to the shadows and made my way over to the row of bungalows. From there it was a relatively easy matter to ease around to the front, open the door, and then slip inside.

I kept the blinds down all the time, so there was no danger of anyone seeing me as I flipped on the lights and headed directly for the bathroom. I turned on the shower and was about to strip down when I had second thoughts.

Don't screw things up now, I told myself, and headed back into the kitchen. I got a large plastic trash bag from under the sink and carried it into the bathroom. I shook open the bag and then arranged it on the floor so that I could stand inside it. With the plastic sack underneath me to catch any dried blood that might crack and fall off my clothes, I undressed, stuffing everything that I took off into the bag around my feet.

When I was finished, I stepped out of the bag and into the shower. I felt dirty in a way I'd never felt before and I scrubbed at my skin, flaking off the splatters of dried blood and then scrubbing and scrubbing some more until my flesh was pink with the pressure. By the time I got out, I think I left more than a few layers of skin behind.

I dressed in clean clothes, dried my hair with a towel, ran a brush through it, and then dumped the towel in the garbage bag with the rest of the ruined clothing just to be safe. I bundled up the bag and tied it tight. My plan was to carry it around to the garage and bury it deep amidst the other bags that were already in the dumpster there for pickup later that afternoon.

Before I had a chance to do so, however, there was a loud pounding at my door.

For one heart-stopping moment I was certain I'd been discovered, and I found myself waiting for the shout of "Police!" and the crash of the door being broken in with a tactical ram.

Instead, I got another knock and a muffled shout. "Hunt! Open the door!"

Rivera!

I could think of only one reason he'd be pounding on my door at this hour of the morning, and it wasn't to play Scrabble.

Getting caught with a bag of bloody clothes in my hands was probably not a good idea, so I glanced around frantically, looking for a place to stash them that wouldn't be immediately discovered. The closet was out, as that was too obvious. So was shoving the bag in with the rest of the trash under the kitchen counter. I needed someplace to stash it long enough to get rid of it properly

My gaze fell upon the ceiling tiles above me.

I didn't have time to think about it any longer. I stood on the edge of the tub, popped one of the tiles loose with my left hand, and stuffed the bag inside with my right. I was just pulling the tile back into place when I heard him again.

"Open the door, Hunt, or I'm coming in!"

I hopped down from the tub, hit the flush on the toilet to give me a reasonable explanation of delay, and then hurried over to open the front door.

Rivera gave me a suspicious glare when I did so, but with the sun coming up I wasn't supposed to be able to see it and so I didn't respond. Nor did I react when he peered past me on either side, clearly looking for something, though I didn't know what.

Instead, I went on the offensive.

"Rivera? Do you have any idea what time it is?"

He studied me for a moment before responding. I expected some wiseass remark from him, as he usually felt the need to assert his superiority in such situations, but this time all he said was, "Fuentes wants you."

That was all.

"Now?" I asked.

"Yes, now."

His tone was flat, devoid of emotion, and I recognized it as a sign of intense anger. Rivera barely seemed to be in control, and I knew it wouldn't take much to set him off. With that in mind, I decided to tread lightly and dropped the irritated act.

"Let me get my cane."

I left the door open so he could see me as I stepped back inside and grabbed my cane off the kitchen counter. Unfolding it, I returned to the door and said, "Ready."

Without another word Rivera turned and strode off in the direction of the main house.

I followed.

A few minutes later he was ushering me into Fuentes's office. The boss man sat behind his desk, watching me closely as I entered. I pretended not to notice, felt for the chair I knew was there, and then stood beside it.

"Sit down, Hunt."

I sat.

He stared at me; I pretended not to see him.

Outside I was as cool as a cucumber, but inside my thoughts were churning a mile a minute. *What did they know? Who had they talked to? What had they seen?*

I didn't have any idea.

It was the not knowing that was making me nervous.

After a moment, Fuentes said, "We have a problem, Hunt."

I considered his words and the tone in which he said them very carefully. Taken one way, his statement could mean that he and I had a problem between us. Taken another, it could mean that there was a problem that the two of us, together, needed to solve.

There were miles between the two statements.

I fought to keep from tensing as I replied, "Something I can help with?"

"Grady's dead."

I froze, intentionally, trying for stunned surprise. I shook my head, as if I hadn't heard him correctly.

"Come again?"

I could see that he was still studying me intently and I tried not to let it bother me as I waited for his answer.

"Sean Grady was killed by an intruder at some point last night."

"Here? On the property?"

Fuentes shook his head. "No, it was . . . elsewhere."

Elsewhere? That was a strange way of putting it. "Any idea what happened?"

Fuentes waved a hand; not important, the gesture said. "Rivera found the body about an hour ago."

Most people would have glanced back toward Rivera at that point, a physical way of acknowledging that the other man had been mentioned. I'd been blind a long time and thought such instinctive behaviors had gone by the wayside long ago, but my newfound ability to see, even if it was through an unwanted passenger's eyes, had me repeating them like I'd never lost my sight. Thankfully, I caught myself in time and turned the motion into a simple adjustment of my position in the chair.

Fuentes wasn't finished. "He's going back to the crime scene in a few minutes. I want you to go with him. Do what he tells you to do. Is that clear?"

Crystal, I thought dryly, the sarcasm dying to fall from my lips, but I managed to hold my tongue and just nodded instead.

The thought came to me that this might actually be a better turn of events than I had hoped for. Fuentes wouldn't want the police nosing about in Grady's business because that might bring to light the thief's connection to Fuentes and the activities he'd been performing on Fuentes's behalf. I suspected that Rivera and I were headed back to the crime scene to do some cleaning up of our own before the authorities were brought in, if they were even brought in at all. It was more likely that Grady would be taken care of in the same manner that Perkins had: a quick disappearance and an unmarked grave somewhere remote that would quickly be forgotten. I assumed my presence there was due to my previous work with the homicide team out of Boston; Fuentes wanted to tap my knowledge of crime-scene investigative techniques to make sure that Rivera didn't overlook anything the police might find significant.

The magister's next words confirmed my guess.

"You've had some experience with this kind of thing, so feel free to speak up where you think it necessary, but follow Rivera's lead. I've given him my instructions and expect them to be carried out."

"I understand."

I don't know exactly what Fuentes had been looking for on my face this whole time, but apparently my answers had satisfied him. He grunted once, softly, as if to himself, and then nodded. "Good. You're doing well, Hunt. I'm pleased with how you're fitting in here."

I wanted to tell him I didn't give a rat's ass how well I was fitting in and that I would doing everything I could to screw him royally as soon as I had the chance, but I simply nodded, once, and then rose from my seat to follow Rivera out the door.

29

That's how I ended up riding in the passenger seat of Denise's Charger as Rivera retraced almost the exact same route the cabbie had taken to bring me back just a hour or so again, but in reverse. For the longest time he didn't say anything and then, almost casually, he said, "Why was your hair wet?"

It was such an innocuous question that I was taken aback at first and had no idea what he was talking about.

"My hair?"

"Yes, when I came to the door, your hair was wet. And yet it took you several minutes to open the door, as if I'd woken you up from sleep."

I looked over at him, knowing not to do so would be more suspicious. It didn't matter that I was blind and couldn't see him; when someone accuses you of something, even if they don't come right out and say it, you turn and look at that person.

"What, exactly, are you implying, Rivera?"

"I'm not implying anything," he said. "I'm asking you a question. Why was your hair wet?"

I laughed in his face. "My hair was wet because I'd just gotten out of the shower." Anticipating his next question, I continued. "When I can't sleep, a hot shower usually calms my brain down enough to let me get some rest."

It was a simple enough explanation and one that he couldn't disprove, not unless he'd seen me coming or going from the bungalow, which I didn't think he had. My first instinct had been to tell him that I'd showered as a result of another long and satisfying bout with Ilyana. I was confident that she'd back me up, but I didn't know what she'd been doing all evening; for all I knew, she could have been with Rivera when he'd discovered Grady's body and I'd have gone from the frying pan into the fire in the space of a heartbeat.

He didn't say anything to that and so we rode in silence for the rest of the way to Grady's apartment building. He parked the car and got out, then started walking away across the lot toward the entrance to the building. Refusing to be drawn into his game, I stood beside the car, listening to the ticking of the engine as it cooled and the activity on the street nearby. After about thirty seconds I could see him walking back over to me.

"Don't fuck with me, Hunt," he said, his voice low and deadly.

I put on my most innocent expression, smiled, and said, "Fuck you, asshole." I put just the right amount of irritation and annoyance into it; that shit should have won me an Academy Award. But I wasn't close to being done. "I'm blind, remember? Or did that little fact slip beneath your radar? You can't just walk off and expect me to catch up if I have no idea where you've gone. If you want my help you're going to have to find some common courtesy in that sorry excuse for a brain and help me."

He didn't know it, but I could see him perfectly fine, and I had a few gleeful moments as I watched the war of emotions spill across his face. He was furious at being spoken to that way but trapped by the fact that he needed me in order to accomplish whatever it was that Fuentes wanted me to do inside Grady's apartment. His fists clenched, his face grew red, and his eyes bore into me like twin spikes of black lightning. All the while I stood there, playing innocent and looking off into the distance the way I normally did when talking to someone I couldn't see.

After what felt like minutes but was probably no more than twenty seconds, he said begrudgingly, "This way," and then waited for me to unfold my cane and follow along beside him.

Once inside, Rivera led me over to the elevator, then held the door so I could get inside without trouble.

Maybe you can teach an old dog new tricks. Who knew?

We were on our way to the twenty-fourth floor and the apartment I'd left Grady's corpse in two hours before when a question occurred to me.

"Why did Grady have an apartment?"

Rivera didn't say anything.

That didn't stop me, however. "The rest of us—Perkins, myself, Ilyana, hell, even you—have living quarters of one kind or another on Fuentes's property. And yet here we have Grady, a thief no less, living out from under the boss's, and by extension, your own, thumb. What's up with that?"

I really hadn't expected him to say anything; after all, what incentive did he have, aside from assuaging my curiosity, and he really didn't give two shits about that, I knew.

But Rivera surprised me. "He was assigned a bungalow just like the rest of you."

Interesting.

"So this isn't his apartment?"

Rivera shook his head. "No, it's his apartment all right."

"How do you know?"

The elevator came to a stop and we got off on the twenty-fourth floor, turning left toward Grady's apartment. At the end of the hall was the stairwell that I'd gone down earlier.

"We know. That's all."

From his tone I decided not to push. There were a hundred different ways of confirming the information, from something as simple as a search of public property records to something more esoteric like a scrying or other mystical ritual.

Rivera stopped in front of the door to Grady's apartment, took a key out of his pocket, and turned to face me.

"You might want to brace yourself if the smell of blood bothers you."

If you only knew . . .

Rivera unlocked the door and stepped inside. "This way," he said.

I followed, pulling the door closed and then locking it behind me. As I turned around, I saw that Rivera had stopped in the middle of the living room and was looking out at the city through the floor-to-ceiling windows, his back to me.

In that instant I was overwhelmed with an almost murderous rage that swept over me like a forest fire. In my mind's eye I imagined wrapping my hands around his throat and squeezing the life from him, of being close enough to watch his eyes bulging out of their sockets, feel his legs kicking and jerking as he fought for air . . .

I turned away, breaking the line of sight between us, and it was like drawing the curtain at the end of a play; the thoughts disappeared and the thing in my head settled back down into silence for the time being. I breathed a sigh of relief. Taking on Rivera bare-handed was not my idea of a fair fight. It seemed I had dodged a bullet for the time being, but I had no doubt that presence would rear its head again before all this was through.

Rivera led me to the bedroom in the back of the apartment, where I was once again treated to the sight of my handiwork. I tried not to flinch and pretended to listen as he explained what was in the room with us.

"So why am I here?" I asked, when he was finished.

Rivera's gaze was locked on the writing on the wall as he said, "I want to know if Grady's ghost is still hanging about here somewhere. If it is, I want you to talk with it, find out what happened and who did this."

Ghosts didn't talk, at least not in the way that Rivera was suggesting, but I knew what he was asking just the same. It was a testament to how focused I'd been on covering my tracks when I came to on the kitchen floor earlier that I hadn't even thought to look for Grady's lingering presence.

"Got it."

I had no idea what would happen if I tried to access my ghostsight with this thing in my head, but now was as good a time as any to find out, I thought. I closed my eyes, flipped the switch in the back of my head, and opened them again to a new reality.

The physical world faded into the background, growing

fainter and less substantial. At the same time cracks and black pockets of decay spread across what remained, like a time-lapse presentation of the effects of entropy on a living world.

I glanced at Rivera.

With my ghostsight, I see the world's true face. Nothing can hide from me; nothing can defeat the purity of my gaze. I can see through magick and glamours to reveal the real creature underneath as easily as I can see the state of a person's soul.

Rivera's soul was as black as pitch and twice as dark. He was surrounded by the same dark aura of power that I'd witnessed the first time I'd looked at him this way and so I didn't linger there, knowing that delving into the depths of Rivera's secrets was not on my current agenda. Instead, I let my gaze move about the room.

Grady came into view almost immediately, as if he'd been waiting for me. He stood in the corner, his ghostly form outlined in a silvery, luminescent glow that made him pop out against the background decay, and pointed a finger in my direction.

I tensed, waiting for an attack, but he did nothing more than glare at me with an angry expression.

Sorry, Grady, I thought in his direction and then turned slowly as if examining the rest of the room.

"Well?" Rivera asked.

I paused. I knew very little about Rivera and had no sense at all of the extent of his powers. He could be staring at Grady right now, fully aware of his presence and just waiting for me to say the wrong thing. Hell, for all I knew he might have been able to detect my earlier presence in the apartment and had set all of this up as an elaborate scheme to get me to betray myself through my own actions. Sure, it was far-fetched, but when dealing with the Gifted I'd come to learn that far-fetched most certainly didn't mean impossible.

Did I dare lie?

Yes, I decided finally. Rivera was a come-straight-at-you, in-your-face kind of guy. Fuentes might try to trip you up with your own words and actions, but Rivera didn't have the subtlety for it, I thought.

I covered my indecision by glancing around the room again, and this time I saw something I hadn't noticed before. There was a sheen of luminescence in the shape of a rectangle on the interior wall of the room, opposite the bed. It reminded me of seeing a light peeking out from beneath a closed door, but on all four sides instead of just one.

Grady, it seemed, had even more secrets to hide than we knew.

30

Rivera was growing impatient at my lack of response, so I figured I'd better say something before he totally lost it.

"No sign of Grady's ghost," I told him and watched him visibly relax at my words. Apparently he was just as sick and tired of facing off against angry ghosts as I was. "No ghost, but I did find something interesting."

"I'm listening."

I walked over to the wall and rapped right in the center of the luminescent rectangle.

"I think there's a safe behind this wall."

A look of eagerness crossed his face and he hurried over to stand next to me. He put his palms flat against the wall at roughly the same place where my hand had been and then closed his eyes. As I watched, black, ropy wisps of smoke rose from the back of each hand, twisted and twined about each other, and then stabbed downward at the wall in front of us with the blink of an eye. A few seconds passed and then Rivera stepped back, pulling his hands away from the wall, and opened his eyes.

"I think you're right. We need a sledgehammer," he said.

The two of us hunted around for one, but the best we could come up with was a meat tenderizer from the kitchen. I was ready to begin pounding away when Rivera walked out of the apartment, only to return a few minutes later carrying a fire extinguisher he'd taken from somewhere out in the hall.

I eyed it dubiously and then said, "Can't you just blast the wall to expose the safe?"

He shook his head. "Not without possibly damaging the safe, and I don't want to do that until I know exactly what I'm dealing with here. I don't know about you, but I'm very curious what Grady considered important enough to hide away behind a wall."

I hated to admit it, but I agreed with him completely. I wanted to know just as badly as he did.

Rivera raised the extinguisher and brought it smashing down on the wall about six inches to the right of where he'd placed his hands earlier. The double layer of Sheetrock crumpled and split, leaving a battered dent in the wall. Rivera did it several more times, creating a rectangle of crushed Sheetrock. When he put the extinguisher down and began tearing at the Sheetrock with his bare hands, I stepped in to help him. In just a few minutes we had the object Grady had hidden behind the wall exposed to view.

It was a safe.

One of the old-fashioned kind made of solid cast iron, with

a fat combination dial and brass handle jutting out from the center of its face. Two-by-fours had been cut and fitted together to form a framework that supported the safe at a height of about five feet off the ground.

Rivera stepped forward and reached for the handle.

"Wait!" I cried.

When Rivera stopped and looked in my direction, I asked, "What if Grady booby-trapped the safe?"

He shrugged. "If he did, we won't live long enough to know it," he said. He paused, considering, and then said, "Why don't you go wait for me in the living room?"

I shook my head. "I'm fine where I am. What if Grady's ghost suddenly turns up and attacks while I'm in the other room?"

He glanced around, then back at me. "Is that likely?"

"I don't know. Does he have reason to?"

I knew Rivera would see that as an accusation that he'd been the one to kill Grady and I threw it out there intentionally, wanting to see what kind of reaction in provoked. He wasn't as easily set off as I'd hoped, though. He just scowled at me and said, "Fine. Stay here. Turn off your Sight though; I'll let you know if you need to see what's in here."

"Kinda hard to for me to see if Grady's ghost is waiting to pounce without my Sight, but if that's what you want . . ."

"Yes. That's what I want."

"Okay." I paused. "Done."

"Good, now wait over by the door."

"Right." I did what I was told, but kept my head up and pointed in his direction, as if listening closely to what was going on. In reality, dropping my ghostsight had simply brought my rider's sight back over my own.

I watched everything Rivera did.

He waited until I was across the room and then pulled the handle of the safe.

I cringed, fully expecting the worst. I had visions of an explosive charge going off, blowing both the safe and the two of us into smithereens, Rivera's fatalism be damned, but nothing happened.

The handle was locked and simply made a clicking noise when he pulled it down.

Even I would have recognized that sound. "Now what?"

He didn't respond. Instead, he kept one hand on the handle and put the other over the dial beside it. There was a flash of red green light accompanied by the scorched-metal smell of ozone. When he took his hand away, the dial was revealed to be bent and blackened as if it had just been through a massive fire.

"What have you been hiding, Grady?" Rivera asked himself and then pulled the handle outward.

The door to the safe swung open on well-oiled hinges.

Five minutes later he had the contents of the safe spread out on the table in the living room. It included sixteen stacks of one-hundred-dollar bills, a passport with a picture of Grady in it that had been issued in the name Daniel Stevens, and a thick set of paper files banded together with a short bungee cord.

As Rivera counted the money, all three hundred and twenty thousand dollars of it, I sat across from him and waited as patiently as I could, resisting the urge to take a look for myself by pulling off that bungee cord and leafing through the files. After all, I wasn't supposed to be able to see anything. Within moments I was ready to scream with impatience.

The money didn't matter; I was certain of it. The mystery was in the files.

Convinced I was blind, Rivera saw no need to hide the contents of the files away from me as he began to leaf through them. By keeping my head in one position, I was able to observe a fair amount of the files he was looking through. I wasn't the greatest at reading upside down, but I made do and it didn't take all that much effort to understand just what was in front of us.

Grady, it seemed, had been working undercover for someone else.

The files contained notes and observations on many of Fuentes's senior lieutenants, including both Rivera and Ilyana, detailing what they had been doing, who they had been meeting with, and what they were expected to accomplish for any task assigned to them over the last six months. The information appeared to have been meticulously collected and had been cross-referenced with the names of those who supplied it as well as those who had corroborated it. If a piece of information couldn't be corroborated, Grady had made note of that and marked the data as questionable.

He'd been thorough.

There wasn't that much that was marked questionable, as far as I could see.

Rivera seemed to grow calmer as he worked through the thick file, as if each new revelation of betrayal was simply confirming something he already suspected or perhaps already knew.

I knew I hadn't given the impression I was a particularly patient man, so eventually I spoke up. "Well? Are you just going to leave me in the dark? What the hell was in the safe?"

He might have seemed calm on the outside, but when he looked up at me I saw the fire in his eyes. Rivera was pissed.

"There are some materials here that we need to bring back with us to the magister. I'm going to find something to pack them in and then we'll get out of here."

I stared at that stack of cash for several long minutes once he left the room. A guy could run pretty far with that kind of spare change on hand.

I'd have to take out Rivera in order to get away with it though, and I wasn't sure I was ready to do that.

Yet.

There was still time; we hadn't yet found the third piece of the Key.

When Rivera returned to the room, I helped him pack the cash and stack of files into the duffel bag he'd found somewhere else in the apartment and followed him to the door.

31

The Preacher was waiting for me when I got back to my bungalow later that morning. I stepped inside, felt the biting cold that usually accompanied him like a cloud of Arctic weather, and knew I wasn't alone. When I turned around after shutting the door, he was standing a few feet away, staring at me with those empty eye sockets of his.

"You surprise me, Hunt."

"Oh yeah," I replied, "why's that?"

"The half-breed, Hunt? Really?"

I felt my ears turning red with embarrassment. How the hell did the Preacher know about that?

"Not really any of your business, now is it?"

He laughed. "Au contraire, Hunt. It *is* my business. You owe me a favor, and until I collect on that favor I will take an interest in anything that can limit your ability to deliver it. What will your dear Denise say when she learns of your dalliance with the wannabe demon?"

I took a step toward him, the anger rising from somewhere deep inside and spreading outward like liquid fire through my veins.

"You leave Denise out of this," I told him, my fists clenching by my side. "Ilyana, too."

I'd used physical force against the Preacher in the past and wouldn't hesitate to do so again if it became necessary.

"I'm not the one who pulled either of them into this. That was all you, Hunt. Couldn't just leave them well enough alone, huh? First you dragged Clearwater into your business in Boston and now you're doing the same with the half-breed. One would think the kidnapping of your daughter would have taught you to mind your business."

"Don't you dare bring my daughter into this!"

He grinned and waggled a finger at me.

"Temper, temper, Hunt."

He turned his back, deliberately I was sure, to see what I would do, but I stayed right where I was, unwilling to provoke a confrontation.

He did a little hop, skip, and a jump, then turned back to face me, straightening as he did so.

"Do you have the Key?" he asked, suddenly turning serious.

I shook my head. "Not yet."

He looked at me a moment, and then cocked his head to the side and looked at me some more. I felt like a bug under a microscope and resisted the urge to shift my feet. He was waiting for me to say something, it seemed, but I was determined not to give him the satisfaction.

Eventually, he asked, "Why not?"

I shrugged. "The Key was split into three sections. I haven't found the third section yet."

"But you have the other two?"

Another shake of my head. "Not in my possession, no, but I know where they are and can get access to them when the time is right."

"That's not good enough."

I was starting to grow really tired of all the people in my life who thought they could direct my every move. After the day I'd had, I didn't give a damn whether the Preacher thought that was good enough or not.

"Frankly, I don't care whether you find that acceptable or not," I told him. "It is what it is."

I had the sense that he was glowering at me with those empty eye sockets as he said, "I'm growing impatient, Hunt."

Now it was my turn to laugh. "Impatient? You've got to be kidding me. It's only been a few days since you gave me this assignment! Did you think I could just wave my hands and cause a mystical artifact that has been missing for the last few hundred years to miraculously appear just because you want it to?"

He was nonplussed. "How you do it is your business, Hunt. I just want the job done."

"I'll get it done, just as I told you I would. I simply need more time to do so."

"Fine. I will give you three more days."

"What?!" That wasn't anywhere near enough time. Neither Fuentes nor Rivera had any idea where the third piece of the Key had been hidden and I certainly didn't either. I'd been waiting for them to get a lead on it and had then planned to make my move to recover all of the pieces before Fuentes could do whatever it was that he intended to do with them.

"Three days, Hunt. Not a moment more."

Talk about déjà vu. That was exactly the time frame he'd given me to bring Denise's soul back from Caer Wydyr, the Fortress of Glass in the lands of the dead, when he'd come to me in the midst of the crisis in New Orleans. I'd taken the deal he'd offered and beaten his clock, though not by much. My gut told me he'd chosen the same interval just to mess with my head.

"There's just no way," I told him.

His reply all but tripped over my statement.

"Do you admit defeat? Are you forfeiting the task?"

Just as with the last time he'd visited with me, there was a certain ritual-like quality to his question, as if the answer meant so much more than the words seemed to indicate they did. It would be so easy to tell him that what he was asking me to do was downright impossible, but as before, something stayed my tongue.

I straightened and stared right into those hollow pits where his eyes used to be, had the fleeting thought that we made quite the pair with our twin sets of ruined eyes that could both still see, and pushed the thought away as I answered him in a clear, confident voice.

"No. The task is not forfeit."

I wanted to be sure there was no chance of a misunderstanding.

He stared back at me.

"Three days then, Hunt. Three days."

"Agreed," I replied.

Then I did something that, in hindsight, seems rather monumentally stupid, but made perfect sense at the time.

I activated my ghostsight.

The true face of things, that's what my ghostsight could reveal, and I wanted to know just who, or what, this Preacher was. He looked and talked and acted like a man, but my gut said he was far more than that. No ordinary man, no matter how powerful, could tear open a rift in the fabric of the world the way he'd done in New Orleans. No ordinary man could find me at seemingly a moment's notice. No ordinary man could appear and disappear at will, the way this one did. I was tired of wondering; it was time to know the truth.

For the briefest of seconds I saw beyond the Preacher's mask. Images flashed past the movie screen in my mind, there and gone again before I could fully focus upon them. Still, what I saw in that brief moment was more than enough—a man strapped naked to a nail-studded rack as something invisible slashed through the skin of his flesh, leaving gaping wounds like open mouths screaming in its wake; hot irons being plunged into open eye sockets as a tongueless mouth screamed itself raw; a body being hacked into pieces and tossed from a cliff into a dark sea far below while demons cavorted in the waves— and then there was nothing but a scream of rage so loud and so strong that it literally lifted me off my feet and flung me away across the room as it was filled with a blinding light.

When I staggered to my feet, the Preacher was gone.

32

Midafternoon found me, Rivera, and Ilyana back on the street, rousting anyone we thought might have some information about the Key or Grady's prior affiliations before coming to "work" for Fuentes. It was a slow process.

As I'd suspected would be the case, Fuentes had been furious to learn that one of his own had betrayed him. The magister just didn't strike me as a particularly forgiving individual, and I knew that Grady was lucky he hadn't been caught in the act. If he had, he probably would have suffered even worse than he had at the hands of the thing in my head.

I kept referring to it as the thing, but the truth was I knew exactly what, and who, it was. Durante's ghost. I just didn't have any idea how to get rid of him. I could try and banish him by playing my harmonica, but I didn't have all that much confidence that it would work because the minute he started to feel the pull of the music all he had to do was force me out and take over the driver's seat. I wasn't sure just how much more I could take before he started making his presence there permanent.

So far I'd been lucky; he'd only tried to take control when I'd been sleeping. He hadn't done anything beyond lending me his sight during daylight hours, but that didn't mean he couldn't or wouldn't end up doing something more. Eventually, he'd decide that a certain moment's opportunity was too good to pass up and he'd snatch control right out from underneath my feet.

My unwanted passenger had taken control and killed a man while I'd slept last night. Given the message that he'd left behind, I had little reason to doubt that he'd try something similar tonight. Grady had been an easy target; he'd been human, after all, and didn't have any extra abilities or gifts that would have helped him fight back. What if tonight's target was Ilyana? Or Rivera? Or, heaven forbid, Fuentes himself? Any one of those three wouldn't hesitate to fry me if they considered me a threat, and without control of my body there wasn't a damn thing I'd be able to do about it.

All of which meant I had about twelve hours to come up with a plan.

No pressure.

Our efforts that afternoon to obtain any information about the Key or Grady were ultimately fruitless, and early evening found us in a crowded Mexican restaurant, downing a few beers and waiting on some dinner. After sitting there for a while, I had to use the restroom, so I excused myself and made my way through the diners to the men's room at the back of the restaurant.

I was only a few feet away from the restroom when someone abruptly stood up from a nearby table, bumping into me and knocking me off balance. I would have fallen if others seated nearby hadn't reached out and steadied me. I turned to say something, but whoever it was had already disappeared into the crowd.

It was only a few minutes later, as I stood in front of the mirrored sink to wash my hands, that I noticed a slip of paper sticking out of my pocket that hadn't been there before. I took it out, unfolded it, and read what was written there.

12549 Tamerlane Drive
10:00pm

That was it; nothing more.

Clearly someone wanted a meeting, but who? And why? My first thought was that it was Bergman, but then, remembering the face I thought I'd glimpsed through that SUV's window, I wondered if it might be Dmitri. It wasn't as if he could just call me up and chat, after all.

Whoever it had been, they had waited until I was away from Ilyana and Rivera before making their move, so it seemed logical that they weren't a fan of Fuentes. That fact alone made me want to make the meeting.

I memorized the address, flushed the paper down the toilet, and returned to my seat.

"Everything all right?" Rivera asked, when I sat back down.

"Sure. Why?" I was suddenly worried that he'd seen the whole encounter, but my fears turned out to be groundless.

"You were gone for a while."

I shrugged, then reached for my drink. "Only one stall and the guy in front of me took awhile. Hope it's not the food they serve in this place."

Rivera scowled, unamused.

Ignoring him, I took a swig of my beer and hoped I wouldn't have to put up with him or Fuentes much longer.

>+++<

I left my bungalow around eleven and retrieved the Charger from the garage out back. I typed the address into the GPS, saw that it was less than an hour's drive, and headed out into the night. I was driving without my shades for the first time in years and felt almost naked without them. I had them nearby though, just in case the ghost in my head decided that he didn't want to be looking out anymore and left me alone in my blindness.

I caught the I-5 and headed out of town.

The address turned out to be that of a twenty-four-hour diner on a dark stretch of highway about forty miles outside of L.A. At this hour there were only a few cars and a handful of tractor trailer rigs in the parking lot. All of the rigs were dark, their drivers no doubt curled up in the back of their cabs to catch a few hours of shut-eye before making the return trip back to wherever they had come from. A tall thin man and a teenager in matching Red Sox caps were just getting into a shiny new Lexus as I swung past, but they were laughing together and neither bothered to even look in my direction.

Of the four remaining cars in the lot, only the dark-colored Mustang caught my attention. It was a newer model, parked off by itself near the back of the lot, in a spot that was just on the edge of the sodium-arc lights' reach. As I slowly approached, the driver flashed the lights at me, once, briefly.

I parked a few spots away, with nothing between us, and got out of the car. The night was cold and reasonably quiet, the only sound the faint growl of cars going past on the interstate off in the distance.

The door to the Mustang opened. The interior light didn't come on as one might normally expect, which meant it was either broken or disabled. My money was on the latter.

There was a pause and then a large, hulking individual climbed out of the driver's seat and stood next to the vehicle for a moment, watching me just as I was watching him.

We might have stood there half the night, both of us hesitant to make the first move, if the passenger door of the Mustang hadn't opened at that point to let the woman inside get out.

She looked over at me and even in the near darkness I knew who she was instantly. My heart skipped a beat, maybe more, as I drank her in. The sight of her was like food for my starving soul, for I truly thought I might never see her again. I marveled that she was here at all and was curious about her healing regimen. I wondered if she'd forgiven me yet for shoving an ancient dagger deep into her heart.

Only one way to find out.

I walked toward them.

As I drew closer I could see Dmitri's usually gruff expression crease into a smile. He stepped forward and wrapped me in a literal bear hug, crushing me to him and lifting me off my feet.

"It is good to see you, Hunt," he said, after he'd put me back down and released me. "I truly did not expect it to be this soon."

"It's good to see you too, Dmitri." And it was, too, but I had eyes for just one person at that moment.

Denise Clearwater.

Hedge witch extraordinaire and the woman who had literally shared her heart with me to bring me back from the brink of death.

The same woman for whom I had walked the lands of the dead and whose soul I had brought back from there in fulfillment of the vow I'd made to her.

I opened my mouth to say something but was prevented from doing so as she rushed into my arms, nearly bowling me over in the process. She clung to me and I could feel her heart beating as furiously as mine. I had missed her, I knew that, but the full extent of just how much hadn't hit me until I'd seen her get out of that car. Now I didn't want to let go.

She pulled her head away from my chest and looked up at me. I saw a thousand different emotions in those eyes and wished that the milky orbs that had once been my own pale blue eyes could still communicate in the same way.

If it was true that the eyes were the window to the soul, then I didn't want to think about what mine were saying to other people.

Denise seemed to sense what I was thinking, for she smiled a sad little smile and took a step back.

"I hope . . ."

That was as far as I got. Quick as lightning her right fist shot out and slammed into my solar plexus with stunning force, doubling me over. I opened my mouth to ask what the hell that was for and discovered that I couldn't breathe.

Not even a little bit.

I could feel myself trying to draw a breath, could sense my

muscles trying to obey the commands my brain was sending to them, but it was no use. My entire diaphragm was paralyzed.

My face grew red from the effort and I fell forward on my knees. A white emptiness gathered at the edges of my vision as the ghost inside my head began to pull back from my consciousness in order to protect itself.

Breathe, Hunt. Breathe!

At last my body responded, sucking in a great whooping lungful of air. I coughed, gasped, and fought to regain my breath. All the while Denise stared down at me dispassionately.

When I could at last take in some air without wheezing and gasping, Denise knelt down beside me.

"That's for stealing my car. The knife in the chest I can forgive. Stealing my car? Not so much. So that's not going to happen again, is it?"

I shook my head.

"Good. Glad we understand each other." She patted me on the shoulder and stood.

"Dmitri, get him up. Then let's go get something to eat. I'm hungry."

With that, she headed off toward the diner door.

Dmitri came over and easily lifted me up, placing me back down on my feet like a parent picking up a young child.

I gave him an evil look. "You didn't tell her?" I gasped out as I fought to get my breathing under control.

I was referring to the fact that it had been Dmitri who had given me the keys to Denise's car when he'd helped me escape the police at the hospital back in New Orleans.

"It just never came up," he said sheepishly, while steadying me with one arm.

"Thanks a lot, man."

"For you, Hunt, anything."

We slid back into the banter as if we'd seen each other yesterday, and I felt a ball of tension I didn't know I'd been carrying around begin to break apart in my gut. It was good to be with my friends again.

Maybe together we could find a way out of this mess.

Ten minutes later we were all seated in a booth at the back of the diner. This was my turf; I knew the players to watch for, so I sat facing the door with the other two on the other side of the table. The waitress took our order, brought our drinks and food, and then left us alone, which is just how we wanted it.

"What are you doing here? How'd you find me?" I asked, when the opportunity presented itself, but I thought I already knew the answer, at least to that last question.

Denise shrugged. "I've been dreaming that you're in danger. We would have come sooner if I'd been able to get out of that damned hospital bed on my own before this point. As for tracking you down, we're bonded, remember?"

How could I forget?

While in New Orleans, I'd been shot by a rogue FBI agent and only managed to escape by throwing myself into a canal and hiding in a drainage tunnel. Unfortunately, by the time the cops had left, I'd lost too much blood to pull myself out. I was on the brink of death when Dmitri had found me and carried me back to Denise. Her healing magick hadn't been enough, so she'd cast an ancient ritual that bound the two of us together, soul to soul. She had, quite literally, taken a piece of her soul and bound it to mine so that my soul would remain in my body, giving her a chance to work enough magick to heal the damage done to my body and spirit.

"It was like following a piece of myself across the country; all I had to do was listen to that inner voice and follow where it told me to go."

Dmitri took over at that point. "A number of my past contacts are still active and it was a simple matter to look them up when we arrived in the city and ask if they'd seen a tattooed blind guy roaming around. They were hesitant to talk about it at first, but eventually they let us know that you were working for the magister."

"Working might be too kind a word for it," I told them. "Indentured servitude might be better."

Denise was watching me closely.

"Tell us about it," she said.

So I did.

33

I went back over everything that had happened to me since I'd fled the hospital that night in New Orleans: the long, rambling drive across the country with stops here and there to deal with some errant spirits, my arrival in Los Angeles and the weeks spent lying low, the discovery by Fuentes's cronies and his successful attempt to shanghai me into service by threatening Denise's and Dmitri's lives.

The little information I had on the Key came next, not only its alleged power to open one of the gates to hell itself but also the actions Durante took to hide it away and how Fuentes had already managed to recover two of the three pieces of the artifact.

A pensive expression crossed Denise's face when I mentioned the Key.

"After all this time, the Clavis Sclerata finally surfaces," she said, when I was finished.

"You've heard of it?"

She nodded. "It may be legend to the Preternaturals, but the Gifted, especially practitioners of the Art, have always known that the legend was true. It was fashioned, after all, by one of our own."

"So is Hunt correct?" Dmitri asked. "Can it really open the gates of hell?"

"Gate, not gates," she said. "It will only open one of them. The Bone Gate."

"There's a difference?" he asked, and I was pleased to see I wasn't the only one who didn't know about this stuff. I had no idea there was more than one gate to hell, never mind that each of them had a different purpose.

Denise did, though. "You'd better believe it," she replied. "Choose the wrong gate at the wrong time and all hell could break loose. And I mean that quite literally."

Despite myself, I was intrigued. It's not every day you get the chance to hear a discourse on the gates of hell, after all. "Why is it called the Bone Gate?"

"The pillars that support it are fashioned of human skulls and the gate leads to a plain littered with bones, a plain that stretches as far as one can see, making the killing fields of Cambodia look like a child's diorama."

Sounded like a pleasant place.

But Denise wasn't finished.

"Not too many people have journeyed beyond the plain and lived to tell what they've seen, but those few who have report a great city of demonic creatures, just waiting for the gate to be opened. Some say that whoever opens the gate gains power over the creatures of that city and can order them to do their bidding as long as they return control of the Key, and by extension, the gate."

"Why do I have the feeling you're going to suggest that it's up to us to stop Fuentes from opening that gate?" I asked.

"Do you see anyone else around?"

I was about to point out the nearly four million other people who called Los Angeles home, but to my surprise Dmitri beat me to the punch.

"Screw that," Dmitri said. "We played hero last time, remember? All it did was nearly get us all killed. Fuentes can't hold a threat to our lives over Hunt's head anymore; I say we blow this popsicle stand right here, right now. We could be in San Diego by sunrise. Catch some rays, do a little fishing. Let somebody else save the world for a change."

Right on! I wanted to tell him, but there were a couple of problems with that scenario that I hadn't gotten around to mentioning yet.

"We can't," I said quietly and both Dmitri and Denise turned to look at me, eyebrows raised.

Back in New Orleans I'd been the first to suggest that we cut and run when we were facing something as powerful as the Angeu, the Welsh personification of Death. In fact, I'd been rather miffed that they hadn't seen things my way. Here I was arguing the exact opposite.

Sometimes I confound even myself.

"There's more I haven't told you," I said, and then went on to explain what had happened the night we searched Durante's home for the third piece of the Key.

I tapped a finger against my skull. "I don't think I'm alone in here anymore."

Denise frowned. "Lean closer," she said.

When I did, she put a hand on either side of my head, bowed her own, and mumbled a few words in what sounded to me like ancient Chaldean. I felt the soothing flow of gentle heat moving from her hands and into my head, but only for a moment as something inside me reacted to that heat, jerking away and burrowing deeper in my mind to get as far from it as it could.

The whole room swayed about me like the deck of a ship in a storm and nausea threatened. Just as I thought I was going to lose it all over Denise's lap, she let go of my head.

The dizziness receded and I was left sitting there, panting heavily as I tried to regain control.

"Yep, you've got a rider, all right," Denise said, "Damned nasty one too."

"It's Durante; I'm sure of it."

I explained about Bergman, as well as how Bergman thought Fuentes had tortured and killed Durante.

Dmitri nodded. "We heard the same story, but from a different source. That prompted us to track Bergman down for ourselves."

"How'd you manage that?"

"Denise did a scrying."

I turned to face her. "Fuentes had no luck at all when he tried to scry out Bergman's location."

A clever little grin crossed her face. "That's because he was looking for Bergman directly and his magick was blocked by the wards Durante had placed upon his aide. I scried for you instead."

I knew from previous experience that scrying was an imperfect art. It could just as easily show you where a person had been or would be as where they were currently. Denise had used that to her advantage.

"So it was you that I saw rushing off with Bergman!"

"And just in time, too. If we hadn't, Fuentes's crew would have gotten him." She paused, considering. "Wait. How did you find Bergman in the first place?"

I told them about the fugue states I had been having, how I'd found Bergman in the middle of one, and how Grady had wound up dead after the last episode.

I quite purposely did not mention waking up in bed next to Ilyana. I didn't think it would go over well, even if I hadn't been in control of my body at the time.

"So how does he get rid of it?" Dmitri asked.

"I don't know."

My face fell. I realized then that I'd been expecting her to have the answer I needed, and her lack of information was disconcerting.

"Fine. I'll just share my head with a dead guy for the rest of my life," I said sourly.

Denise grimaced and looked away.

She was too used to me being blind; normally I wouldn't have caught a gesture like that. But this time I had.

"What was that look for?" I demanded, the hair on the back of my neck suddenly standing at attention.

Somehow I knew I wasn't going to like her answer.

I was right.

"I'm afraid you don't have that long."

"Say what?"

"You've already mentioned that the rider is taking control of your body when you go to sleep. You're less alert during those times; it's easier for him to push your consciousness into the background and let his come to the fore."

Right. I'd figured that part out myself. It was what she said next that made me sit up and take notice.

"Obviously you can't stay awake forever, but even if you could that wouldn't save you. Not really. The whole time he's in there he's mapping out the territory, getting an understanding of just where your defenses are and how strong they might be. Eventually, he's going to have your whole head mapped out. Once he does, it will be trivial for him to force you into the backseat while he takes control. Permanently."

Nothing like adding a ticking clock to an already screwed up situation.

"Great. Just fucking great," I said, with no shortage of sarcasm. I'd be the first to admit that I have a habit of getting myself into trouble, but this time I'd really outdone myself, no doubt about it. Fuentes, the Preacher, and now Durante—it seemed that everybody wanted a piece of me. Disappoint any one of them and I was in deep shit. I didn't even want to consider what my life would be like if I disappointed all three. Nuclear Armageddon would probably be preferable to . . .

Wait a minute!

The idea came out of nowhere, as most of my best ideas do, and there was no doubt that it was probably the most cockamamie and outlandish idea I'd ever come up with, but the very insanity of trying such a thing might be the thing that made it succeed where other more sane ideas might not.

Question was, would Durante help?

I realized that the others had fallen silent and looked up to see them both staring at me expectantly.

"What?" I asked.

"You've got that look, Hunt," Dmitri said. "The one that says you're about to dump us into a whole bunch of trouble."

"I have a look?" I asked.

"Yes!" they both answered, simultaneously.

I laughed. In a weird way, their agreement was oddly comforting.

"Okay, fine. I've got a look. But I can do one better than that this time around—I've got an idea."

And I told them how we were all going to get out of this mess.

34

Later that night I stood in front of the mirror in the bathroom of the bungalow Fuentes had assigned to me, watching my reflection, hoping to catch a glimpse, just as I had a few nights before, of the rider I was carrying.

If I could get him to show himself . . .

It wasn't to be, apparently. My reflection looked perfectly normal. Or, at least as normal as a guy with badly dyed hair, tattoos from waist to shoulders, and milky white orbs for eyes could look.

Still, I knew all wasn't as it appeared to be. The fact that I had the lights on and could actually see my reflection at all was proof enough of that; someone else was in my head with me and was looking out through my eyes at that very moment.

It was more than a little unnerving.

Just what the fuck did Durante want anyway?

That was the question of the hour. Judging from everything that had happened so far, I was pretty well convinced that he wanted me to stop Fuentes from getting the Key. Why else would he have led me to where Bergman was hiding?

The same went for his elimination of Perkins, and even Grady for that matter. Perkins clearly had been targeted because he could have pinpointed the location of the third section of the Key if he got close enough to it, and Durante must have recognized that in him. It seemed to me that Grady had been targeted to send a message to Fuentes that he wasn't safe, hiding away in his ivory castle. If Durante could get to one of Fuentes's trusted lieutenants, then it stood to reason that he could get to Fuentes himself. That's no doubt what the message on the wall had meant: I'm coming for you. Literally.

If Durante could cripple Fuentes's operations, he could keep him from reassembling the Key and using it to further his own ends.

I just hoped I was right.

Given that I was basing our entire plan of attack around that answer, I had better be. Otherwise the next forty-eight hours were going to prove to be rather painful in more ways than one.

Only one way to find out.

I squared my shoulders and faced the mirror directly.

"All right, listen up," I said to my reflection, watching it carefully for any deviation in the way I normally looked but not seeing anything.

"I know you're in there. And I think I know what you want. Fact is, I want the same thing."

I paused, waiting to see if there would be any response.

Nothing.

"Fuentes can't be allowed to control the Key. I know that and you know that. So it seems it would make sense for the two of us to work together to keep him from doing so, don't you think? Join our forces to eliminate the need for a counter-attack; get it all done in one fell swoop before he even knows who's hunting him?"

Another long pause.

Another "nothing" result.

"My friends are here now. Good, honest, dependable people. The kinds of people, I suspect, that you might have gotten along with rather well, had you had the chance to meet them under better circumstances.

"All that's water under the bridge at this point, though. What's important is that we want to help you. We want Fuentes to pay for what he has done—to you, to others—and we think we've come up with a way to make him do that.

"But in order to pull it off, we're going to need your help."

I must admit, I felt a bit silly standing there talking to my reflection. Or rather, talking to my reflection and expecting it to make some kind of sign that it had heard what I was saying. That wasn't going to stop me, though. Enlisting Durante's help was the best chance we had of pulling this thing off, and I really hoped he was listening.

"I know you can hear me."

I leaned in closer, staring deep into my own eyes.

"Hell, I probably don't even have to say anything aloud, do I? You're in my head; all I have to do is think it and you'll probably hear it just fine, huh?"

"Let me help you, Durante."

Was that a flicker of movement I saw behind my eyes?

"There's just one thing. If you want our help nailing Fuentes to the wall, you have to leave me in control. No more fugue states. No more nighttime adventures with me waking up somewhere I don't remember going. You could ruin everything. We'll get Fuentes; I give you my word. But we have to do it right."

"Are you listening, Durante?"

My reflection rippled and there, for just a moment, was another face looking out of the mirror at me. Durante stared hard in my direction, the rage and insanity I'd seen nights before now replaced with cold calculation.

I felt my head nod up and down.

The hair on the back of my neck and arms stood straight up and a chill raced down my spine for I knew I hadn't moved of my own volition.

Durante was showing me what he could do. Perhaps even reminding me of what would happen if I didn't follow through on my end of the bargain.

"Don't worry about me; you just do your part and I'll handle my end just fine."

But he was already gone and I was left talking to my reflection again.

I washed up and then headed off to bed, wondering where I would wake up come morning and who might be lying dead beside me.

>++<

To my surprise, I awoke the next morning feeling refreshed and well-rested for the first time in more than a week. I glanced about, taking in the details of my surroundings, and then breathing a sigh of relief when I realized that I was still in my own bungalow.

Throwing off the covers, I got out of bed and headed for the kitchen, my thoughts on where Durante had hidden the third piece of the Key. I hadn't taken ten steps before pulling up short, my mouth open in shocked surprise.

Holy shit!

The information was suddenly just sitting there, right in the forefront of my brain, as if it had been there all along.

I knew where the last piece of the Key was!

I didn't waste any time. I walked into the living room, picked up the phone, and dialed the number Denise had given me the night before when we'd worked out the details of my plan. She'd explained it went to a throwaway cell phone and that she'd dispose of it the moment after taking my call, ensuring that she couldn't be traced through it. If Fuentes was monitoring calls from the bungalows, which, given his paranoia, I was certain he was, all he would see was an extremely brief call to a nonexistent number. If pressed, I'd say I'd reached a wrong number and hung up once I'd realized what had happened.

Before we'd left the diner, we'd worked out the finer details of the plan, so that a simple phone call would set things in motion.

The phone rang once, twice, three times and then, on the fourth ring, was picked up. I waited a moment; if Denise said hello that would mean someone was on to them.

When the silence continued, I spoke a single word.

"Execute."

The phone was hung up on the other end, signaling that my message had been received.

There was no going back now.

So be it.

35

My intention was to slip off the property, grab a cab to the place where Durante had hidden the final portion of the Key, and return with it before anyone even knew I was gone. I would then find a decent place to hide it until it was time for the next stage of our plan.

I should have known it wouldn't be that easy.

No sooner had I left the bungalow than Rivera intercepted me and put me to work. I accompanied him back and forth across the property and throughout the house, using my ghost-sight to examine all of the arcane wards and defenses that had been erected in the wake of Grady's murder. We were still at it, several hours later, when we were both summoned to Fuentes's office.

When we arrived, we found Ilyana already there and Fuentes pacing back and forth behind his desk. The atmosphere in the room was tense, and as I pretended to feel my way to my seat I could feel my heart rate kicking up.

Here we go.

Fuentes got right down to business.

"A courier just delivered a priority letter from Jack Bergman. He's offering to turn over the final piece of the Key in exchange for his life. He has asked for a meeting at nine this evening, at a location he will reveal closer to that time. Thoughts?"

Ilyana was the first to speak up. "It could be a trap. We know Bergman was taken from the motel by person or persons unknown; perhaps they are trying to set you up, take you out."

Rivera seemed to consider this for a moment and then shook his head. "I just don't see it. With Durante's death there isn't another practitioner in town that could challenge your power. We've eliminated or driven off any serious challenge to your authority and we would have known if anyone of that caliber had entered the city, especially in the last few days. Bergman's not a player; I think he's just scared out of his mind and is looking for a way out."

"Hunt?"

I was surprised that Fuentes bothered to ask my opinion, but we'd planned for it just in case.

"Strong emotions can often stick to an object, leave a kind of emotional trail if you will. If the letter truly is from Bergman, and if he is truly scared out of his wits the way Rivera suggests he would be, then I should be able to see it using my ghostsight."

Fuentes glanced at Rivera and raised his eyebrows, questioning what I'd said without coming out and saying so. I had to resist the urge to laugh in his face when Rivera nodded.

Gotcha, I thought with smug satisfaction.

"Excellent idea, Hunt," Fuentes said. "Please, take a look. I'm placing the letter directly in front of you on the edge of my desk."

I could see it just fine, but of course he didn't know that. I pretended to give it due consideration and then sat back, clutching my head as if the effort had been a bit much.

"Fear. Definitely fear. A little bit of hope, too, but mostly fear. Whoever wrote that letter really doesn't think they're going to come out of this alive."

It was all bullshit, plain and simple. Denise had written the letter and paid the courier to deliver it as a priority parcel. When Fuentes arrived with his two pieces of the Key, Denise and Dmitri would be waiting to help me with the final part of our plan. And though he didn't know it yet, the Preacher was going to help too.

Willing or not.

But first I had to get the targets to the meeting place.

And pick up the final piece of the Key somewhere along the way.

"All right, that settles it," Fuentes said. "The three of you will be my escorts. I want this thing to go off without a hitch."

"Yes, sir," Rivera replied.

"What about Bergman?" Ilyana asked.

Fuentes laughed. "I'm surprised you even need to ask. Once he turns over the remaining piece of the Key, kill him and anyone who's with him."

36

Once the decision had been made to meet with Bergman, Fuentes kept the three of us busy throughout the rest of the afternoon, which proved even more frustrating than the morning had been. Every time I would try to find an excuse to leave the property, even for only a few minutes, Rivera would be there, giving me a new task to perform. My paranoid nature told me he was intentionally keeping an eye on me because he and Fuentes knew the truth, knew I'd been the one to kill Grady, knew I was setting them up for a fall. Then my rational side would rear its head, reminding me that these guys were paranoid to begin with and they didn't have to know anything about what was really going on behind the scenes to want to keep me in their sights. I was, after all, an outsider and, to top it all off, here against my will.

I was ready to scream in frustration by the time the call from "Bergman" came in that afternoon. The meeting site turned out to be a warehouse along the docks in Long Beach, some thirty miles away. Of course L.A. traffic being what it is, we needed at least an hour to get there at this time of day, leaving us with just enough time to get our things together and get on the road.

Fuentes had wanted to get there ahead of time, in case Bergman changed his mind and tried to bolt at the last minute, but their strategy of keeping us in the dark until the last minute would make that difficult to pull off. I knew there was no chance of Bergman getting cold feet, particularly since Bergman wouldn't be anywhere near the place, but there was no way I could talk them out of the frantic rush to leave without making it obvious I knew something they didn't.

Thankfully, Rivera demanded we take two different vehicles for security reasons, and when he put Ilyana and me in the same vehicle and he and Fuentes in the other, I wanted to shout in satisfaction.

Now, at least, I had the means to retrieve the final piece of the Key. All I had to do was convince Ilyana to play along with me for the ruse I had planned. Given her previous comment that her presence here wasn't entirely voluntary, I was hoping I could appeal to her desire for freedom and enlist her help in pulling all this off. If she disagreed, I was going to have to find a way to take her out of the equation, perhaps permanently.

That was a task I wasn't looking forward to.

I would have preferred leaving the final piece of the Key right where Durante had hidden it. It would have been safe there and there wouldn't have been any chance of it falling into Fuentes's hands. But in order to fulfill the letter of my bargain with the Preacher, all three pieces of the Key had to be present when he arrived to collect. That meant I had to retrieve the final piece or deal with the Preacher's wrath, and something told me that I didn't want to default on the terms of our agreement.

All of which meant I had no choice about what I had to do next.

"I know where to find the final piece of the Key," I said to Ilyana, as we began the journey to Long Beach with the last of the day's sunlight.

Ilyana was driving and she barely glanced in my direction as she said, "Not funny, Hunt."

"I'm not trying to be," I said, matter-of-factly. "I know where it is. I need your help to get it. If we do, I promise that you won't have to worry about Fuentes or Rivera any longer."

She started to laugh and then stopped. "You're serious," she said, her voice trembling slightly.

"Of course I am. Did you think I would make something like that up and dangle it in front of you, of all people? Give me some credit."

She was quiet for a time and then, "Where is it?"

Her voice was full of need, of longing. Maybe even anticipation.

"I can't tell you that. Not until you give me your word that you'll help me take down Fuentes. Are you with me or not?"

Her brow creased in confusion. "You'd take my word as bond? Even knowing what I am?"

"You're not that different. You want your freedom as much as I do."

To her credit, she only took another thirty seconds to think about it. "Done. I give you my word that I will help you break free of Fuentes's control and influence."

That was good enough for me. "We need to go to the Hollywood sign. We need to do it alone and we need to go now."

She didn't question it; she just picked up her cell phone and pushed a speed dial number. When whoever it was on the other end answered it, she said, "I think we've picked up a tail. Keep going; we'll check it out and then hang back a bit to discourage any others that might be out there."

Ilyana listened for a moment and then said, "Relax, Rivera, I've got it. Better to deal with it now than to lead them all the way to Long Beach and the meet-up, right?"

Rivera must have agreed, for Ilyana killed the connection and then took the next turn we came to, cutting off the car beside us and banging a hard right in the process.

"This excuse should be good for twenty, maybe twenty-five minutes. Beyond that we're going to face some serious scrutiny when we catch back up with them."

"That should be more than enough time," I told her, while secretly hoping I was right. Ghosts could be fickle creatures and the one we were going to visit had more reason than most.

37

The sign.

Or, as the locals call it, the Sign.

Perhaps one of the most famous landmarks in the entire world, right up there (at least Los Angelinos think so) with the Eiffel Tower and the Pyramids of Giza. Built on the edge of Mount Lee in Griffith Park, the Sign looks down on the city of L.A. with casual indifference, the perfect attitude, I thought, to match the very thing it now stood for, the hope and misery forever bound together in the Hollywood entertainment industry.

Originally built in 1923 as an outdoor ad for a suburban housing development known as Hollywoodland, the Sign has become the symbol of something that's hard to define. Like the section on an old map marked by the warning, "Here be dragons," the Sign seems to shout a message all its own, one that on the surface screams "Dreams are made here," but underneath breeds the harsh cynicism of an industry that can chew you up faster than a spectre-eating demon, present company excluded.

We were here to meet with someone who had experienced that cynicism firsthand and who had succumbed to the dark allure it exuded.

In years past it was possible to scramble up the steep face of Mount Lee to reach the fifty-foot-tall letters fashioned of wood and sheet metal, but erosion, vandalism, and concern for the welfare of those stupid enough to attempt the stunt eventually resulted in a fair amount of changes.

The sign was restored in 1978 and the original letters were replaced by forty-five-foot steel behemoths, designed to last for decades to come. The sturdiness of the structure would make what I had to do here tonight easier, so I was thankful for that, but the increased security that went along with it didn't have me jumping for joy. I couldn't blame those in charge, though. The sign had a long history of incidents surrounding it, including the one that had brought me there that night.

In September 1932, an English stage actress named Lillian "Peg" Entwistle used a workman's ladder to climb to the top of the letter *H* and then threw herself off the top, the first person to commit suicide from the sign.

Durante had given the last piece of the Key to Peg's ghost. She was the one we came here to find.

After we gained entrance to the place, of course.

In 2000, the L.A. police had hired Panasonic to install a rather intricate security system designed to stop trespassers like me. The system consisted of a perimeter fence topped with razor wire, twenty-four-hour surveillance cameras, infrared detectors, motion detectors, and regular foot and air patrols by the Los Angeles Police Department.

Overall, it was both a comprehensive and effective design.

Thankfully, I had Ilyana on my side and we were going to make short work of the security. Get in, get what we needed, and get out again, all without being caught. That was the mission protocol for the evening and we were ready to carry it out.

Time was at a premium, so we couldn't make our way down to the sign from above as I would have preferred. Instead, we parked on a side street, cut through several yards to reach the base of Mount Lee, and then began climbing upward.

It didn't take long to reach the fence.

"Would you mind?" I asked.

"Not at all."

Ilyana walked forward, grabbed a section of the chain link and tore it free of the pole to which it had been secured. From there it was a simple matter to hold it open long enough for both of us to slip through to the other side.

Knowing an automated call was already going out to the L.A. police, I didn't waste any time, hustling forward and climbing up the last hundred feet to stand level with the base of the letter *W* as quickly as I could. Ilyana followed, with, I must admit, a bit more grace than I. Once she joined me, we both moved over to the letter *H*.

The feed from the surveillance cameras surrounding the sign was visible from several different Web sites and I wondered how many people were chatting about me on the Internet as I made my way over to the access ladder at the back of the *H* and began climbing upward. Hopefully we'd be long gone before someone tied my image to that of the man wanted for multiple murders by the FBI and Boston PD.

Otherwise, things might get a little uncomfortable up here.

Peg Entwistle had thrown herself off the top of the *H*, so if I wanted to meet her ghost that was where I had to go as well. The wind whipped and picked at me as I made my way up the ladder, and I knew it would be even worse once I reached the top, but there was nothing to be done for it. Hand over hand, foot after foot, I went up that ladder.

Reaching the top, I paused to catch my breath with the city of Los Angeles spread out below me. Lights gleamed and glistened and from here the town looked like a jewel in the night. It was a beautiful sight and I took a few seconds to drink it in.

Then, just to remind myself that all is not as it seems, I triggered my ghostsight.

The city below me was transformed. Angels warred over downtown, riding the air currents like massive eagles, swooping and diving as they slashed and hacked with the weapons in their hands, spilling blood onto the streets below. Darkness lay about much of the city, creeping insidiously into areas that had previously been bastions of light and power, now grown cold and dark with the futility of their inhabitants. I stood there, a watcher of the dark, and felt it watching me in turn.

It was enough to make me shudder and turn away.

Enough dillydallying, Hunt, I scolded myself, and dug my harmonica out of my pocket. Putting it to my lips, I began to play a summoning song.

It was a soft, gentle melody, a wistful song of lost hopes and dreams, of desires unfulfilled. I'd never heard it before, but I knew it was right just the same, just as I'd known that the ghost of the long-lost actress was the final piece needed to solve the puzzle.

I played until the smell of gardenias washed over me.

It was Peg Entwistle's favorite scent of perfume and one of the signs I was looking for.

Slowly I turned around and there she was, standing about five feet behind me. She was slim and good-looking, with short-cropped blond hair and a crooked little smile. She was dressed in a skirt and top; her jacket, shoes, and purse had been left behind on the ground, neatly folded.

At first I thought she'd seen me, for her attention was focused completely in my direction, almost unnervingly so. But then she started walking toward the edge and I realized what was happening; she was going to throw herself off the *H* just as she had some eighty-odd years ago. If she did, it would be nearly impossible to get her to manifest herself again in time to make the meeting. I was going to get one chance at this!

I pulled out my harmonica and began to play, letting the full force of my emotions pour into my music. Peg managed a few more steps, closing roughly half the distance to the edge. I tried different styles and tunes as I searched for the right one.

So focused was I on getting it right that I nearly jumped out of my skin when a police helicopter came roaring over the hill behind us. A spotlight speared down from above and it didn't take long for it to find me standing there atop the *H*. I knew they couldn't see Peg and wondered what was going through their minds as they looked down from above to see me swaying there, harmonica to my mouth and weird strains of music pouring forth, a modern-day Nero fiddling while the city below me was lost to darkness rather than fire.

My question was answered seconds later as the booming

voice of the chopper's PA system split the night. "This is the Los Angeles Police Department. You are trespassing on private property. Climb to the top of the hill behind you and wait for the arrival of other officers now en route."

I didn't bother to acknowledge them in any way; I was focused only on the song pouring out of my instrument, knowing that if I were to be distracted now I'd lose my tenuous hold on Peg's ghost and destroy any chance we had of getting free of Fuentes.

The music was working, there was no doubt about that. Peg had stopped her inexorable walk toward the edge of the sign and was standing there, as if in indecision. A few more minutes and I'd have the link I needed to get her to release the rest of the Key.

The voice boomed again, the spotlight still holding me in its grip. "I repeat, this is the Los Angeles Police Department. Continue to ignore our instructions at your own risk. Officers are on their . . ."

There was a shattering of glass and the light went out. The PA boomed a final time, "Shit! Shooting at us!" and then went silent as the chopper banked away.

We were in deep trouble now.

Can't be helped, I thought. *Focus on the music, nothing but the music. Get the Key . . .*

As I continued to play, Peg stopped, turned, and looked at me, really looked at me, for the first time since I'd arrived. There was an intelligent spark in her eye, an awareness to her features that hadn't been there before.

She stared at me, opened her mouth, and spoke.

"Do I know you?"

The music faltered, then stopped. Ghosts don't normally speak, and I'll admit it caught me off guard.

"Ah . . . no, no you don't know me," I stammered out nervously. "I'm a friend of Michael Durante's though."

"Oh, that Michael," she said, smiling and blushing as if they'd done something more than a little risqué together.

I really, seriously, didn't want to know.

"Michael gave you something to watch over, didn't he? He's asked me to come collect it for him."

I blinked and she was holding the final part of the Key, turning it over in her hands as she looked at it curiously.

"Doesn't seem like much," she said.

I agreed. It didn't seem like much. Sometimes the smallest, most inconspicuous things can cause us all to stumble.

I hoped like hell this wasn't one of those times.

"May I have it?" I asked.

The chopper was still hovering out there in the darkness, the thump of its rotors pounding out a rhythm in the sky above. Sirens could now be heard in the distance too, growing closer with every passing second, and I knew we were just about out of time.

Now or never.

Peg was still lost in thought, turning the piece of thick metal over and over again in her hands, as I stepped forward and snatched it out of her grasp.

The minute my hands touched the metal, Peg vanished.

Leaving me the proud possessor of the final section of the Key.

A key that was our ticket out of this mess.

I jammed it into my pocket and ran for the ladder.

Ilyana was waiting for me at the bottom.

"Do you have it?" she asked, over the ever increasing sound of the sirens.

"Yes. Let's go!"

I turned to do just that but apparently Ilyana had something else in mind. I hadn't taken two steps before she snatched me up, slung me over one shoulder like a potato sack, took off down the hillside while the just arriving police officers at the top of the bluff looked down and watched us go in sheer disbelief.

I wanted to wave, but decided not to press my luck.

38

The warehouse chosen for the meeting stood by itself at the end of a long pier opposite a massive container ship. Stacks of cargo containers stood nearby, piled eight high and five deep. Next to the front rack were two of the oversized cranes that were used to load the containers onto the ships, silent and watchful.

Fuentes's Escalade was parked in front of the warehouse, as if flaunting his presence and daring someone to make a move against him when he was this far outside his sanctuary. I nearly smiled to see it; after all, I knew what lay in store for him.

Ilyana pulled the car to a stop a few yards away from Fuentes's and we both got out. I had my harmonica in my pocket but had stashed the final piece of the Key inside the cushion I was sitting on. I had no idea if Fuentes would be able to sense its presence if I carried it into the warehouse with me, nor how it might react when it was brought into close proximity of the other sections. Better safe than sorry; I could always retrieve it later if and when I needed it.

"Let me handle the explanations," Ilyana said and I nodded in agreement. She turned away, headed for the entrance, but when I moved to follow I was nearly overcome by a wave of dizziness so great that it threatened to bring me to my knees. I shook my head to clear it, took a few tentative steps in the direction Ilyana was headed, and then hustled to catch up.

As I came through the door to the warehouse, I saw Fuentes and Rivera standing together in the center of the room watching the door expectantly, each with a smug expression on his face. When Rivera's gaze shifted to something over my shoulder, I knew I was in trouble.

There was motion in the shadows to my left and I had a split second to wonder where the heck Ilyana had gone as what felt like a twenty-pound sledgehammer slammed into the side of my face. I went down like a side of beef, my face bouncing off the cold cement floor of the warehouse practically before my brain even registered that I'd been struck.

I lay there, dazed and most definitely confused, blood leaking from my nose and mouth and dribbling down the side of my face to the warehouse floor. I thought I heard male laughter coming from what sounded like very far away, but I couldn't seem to get a fix on it any more than I could get my arms to push me back up off the floor.

I heard footsteps approaching and then someone squatted down in front of me. A hand reached out and patted my cheek affectionately. It took a moment for Ilyana's face to come into focus.

She smiled at me, then said, "You may be a good fuck, Hunt, but you are one naïve son-of-a-bitch."

Another pat on the cheek and then she stood.

"Oh, one more thing. This is going to hurt. A lot."

With her laughter ringing in my ears, I watched, unable to move, as her booted foot drew back and then came flying forward again, connecting with the side of my skull and sending it right down into the darkest oblivion.

39

When I came to I found I was lying on the floor in the corner of the warehouse, my hands and feet trussed like a Christmas turkey with bailing rope and my head pounding as if the entire drum line for the John Sousa Marching Band was parading through my skull.

I turned my head and discovered Fuentes, Rivera, and Ilyana bustling about in the center of the warehouse floor about twenty feet from me, making provisions for some kind of ritual. I could see that they had laid out a circle of protection on the floor in salt. Fuentes stood in the center of the circle, a small podium-like stand in front of him. On the stand rested a very old and very thick-looking book. He was muttering to himself while flipping through its pages, no doubt refreshing his memory about what he had to say and do to find success. On a small card table to his left were the three separate pieces of the Key.

They didn't look like much through human eyes, just three oddly shaped pieces of metal, each about six inches long. I knew perceptions could be deceiving; when I viewed the pieces of Key through the borrowed eyes of the ghost in my head they shone with a light as black as midnight and twice as deep.

Seeing them there, all together in one place, reminded me that I'd been betrayed. I glanced at the three of them bustling about and felt Durante's rage explode inside me. His emotions shot like quicksilver through my body, igniting every nerve ending and setting my muscles vibrating so hard that I felt as if I could run a marathon in mere moments. It was like switching from smoking cigarettes to mainlining pure heroin; one moment I was trying to make sense of what had happened to me, the next I was roaring with rage and bloodlust.

I've never wanted to kill three people more than I did at that very moment.

And yet . . . something held me back. Durante might control my emotions, but I still controlled the centers of reasoning and self-restraint inside my head and I used them now to try to calm my errant passenger down. I knew if he attacked now all our efforts would be for naught; Durante, Rivera, and Ilyana combined were no match for the former sorcerer.

Not yet, I cautioned, knowing Durante could hear me just fine inside my head. *Not yet. I promise that you will have your revenge, but the time isn't right. Just a bit longer.*

I kept repeating the same refrain, over and over again, until I felt all that raw anger recede. It was nice to know it was there for when I needed it, but right now cunning was more important than uncontrolled rage.

I moved my head slowly, looking around as surreptitiously as I could. The doorway I'd come through was along the rear wall. The section of the warehouse to my left held palates of packaged goods wrapped in opaque plastic stacked nearly to the ceiling. Across the room, on the other side of my enemies, was a series of offices stretching down the far wall. All of them were dark.

All but one was empty.

Or at least that was the case if everything went according to plan. Dmitri had been familiar with the warehouses from some point in his past and he'd been able to hack into the city servers and call up blueprints on his iPad for us to examine at the diner last night. The offices were determined to be the easiest place to hide, as well as the most defensible location should they be discovered ahead of time. Fuentes and Rivera had been too intent on capturing me, never mind the third piece of the Key, to do a thorough check it seemed.

I was just about to turn away when a flash of movement behind the window in the second to last office caught my attention. For just a moment I thought I'd seen a young girl go running past, her hair in pigtails and bouncing against her back.

Whisper.

That was where my friends were hiding; I was certain of it. It put them less than twenty feet from where I now lay at my end of the warehouse, which was going to make things easier when the shit hit the fan.

The trio in charge of the ritual appeared to have just finished their individual preparations when a rather significant look passed between Fuentes and Rivera. Unfortunately for Ilyana, she was looking in the other direction at the time and didn't catch it.

Without warning Rivera stepped closer and grabbed her

by the back of the head. Sparks and wayward tendrils of power flew out from beneath his hand while the rest burrowed themselves deep into Ilyana's skull. Her limbs danced about spasmodically for a moment, a puppet doing a Saint Vitus dance, and then she collapsed to the floor, unconscious. The smell of burnt hair filled the room.

"Careful, Rivera," Fuentes scolded. "We need her alive for the sacrifice; without that demon blood in her veins, there's no way to hold the gate open permanently."

Rivera shrugged off the admonition. "She's tougher than she looks. She'll be fine."

He bent over her, did something to her hands, and then stepped away again, revealing the iron chains that he'd secured about her ankles and wrists.

Even as I looked on, thin wisps of steam began to rise from her flesh, as the cold iron worked its magick on her nonhuman flesh and began to eat away at her like a very slow acting acid. Iron was anathema to demons and ghosts alike. Even if she woke up, Ilyana wasn't going anywhere now.

When he was finished binding her, Rivera picked Ilyana up and dumped her inside the circle. Then he, too, stepped inside it and "sealed" it behind him with a cup of salt that had been laid aside for that purpose. I wasn't an expert on circles by any stretch, that was Denise's department, but I seemed to recall that the circle would protect the summoner from whatever it was that he summoned. It wouldn't do squat against an earthly foe, such as myself, but if something came through the gate and decided not to listen to Fuentes, he and his companions would theoretically be protected.

I'd be fair game, but they obviously weren't too concerned about my overall welfare anyway.

"Let us begin," Fuentes intoned.

"Let us begin," Rivera replied.

The two men stripped to the waist, revealing an intricate series of tattoos covering their entire upper bodies: chests, backs, and arms. Fuentes picked up a gold-plated dagger from the podium beside him and then made a ritual slash across one shoulder with the blade. The fine network of scars already there told me this was a regular occurrence. Fuentes handed the blade to Rivera, who did the same thing to himself before picking up a silver goblet off the table nearby and advancing toward Ilyana, knife and cup in hand.

He's going to slit her throat, I thought.

But it wasn't to be. Holding her up by the hair, Rivera instead slashed the edge of the knife across her forehead. For a second nothing happened, so fine was that knife blade, but first drops and then streams of blood began pouring out the wound.

Rivera positioned the cup to catch most of it, then dropped Ilyana's head back down against her chest and carried the blood-filled cup over to Fuentes.

Accepting it, Fuentes poured the blood over the three pieces of the Key. The strange metal sucked up the blood instantly, the way the earth will consume a rain shower in the midst of a drought. Within seconds there was no sign that blood had even been shed.

Satisfied with what he'd seen, Fuentes arranged the pieces so that they resembled a three-sided star and then pushed them together. There was an audible click, and a low-grade hum filled the room. At first I thought the sound was coming from Fuentes, but after watching for another moment I realized that it appeared to be coming from the Key.

That's it? I thought. *All that effort for three pieces of metal and a disembodied voice?*

Fuentes picked up the Key, spun it several times between his hands, and then placed it in the air directly in front of him as if putting it on a shelf.

It stayed that way, hovering above the floor at a spot about five feet off the ground.

Then Fuentes spoke a command in a loud voice in a language I didn't understand and the three-sided Key began to replicate itself.

Click, click, click, click—each piece would split off and form a new piece, slotting itself in place and then repeating the process until that simple, three-sided structure had grown into an intricate combination of elements with a gleaming Tau Cross in the center.

The Key hung there in the empty air and seemed to taint the very air around it with a malevolent presence.

Fuentes began chanting. Softly at first and then with increasing rapidity, he called out in a deep, guttural language that didn't belong to this reality but to another, darker one just beyond. Rivera waited until he'd been through one entire sequence of the chant and then joined in, his voice rising in eerie counterpart to his master's, pushing the sound to newer, greater heights.

Within minutes the sound grew so loud that it was no longer possible for something of that volume to be produced by human lips, and I knew then that this was why they had slashed themselves and drawn their own blood. Death mages can't work a major working without shedding blood, and using their own blood in a ritual powered it up in a way that few other things could. The room soon filled to bursting with the magick they were pouring into the heart of the chant. Tension flailed about like an angry child, and if they didn't do something soon I was certain the room would explode.

As if hearing my thoughts, Fuentes reached out, grasped the Key around the cross in its center, and gave it a sharp twist.

A deep groaning sound seemed to rise from the earth beneath our feet and then the very fabric of reality seemed to shiver and shake for a long, gut-wrenching moment.

When it stopped, the rear section of the warehouse was just . . . gone.

Standing in its place was the Bone Gate.

40

I laid there stunned, not quite believing my eyes.

Twin columns rose on either side of the structure, giant gateposts made of human skulls piled nearly one hundred feet high. Some of the bones were fresh, their gleaming white surfaces reflecting the warehouse lights, while others appeared centuries, if not millennia, old, yellowed and cracked with the inexorable passage of time. All those empty eye sockets staring down at you was chilling and, when combined with the unmistakable aura of malevolence that surrounded the structure, it was enough to make me want to turn around and run like hell to get as far away from this place as I possibly could.

Unfortunately, I didn't have the luxury.

Between the skull posts was the gate proper, a glistening metallic structure consisting of horizontal arms at vertical intervals, reminding me of a whale's rib cage turned sideways and welded into place. The metal of the crossbars seemed to pulse and breathe with a life all its own. I was instinctively repulsed by its very existence. It was just . . . wrong somehow, and my very being seemed to cry out against it.

Beyond the gate a dusty, bone-strewn plain seemed to stretch on forever under a dark and thunderous sky. Nothing moved on its surface and no structures broke the plain's seemingly endless march to the horizon. Nothing but skulls and bone fragments as far as the eye could see.

I tore my gaze away from the gate and looked to where Fuentes stood, staring through the gate into the strange land beyond, still chanting his summoning ritual. Rivera stood nearby, guarding his back now that the gate had appeared, but he was no longer adding his voice to Fuentes's. At Rivera's feet lay an unconscious Ilyana.

Just like the Angeu, and the shade of the sorcerer Eldredge before him, Fuentes and Rivera underestimated me from the very beginning.

Directing my thoughts inward, I called out to Durante in the same way that I'd been calling to Whisper and Scream for years now.

I need your help, Durante. I need your strength. I need your rage, but I need it controlled. Can you do that?

Involuntarily, my head nodded up and down.

Goose bumps raced across my skin; not being in control of my own body was a horrifying situation and one I would be happy to be free of once we dealt with Fuentes.

A voice in the back of my mind that sounded like me but very definitely was NOT me echoed the sentiment.

When we've dealt with Fuentes. And his pet sorcerer.

I tested the bindings holding my wrists together behind my back. They were too tight for me, but maybe not for him. I would definitely need my hands free for what came next.

Can you get these bindings off my wrists?

I felt the equivalent of a mental shrug and then my arms tensed and kept tensing. I could feel the cord biting into my skin, could feel blood starting to run down my wrists, and then he was there inside my head, blocking the pain and goosing my muscles with his own ghostly power until with a snap the bindings broke.

I reached down, grabbed the bindings around my ankles and, with another surge of help from Durante, tore those loose as well.

I was still a bit dizzy from the blow to the head—bitch gave me a concussion, no doubt—so rather than getting up I just stayed where I was for the next part of the plan.

All of us were present save one. It was my job to get him here.

I grabbed my harmonica and brought it to my lips to play a summoning of my own.

The music was sharp, discordant, full of strange key changes and unusual riffs, but it was perfect for what it was designed to do.

The music from my harmonica warred with the chant coming from Fuentes's mouth. He cast a withering glance in Rivera's direction that didn't need much translating; "Get rid of him," it said.

Rivera smiled.

He brought his hands up in front of him and began a series of complicated gestures. Still playing, I watched as a ball of green fire began to form between his palms, growing with each sequence of his hands. It started about the size of a golf ball and then began to grow, hissing and spitting sparks and magick in every direction, until it was about the size of a basketball.

He paused, as if savoring the moment, and then flung the ball of fire directly at me!

I didn't move.

Didn't flinch.

Didn't stop playing.

Fuck you, Rivera, I thought.

The fireball sailed through the air, perfectly on target, and I had to force myself to remain stock still and not move, no matter how much my instincts were screaming at me to get the hell out of the way.

My playing got a little louder, but that was the only external sign that I was at all concerned about the crackling ball of energy that appeared about to incinerate me.

I hit the last, strident note of my summoning call and held it, letting the sound blare in defiance as the fireball came thundering in with point-blank precision . . . only to splash harmlessly about a foot away from me on the dome of blue gray energy hanging there in the air and surrounding me in a dome of protective magick.

"Gaia bless you, Denise," I muttered as I climbed to my feet and faced Rivera.

He was not a happy camper. He glared across the space separating us, his fury readily apparent, and I couldn't resist giving him the finger.

Childish, I know, but ultimately very satisfying.

Rivera's response was to fling four more fireballs in my direction.

Simultaneously.

I had a few seconds to wonder if Denise's shielding was going to hold as they came sailing toward me, and then the flames were crashing against the barrier, hitting it and splashing outward like some kind of arcane napalm, trying to overwhelm the magick that held the shielding in place.

After a few seconds, when I realized I hadn't been burned to a crisp, I opened one eye and looked about. I was still whole, still protected behind a shimmering blue gray dome of mystical energy, and still in this fight.

Rivera, however, was no longer paying attention to me, but was staring out across the Plain of Bones with a queer expression on his face. Fuentes, too, had seen something out there, and as a result his chant stuttered and then fell silent. I strained to see what it was they were starting at.

At first I saw nothing, just that flat, seemingly endless expanse of dusty plain, but then a figure gradually emerged from against the background, coming toward us.

As the figure drew closer two details became readily apparently.

The figure was human.

And, above his hand-sewn white shirt, dark trousers, and black frock coat, he wore an old-fashioned wide-brimmed hat.

A preacher's hat.

41

The Preacher walked up until he stood just a few feet away from the gate and casually examined those of us on the other side. He let his gaze pass over Fuentes and Rivera rather quickly, let it linger a bit longer on Ilyana, and then turned to face me directly.

"Where's the Key you promised me, Hunt?"

Even though those were the very words I'd been hoping to hear from him, I was kind of surprised that he even bothered to ask. Couldn't he see the Key was right there in front of him, in the center of the gate?

I pointed to the spot where the Key now hung in its strange, home-grown lattice setting.

"It's right there in front of you, Preacher. All you need to do is take it."

Fuentes was standing there, staring at the Preacher with his mouth wide open, trying to process this new chain of events. I think it was solely the fact that something that just walked out of the Plain of Bones, seemingly out of hell itself, not only knew my name but was talking with me as if we were old friends, that kept Fuentes from trying to blast the Preacher where he stood.

His hesitation didn't last for long, though. Fuentes controlled the gate by virtue of controlling the Key, and he wasn't about to let either one go easily. He gestured with one hand and the gate swung inward, allowing him to see the Preacher more clearly. He stepped in the other man's path.

"I don't know who you are or where you came from, but the Key is mine. It is not Hunt's to give."

The Preacher fixed those eyeless sockets directly on Fuentes and slowly looked him up and down. The dismissive expression that crossed his face clearly showed what he thought of Fuentes's opposition.

"Then I suppose I will have to take the Key from you, instead," the Preacher informed him.

Fuentes grinned. "You can try."

The two stepped forward, like Old West gunfighters about to have a showdown in the middle of the street.

Until that moment Rivera had been standing as idly by as the rest of us, watching, waiting to see what Fuentes would do. The minute Fuentes went on the offensive, Rivera did too.

He waved his hands again, just as he'd done earlier, and another ball of mystical plasma began to form between his palms.

The man sure does like his fireballs, I thought, and was opening my mouth to call for help from my two hidden companions when a couple of things happened simultaneously.

Ilyana rolled over, snatched the dagger from the table where it had been discarded by Rivera earlier, and plunged it directly into the latter's leg about midthigh.

Rivera screamed in surprised pain and the fireball he'd been working with shot free of his hands, narrowly missing me by scant inches. I ducked as it shot overhead and smashed into the wall behind me. When I looked up, Ilyana had managed to pull the blade free of Rivera's leg, but he had hold of her now and flung her across the room to slam into a pile of packing crates even as I looked on.

So much for that diversion.

He snarled something at me in Spanish, then paused to pass a hand over the wound in his leg. It stopped bleeding and sealed itself in a matter of seconds.

With abilities like that he was going to be damned hard to take down. Thankfully, I didn't have to do it on my own.

A roar filled the confines of the warehouse and I knew Dmitri had entered the fray. Dmitri was a berserker, one of the few who could take on the form of their totem spirits and reap all the benefits of being in that form while still retaining their ability to think clearly. Dmitri's totem spirit was a polar bear; I don't care who you are or what powers are at your disposal, when a polar bear roars at you in rage it puts a bit of a quiver in your boots.

Rivera wasn't any different than the next guy down the line. He quaked at the sight of Dmitri charging toward him and quickly whipped up some magick to try to deal with the annoyed beast now bearing down on him, but what he hadn't counted on was the short, red-haired woman who rode astride Dmitri's back, her legs clamped tightly around his sides.

Stealing a page out of Rivera's own playbook, Denise began to fling bolts of power in his direction, brilliant red flashes that slammed into the floor and walls around him, but never seemed to touch his body directly.

Normally I'm pretty useless in a fight; it's hard to take action when you can't see much of anything, but as long as Durante was inside my head I should have been able to contribute something valuable.

Except when I tried to go to Denise's position and offer some aid, my body moved in exactly the opposite direction.

Not now, Durante. Not now.

But he wasn't listening, not anymore. He would be denied his vengeance no longer.

He headed straight for Fuentes, who was still involved in an arcane battle with the Preacher. Mystical energies were flashing about with no thought at all as to what they might hit if they missed their target, and I knew that if I got into the middle of that I was going to be in serious trouble.

I thrashed about inside my head, metaphorically throwing myself around in an effort to break free of Durante's control. I planted my feet against his efforts to move me forward. I pushed when he pulled, pulled when he pushed, and let my general stubbornness out to play in his sandbox. I had almost reached the gate itself when he must have decided the fight to stay inside my body wasn't worth it anymore.

He abandoned it, bursting free without warning, leaving me to stumble and crash to the floor as he released control of my limbs. He took his sight with him as he left, so as I picked myself up off the floor I realized that all I could see around me was an endless sea of white.

With no other choice available to me, I activated my ghostsight.

I was just in time to see Durante's spectral form plunge inside Fuentes's human one.

There was a moment when everyone around me seemed to freeze, when the world went past my eyes in ultraslow motion, and then in the next instant Fuentes literally exploded right before my eyes. Flesh, blood, and brains were flung outward in a hundred different directions, leaving me staring through the space where Fuentes had been into the surprised face of the Preacher.

Remembering what had happened the last time I'd viewed him with my ghostsight, I quickly turned away.

Across the room, Ilyana had hauled herself to her feet and she, Dmitri, and Denise were fighting it out with Rivera. The trio seemed to be gaining the upper hand; all of them had injuries of one kind of another but Rivera seemed to be slowing down, his energy fading. It didn't look like it would last much longer . . .

"Hunt!" Denise cried. "Behind you, on the plain!"

I turned to look, expecting to see the Preacher, but found he too was staring off into the distance.

One look was all I needed and even that was too much, for there was now no way of wiping what I saw out of my memory, and memories live a long time in our hearts and souls.

Far across the plain, out on the edge of that horizon, what looked like an army was moving in our direction. I couldn't see them clearly yet, they were too far away, but what I could see was that there were literally hundreds, if not thousands of them, and that they all carried the taint of the dead and the damned about them. If they got loose on this side of the gate, the world as we knew it would come to an end, I was certain of it.

I had to shut that gate.

Not only shut it, but send it back to wherever the hell it came from too, before those things got here.

The Preacher apparently put two and two together as quickly as I did. He looked at the gate, then at me.

"Don't you dare . . ." he said, fury building on his face.

I dared.

I ran across the cement floor of the warehouse as quickly as my legs could carry me, skidding to a halt in front of the gate while the Preacher still had at least half the distance to go. He tried to intimidate me one final time . . .

"Hunt! I'm warning you!"

I didn't care what he would do to me when this was over. Right now the literal fate of the world hung in the balance and I wasn't going to be found wanting. Not this time.

My ghostsight lets me see things as they really are and so it was a rather simple matter for me to see that if I were to turn the Key like so and then again like so . . .

The massive gate began sliding slowly, ponderously shut.

I watched the Preacher begin to close the distance.

Twenty-five feet.

Twenty.

Ten.

He was going to reach me before the gate was shut; even someone as math challenged as I was could see that. He was going to reach me and take control of the Key and then those things out there were going to wreak havoc . . .

Five.

I stepped up, ready to do what I could to try to stop him . . .

With less than a foot to go before the gate closed, locking the Preacher on the other side, he reached the entrance's edge and started through it.

A roar sounded in my ear, horrifyingly close, and then a massive white paw slipped past my shoulder and slammed into the Preacher with stunning force. He was flung backward a good ten feet, landing on his butt in the dust and bone fragments of the plain.

Our gazes locked as the gate swung ponderously shut.

"Hunt!" he screamed.

I grabbed the Key and pulled it free of its mooring.

A great whooshing sound filled the structure, and reality did that shifting thing again. The world blinked . . .

When it was over, Denise, Dmitri, and I stood in an empty warehouse. The gate was gone and with it the Preacher as well as that army of creatures that had been headed in our direction.

I didn't see Rivera anywhere and asked Dmitri what had happened.

"He hit me with a fireball," he said, turning to show a spot on his shoulder where his shirt had been partially burned to his skin. "Bastard got away while I was trying to keep my fur from going up in flames."

"And Ilyana?"

She too was gone, though neither Denise nor Dmitri had actually seen her go. She must have slipped out during the final few minutes of the battle with Fuentes, though whether she had done it on her own or had left with Rivera's help, we didn't know. I suspected we hadn't seen the last of her.

Fuentes was dead; that much, at least, we'd achieved without too much difficulty.

Perhaps most importantly, I was free of the spectre of

Michael Durante and could get back to normal. Or what passed for normal in the lives of three interstate fugitives, anyway.

"What are we going to do about this?" I asked, holding up the Key.

Denise smiled. "I know just the person to guard it for us," she said.

42

The sun was still below the horizon by the time we reached our destination in the desert outside of Palm Springs. We'd left the L.A. area immediately following the confrontation with Fuentes and the Preacher in Long Beach and, aside from a short stop in a rest area for Denise to make a call, had driven straight through.

I wasn't sure what the hurry was; no one had been living here for years. This place had clearly been deserted for a long time; the few buildings that were still standing were all in various states of disrepair, everything from broken windows and doors to sagging roofs. A chain-link fence surrounded the property, and there appeared to be a padlocked chain holding the gate closed, but when Dmitri pulled on it, the chain was revealed to be nothing more than window dressing, draped there to chase away unwanted visitors but not actually locked.

I drove the car forward and waited for Dmitri to close the gate again behind us. Denise was lying down in the backseat, asleep for these last four hours while the desert highway had rolled beneath our wheels, and I almost felt sorry for having to wake her up at this point.

Almost.

"Hey, wake up," I told her, leaning over the back of the front seat and gently shaking her shoulder.

She came awake with a start, her hands out in a defensive posture, and it took a few seconds of soothing talk for her to calm down enough to recognize me. I wondered what she'd been dreaming about.

"We're here," I told her, when she was coherent enough to follow what I was saying.

While I'd been concentrating on getting Denise up, Dmitri had driven through the maze of half-ruined buildings and come out at the edge of a short runway. He parked in the shade of a nearby hangar and turned off the ignition.

"What is this place?" I asked, looking around into the darkness as the three of us got out of the car.

Dmitri sounded amused as he said, "Old smugglers' strip. Used to provide a quick, easy way to take product across the border into Mexico."

"What kind of product?"

He shrugged. "You name it. Drugs. Money. Talking Elmos. Whatever was in demand."

Talking Elmos? I let that one go without asking any further. Something told me I really didn't want to know.

"What happened to it?"

"DEA sold half a dozen armed surveillance drones to the Mexican government. Two of the Cessnas the smugglers used were shot down, all hands lost, and that pretty much took the heart out of the entire group."

"And you know this how?"

Dmitri smiled. "Oh, you know, word gets around. A person hears things, if they know how to listen."

Right.

Dmitri's past was still a big mystery to me, at least the part before I'd met him as the owner-bartender of my favorite drinking hole in Boston, Murphy's, and local fixer. If you needed something and couldn't get it through normal channels, Dmitri could often get it for you, for the right price.

I was just about to deliver a scathing reply when Denise said, "Shhh," and cocked her head as if she was listening to something.

It took me a minute, but eventually I heard it too: a faint sound breaking the stillness of the early morning. Gradually it grew louder as it grew closer, until the sound resolved itself into the *whomp-whomp-whomp* of a helicopter's rotors.

The sun was just peeking over the horizon and soon I wouldn't be able to see anything again, lost once more to the ocean of white that was my everyday existence; I just hoped we'd be able to conclude our business and be on our way before that happened. I slipped my shades on my face, hoping to buy a few extra minutes when the time came.

As the sound grew louder, we stepped out into the open and started looking around. It was Denise who saw it first, a dark splotch against an even darker near-morning sky, angling in our direction. Eventually we could see the shape of the helicopter, and I was surprised to see that it was a military, rather than civilian, model. A Blackhawk or Apache, one of those kinds of birds. The cargo bay door was open and even from where I stood I could see the soldier manning the mini-gun, keeping it trained off to one side of our little party but ready at a moment's notice.

The chopper circled once, checking the area out, and then set down in the middle of the old runway. As we watched, a tall black man in a military-looking gray jumpsuit and combat boots stepped out of the open door, automatic rifle in hand. Even through the jumpsuit it was clear he was in excellent shape. If I had to guess I would say he was a few inches over six feet. His head was shaved and he wore a neat-looking goatee. He took up a position beside the helicopter, his weapon pointed at the ground and not at us, but ready at a moment's notice.

He glanced around and then nodded.

At his signal, a second man emerged from the helicopter behind him.

The newcomer was white and was dressed the same as his companion, but he had a sword strapped to his back instead of an automatic rifle in his hands. He looked just as fit as his companion did, with hair that was long in back and a pirate-style eye patch covering one eye.

He strode toward us without hesitation.

Denise stepped out to greet him.

I didn't like the idea of Denise meeting with this guy alone, so I moved to join her. Quick as a snake Dmitri reached out and grabbed my arm, stopping me.

"I wouldn't do that, if I were you."

"Why not?"

"You've got the Preacher's taint about you and the Templars won't take kindly to it. No need to provoke them. They've been hunting our kind down for centuries. Little thing known as the Inquisition."

"All the more reason not to leave Denise out there alone."

Dmitri shook his head and that was when I realized he still hadn't taken his gaze off the knight standing beside the helicopter. Not once.

"She's not in any danger. Not from him, at least. She helped him out in the past; something to do with his wife, if I remember correctly. Now it's his turn to pony up and help us."

Sounded fair to me, but I kept my eyes on Denise just the same. I trusted Dmitri's assessment, but there was something to be said for remaining diligent just the same.

The two spoke for a few more moments and then Denise handed over the case to the other man. After accepting it, the two quickly embraced and then turned in opposite directions, with Denise coming toward us and the Templar headed back to the chopper.

"Everything all right?" Dmitri asked as Denise rejoined us.

"Cade intends to bury it deep among the artifacts kept locked away inside the vaults of the Templar reliquary. It should be safe there."

The news was reassuring, in an odd way. The Key had been fashioned by a senior member of the church, and it made an odd kind of sense that the church would take responsibility for its creation and lock it away where it couldn't be used to stir up the denizens of the netherworld against them and the rest of humanity.

The chopper started up, the growling of the rotors making it impossible for us to talk for a few minutes, and then it took to the sky, forcing us to shield our eyes from the dust and rocks and debris that the rotors kicked up on lift-off.

WATCHER OF THE DARK

We watched it head off toward the horizon until it was out of sight.

I couldn't hold back my annoyance any longer.

"So that's it? That's the great plan, Denise? We hand the Key over to some eye-patch-wearing dude in a jumpsuit and hope for the best?"

I didn't know what was making me so obstinate. Lack of sleep? The fact that I'd just consigned the Preacher, a seriously creepy dude if there ever was one, to spending an unspecified amount of time trapped in a hell that was most definitely not of his own making? Maybe crankiness was a side effect of being possessed for longer than three days?

Denise, it seemed, wasn't going to take offense.

"That 'eye-patch-wearing dude' as you so quaintly put it," she said with wry amusement, "is a senior Templar commander, which is why I called him in the first place. The Templar Order has been safeguarding such artifacts for centuries now, and I have complete confidence in their ability to keep the Key out of the wrong hands well into the not-so-foreseeable future."

Okay, fine. I guess I could live with that. After all, Fuentes was dead and the Key was now in safe hands, but there were still a lot of questions for which I didn't have any answers and that made me uneasy.

Ilyana was out there, somewhere, and apparently so was Rivera, unless she'd caught up to him and dealt with that problem. Would I see her again? I wondered. Did I even want to? I didn't know. I did know that I'd be perfectly happy if I never saw Rivera's face again, but something told me I wasn't going to be that lucky. I'd not only made him look like a fool, but I'd managed to get the person who was the closest thing to a father that he'd ever had torn to pieces from the inside out.

299

I didn't think forgiveness was an inherent part of Rivera's nature.

And, of course, there was the larger question of the Preacher. Who the hell was he? What did he want with me? Why did he keep popping up in my life? He was clearly maneuvering me toward something, but what?

I didn't have any answers.

Thoughts of the Preacher made me wonder just what had happened to him when I'd pulled the plug, so to speak, and sent the gate, plus those on the other side of it, on an all-expense-paid trip right back to whatever backwater section of the netherworld Fuentes had dragged them up from. Would the Preacher be looking for revenge now too?

When you added in the Boston Police Department, the New Orleans Police Department, and the Federal Bureau of Investigation, it was pretty daunting thinking of all the people who were hunting me for one reason or another.

In fact, it was downright depressing.

Which was precisely why I refused to dwell on it. I wasn't going to let my circumstances bring me down, not today. My friends and I had just kept a murderous psychopath from taking command of hell's legions and I thought that was a damned fine accomplishment. It was time to celebrate.

As we turned and walked back to where I'd left Denise's car, there was only one question that I needed an answer to right then and there.

"Anyone mind if I drive?"

ABOUT THE AUTHOR

Joseph Nassise is the author of more than a dozen novels, including the internationally bestselling Templar Chronicles, and, more recently, *Eyes to See* and *King of the Dead,* the first two books of the Jeremiah Hunt Chronicle. He is a former president of the Horror Writers Association, a two-time Bram Stoker Award and International Horror Guild Award nominee, and a life and creativity coach who likes working with people to help them realize their full potential in life.

Born and raised in Boston, Massachusetts, he attended Fordham University. He lives with his wife, four children, six dogs, four cats, and a pair of guinea pigs in Phoenix, Arizona.

Find out more at www.josephnassise.com.